# LUCKY NUMBER

JO COX

Copyright © 2023 by Jo Cox

All rights reserved.

No part of this book may be reproduced in any form or by any electronic or mechanical means, including information storage and retrieval systems, without written permission from the author, except for the use of brief quotations in a book review.

This is a work of fiction. Names, characters, places, and incidents are either the products of the author's imagination or are used fictitiously. Any resemblance to actual persons, living or dead, businesses, companies, events, or locales is entirely coincidental.

# 1
## ABI

The sign marking the football club entrance came into view and caused Abi's heart to flutter with either apprehension or excitement. Like the line between pleasure and pain, it was too thin to tell.

"You can just drop me here," she suggested, reaching into the footwell for her bag while reminding herself that she was glad to be back.

Her pulse steadied until she looked up again a few moments later. They'd rounded the bend towards the car park and were only thirty metres from the clubhouse, but still hadn't stopped or even slowed down.

"Dad. Really. Here."

When a firmer tone didn't work, she threw the bag back onto the floor and then her hand shot out to grip the open window, the other clawing for the door handle. Executing a plunge and roll was dramatic, especially for someone who'd spent months struggling to breathe while upright on the sofa, but she was sure she'd do it anyway and bugger the consequences.

"Don't be silly, love. I need to turn around."

"But!" Abi began. She didn't get any further, though, because a disarming smile accompanied Stanley's reply. It had already forced her shoulders to slump forward, her muscle memory well-honed and used to defeat at the hands of her dad. The only thing that might save her now was plan B, but when she grabbed her bag again and prepared to make a swift escape, the commotion roused her mum.

Petra squinted as she read the screen of a tiny smartphone without her glasses but discarded it with a gasp of excitement when she clocked where they were. The rear window rolled down, her voice climbing in pitch like a slide whistle as she cooed at a bewildered football coach, "Now you are going to look after my girl, aren't you?"

*Fan-bloody-tactic.*

Abi crumpled in on herself, stealing a look in the wing mirror to check there were still crow's feet pinching her eyes. Yep, definitely thirty-three and not thirteen. Definitely in hell.

She frowned as she recounted her recent run of bad luck. Highlights included the decimation of her business, moving in with her parents, a brief period of hospitalisation, and her last tropical fish perishing. This latest blow wasn't a shock.

"Are you feeling alright, love?" The car stopped and Stanley's rough palm landed on Abi's forearm. "You sure you're ready for this?"

Her grip tightened on the bag to keep her hand steady. She still wasn't at all sure, and the humiliation of Petra detailing the most miserable months of her life was once again the least of Abi's problems. With only a friendly and a few weeks of training before the new season began, she should be in peak condition and guaranteed a spot in the starting eleven. Right now, she was unlikely to make the bench. Perhaps trying to play this season was a mistake and it was time to take up something less physically demanding, like crochet.

Abi could never lie to her dad but didn't want to get into it, so only nodded. Then she turned and mouthed an apology to her coach. Jax was supportive and had spent weeks coaxing back her 'star player', but she'd end up in the changing rooms if she retreated any further. Like everyone else, she'd reached her limit with global pandemics and wanted a couple of hours off. Not a lecture from a small, noisy Spanish woman about bed spaces in the local hospital, or how lucky they all were to be alive.

"Ma," Abi interrupted. "We need to warm up soon and Dad wants to get to the supermarket."

It did little to deter Petra because she assumed everyone was her friend, like a dog. The yappy, high maintenance kind who follows you to the toilet and whines outside the door until you hand over your last shred of privacy. Then expects a treat for it.

When Abi slapped her hand down on the roof of the car, Stanley did a better job of taking the hint and threw the vehicle back into first gear. Petra sailed around the bend towards the main road and Abi let out the breath she'd been holding. She loved her parents, but their encroachment on all areas of her life felt like someone had shrink-wrapped her head and she was running out of oxygen. It had been eight months of fussing, force feeding, and futile attempts to snatch moments alone. The last part was impossible, though. Wherever you looked, someone was there, and usually with a snack.

When a comforting arm wrapped around her shoulder, Abi smiled. Then she closed her eyes and leant her head sideways, hitting Jax. For a few moments, the world was still besides the chatter of kids on the field, but then the scent of jasmine and orange-blossom registered. The realisation that it wasn't Jax next to her caused Abi to jolt forward and she tripped on the strap of her bag, narrowly avoiding a face full of gravel.

"Steady on," came the mischievous voice from behind.

Abi turned, her eyes popping as they met Jenna's tiny black shorts. Then they roamed over generous quads, up a stocky frame to Jenna's muscular arms and chest until they reached the area that always undid Abi—messy blonde hair framing beautiful brown eyes. And they were shimmering now, as Jenna sniggered.

"I—" Abi started, with no idea where she was going next. She was too busy mentally nipping along the strip of reddened skin where Jenna's T-shirt had slipped and she'd caught the sun.

"What the hell's wrong with you? Did they take your brain out in the hospital, huh?" Jenna stepped over the bag and pulled Abi into a hug before she could reply, which was a blessing because she didn't know the answer. For a few seconds, she wasn't even sure of her own name. "I'm so glad you're back. I was worried when you didn't show up for the first couple of friendlies."

"You were?"

"Of course! You never miss preseason." Jenna let go but stayed close because she couldn't take a step backwards without also tripping herself.

Abi could've been the one to move, but she didn't want to. Now that she'd acclimatised, she was enjoying the warmth of Jenna's breath on her face and the regular brush of her arm from their forced proximity. The last person who'd touched her for any prolonged period was a nurse, and not the good kind. Jenna, on the other hand, would rock that uniform. Or any uniform. Or no uniform at all.

Realising nothing was wrong with her that banging her teammate up against the clubhouse wall wouldn't cure, Abi bit her bottom lip. She tried and failed to halt a salacious smile, finally pulling herself together enough to ask a sensible question: "How have you been?"

"Oh, y'know. Surviving. Did I tell you I broke up with Cass?"

Abi managed a sympathetic expression and paired it with a head tilt. "Yeah, you mentioned it over WhatsApp once or twice.

I was really sorry to hear that," she lied. Outrageously. Cass was a stuck-up pair of overly starched trousers who looked down her nose at everyone from the football club. Particularly scruffy gardeners like Abi, who wasn't even good enough to trim her bushes. "What happened?"

"The usual." Jenna folded her arms but didn't offer any further information about what 'the usual' entailed. Not that Abi cared. She was just glad to see the back of the woman, however it had happened. "I might resign myself to being single forever. I'm getting too old for this nonsense."

"At twenty-eight?"

"Nine!" Jenna exclaimed, her eyes growing wider.

Abi smiled as she nudged Jenna's shoulder with her fist. "Silly me."

"Don't look at me that way. It's hopeless. No one will ever love me again, so I'm giving up on women forever."

"Until you meet another tall, confident, highly successful dream boat and she sweeps you off your feet?"

"Exactly."

Abi looked down at all five foot five of her unemployed, out of condition self. She wasn't even in the running, but it was a relief to find she could still feel this way. After months of illness, she worried someone had surgically removed her sex drive at the hospital, not her brain. "You're doing better than me. I haven't had so much as a date since getting dumped last March."

"You and the rest of the world. Look on the bright side, though. All those sex starved lesbians will be easy pickings." A devilish smile lit up Jenna's face as she declared, "I'll be your wing woman."

Abi's lips parted. She was about to argue because dating from Jenna's pool of stuffy solicitors sounded like a horrible idea. In the end, though, all she mumbled was a pathetic "mmm, sure".

"Is work at least going okay?"

"What work? I've only got a few regular jobs left, and one of those is mowing my Aunt Ida's lawn for tea and biscuits." Trying to remain positive was tough. Abi had spent years building relationships with her clients and Covid had blown it to smithereens in a matter of months.

Without missing a beat, Jenna replied with characteristic optimism. It was her most attractive feature, if you discounted her legs. "I can help you out with that, too. A few weeks from now, you'll be turning away clients and have more dates than you can handle. Stick with me—you won't regret it."

Shuffling on the gravel, Abi peered around at the new youth players squealing as they raced each other across the eighteen-yard box. Then she turned back to Jenna and frowned. She had a feeling she *would* regret this. Very much. But if she ever wanted to earn money rather than biscuits and move out of her parents' spare bedroom, she was in no position to argue.

\* \* \*

Two hours later, Abi had upgraded herself from out of condition to knackered and ready for the scrap heap. She sat on the grass and stuffed her shin guards into her bag, then laid back and let out a long, low growl.

It only ended when Jenna nudged her foot, as if she were prodding a stricken animal for signs of life. "Coming in for a pint? Looks like you could use it."

"Can't. Van's in for a service and I need to find the energy to walk home. Maybe next week?"

"That excuse is unacceptable. What you *need* to do is collect your new kit ready for Sunday. Jax has gone to grab it from the shed, so hang around and I'll drop you home later."

Abi emitted another strangled noise she hoped Jenna would

recognise as agreement. Then she sat up and pulled away the streak of hair matted to her cheek. What had once been a lustrous chestnut brown must now look like a North Sea oil slick. "I'm expecting Greenpeace at any moment," she mumbled to herself, shaking her head when Jenna looked understandably confused. "Never mind. Has Jax said anything about the team yet?"

"Only that she'll post the squad on WhatsApp by the end of Friday. Why…? Are you worried?"

"No, of course not," Abi shot back. Then she really gave the game away by glancing at the teenagers from earlier. They'd stopped squealing and huddled in a group by the entrance to the clubhouse, pulling ID out of their purses and pooling loose change.

"Liar," Jenna scoffed, kicking Abi's foot a little harder. "I've never seen this insecure side of you before and I'm not sure what to make of it, but at least you're back."

"You really missed me, then?"

"Of course! Who else would make me look like Ronaldo by comparison?" When Abi scowled, Jenna laughed and held out a hand to hoist her from the ground. "Fair enough. I guess you're more like him than I am, what with the whole European thing."

"The *European* thing?" Abi frowned and bashed away the grass stuck to her bum. "You know Europe is a continent, right? And I'm half Spanish, not Portuguese."

"Of course I know Europe is a continent. Spain is in it. Or on it. Or whatever." Jenna grabbed both of their bags and strode towards the clubhouse but stopped, turned, and frowned when Abi took only a few wobbly steps. "You look like a baby calf."

"As opposed to a fully grown one, otherwise known as a cow?"

"Have you always been this grumpy? It's hard to remember, given you wouldn't let me visit when you were ill." After thrusting Abi's bag at her, Jenna glared at the teenagers. "Don't think you can change the subject. You're worried one of them is taking your place, aren't you?"

"No!"

"You're a terrible liar, do you know that?"

It was safer not to reply. Instead, Abi continued to limp towards the clubhouse, a large red brick building in an L-shape with changing rooms in the sticky-out bit and an adjacent bar. It had shut during the first lockdown and stayed that way for almost a year-and-a-half, but finally reopened for preseason training. The committee had used the time to give it a revamp, with a fresh coat of white paint and a new carpet to match the royal blue of the team colours. There was also a sixty-inch 4K television ready to show all the Premier League and Women's Super League games. Or so Jenna was saying, but Abi was only half listening.

By the time they reached the slab of concrete patio which butted up against the field, a film of fresh sweat coated her palms and her mouth had run dry. Jenna held open the door and Abi stepped inside, fiddling with the zip on her bag and gawping at the transformation, then swallowed hard against the lump in her throat. They'd done a good job, but seeing it so changed was tough. She'd imagined being back all the time during lockdown, and especially when she was sick, but it didn't feel quite right without crisps matted into the carpet or the faint smell of sweat.

"Wow, this is… great," she just about got out, her parched tongue sticking to the roof of her mouth.

"Uhuh. Try to sound a bit more convincing when you speak to Jax. She was up here for days helping and won't shut up about it." Jenna lobbed her bag on a chair, then pulled up a stool at the bar which intersected the rectangular room, splitting it into two squares, and squinted into the row of fridges.

"It *does* look good, it's just... different."

Abi shuffled onto the stool opposite Jenna, dumped her bag, and rolled a beer mat between her fingers while she surveyed the room. On the other side of the bar was a new pool table, and behind that was a wall of old team photos dating back to when The Blues formed in the 1980s, along with snapshots from tournaments and nights out. It would be good to get back to that again, and Abi's features finally softened as she pointed to a picture from the last pre-Covid Christmas party. It felt like a million years ago, even though it had been less than two.

"Do you remember that night?" she asked, smiling at the shot of Jenna arriving in a full Santa suit with a toy reindeer tucked under her arm. There was always someone who took the Christmas jumper competition too far, and it was usually her.

Jenna laughed. "God, I'd only been with Cass for a few months and I remember her being mortified dropping me off in that costume."

"You reckon you'd have stayed together if things had been normal?"

"Probably not, and it's done now anyway so why bother worrying?"

That was a level of acceptance Abi hadn't quite ascended to yet, no matter how hard she tried, because the first lockdown had also smoked her own relationship. "I guess. Are you doing okay with the breakup, though?"

"Yeah. Things don't feel all that different, to be honest. We're trying the whole friends thing and still spending time together. We're just not having sex." Jenna scrunched her face as she added, "...mostly."

Abi joined in with the laughter that followed but was unsure why because the idea of Jenna and Cass having casual sex had caused her chest to swell with yet another unhappy emotion. It became difficult to pin them down when you had so many. "Friends? That's the most lesbian thing I've ever heard."

"I know, right? I've never done this before, but it makes sense from a work point of view if we can play nice, and she assures me we're mature adults."

"Maybe *she* is."

Jax interrupted Jenna before she could shoot back a reply, throwing a shrink-wrapped package of kit so that it skidded across the bar. Then she hurled another and it smacked a teenager on the back of the head. They were about to retaliate until they realised who their assailant was; no one messed with Jax before match day.

Abi yelled a quick "thank you" and then held up the package. "How come we've got a new kit?"

"New sponsor."

Jenna took the bag and ripped open the top, pulling out a shirt to show the company logo plastered across the front. Lo and behold it was for Cass's firm of solicitors. So much for being rid of the woman.

"They're allocating kit to everyone this season," Jenna continued, turning it over to show the back. "Something to do with ongoing Covid protocol, but as someone on the committee with insider knowledge, I think it's just so we have to wash our own."

She went to put it down on the bar, but Abi stopped her. "Wait, what's this?" Her heart raced as she took the shirt from Jenna and held it out to her side, checking she hadn't misread the number. "This isn't mine. I'm number eleven."

Everyone knew that. She was their left winger and had worn the number eleven shirt for the past six seasons. It'd been her lucky number ever since her third game for the club, when she'd scored a legendary goal from the halfway line.

"I don't know. Does it matter?" Jenna fussed over the wrapping, balling it up and lobbing it at a bin behind the bar.

"Does it matter?" Abi repeated, the shirt wringing in her hands.

Her bottom lip trembled and her foot tapped on the footrest of her stool as she watched the teenager hold up her coveted number eleven shirt. It was a ridiculous overreaction, but she had a feeling she knew what it meant and once again struggled to keep her emotions in check. The world had felt overwhelming and scary since it started reopening, like she couldn't quite trust she was safe. That shirt was a familiar comfort blanket. A thread which tied her to the past when she was carefree and healthy. Now she felt like it was going to snap. That *she* was going to snap.

*It's over. You're safe. You got through it.*

She repeated the same mantra, but no matter how many times she told herself that she was lucky, normal no longer felt like normal. She didn't know how to get back there and sometimes she wasn't even sure who she was anymore—she only knew she didn't want to be number four.

"I'll be back in a sec." Abi discarded the shirt, slipped off her stool and jogged to the toilets on the far side of the room. When she was safely inside, a lungful of pine scented disinfectant almost made her retch. She was in a manic state somewhere between laughter and tears as she gripped either side of the little white sink.

"What has the world come to?" she asked herself as she peered into the square mirror above and realised it was clean for the first time since 2008.

"Are you talking to me or yourself?"

A whoosh of running water followed, and then the click and clunk of the cubicle door opening. Even before she appeared, Abi knew it was Jax. Her American accent had lost its edges over the many years she'd spent living in a small Oxfordshire town and it had ended up as a hybrid, slipping from Midwest to Middle England depending on how much you'd pissed her off, but the low drawl was ever present and unmistakable.

Jax placed a hand on each of Abi's shoulders and also stared into the mirror. "How are you doing, champ?"

"Fantastically... fine..." Abi's face contorted. She knew she'd convinced precisely no one.

"I can see that. If anyone had asked me, I'd have said *that Abi, now there's a gal who's fantastically fine*. You're not feeling ill, are you? Because Petra will kill me if I've broken her girl."

Willing her jaw to unclench, Abi eased her tight grip on the sink. "No. I mean, I'm obviously fucked, but..." She trailed off, not wanting to give Jax an excuse to leave her out of the team on Sunday, but couldn't think of anything else to fill the void.

After a few moments of silence, Jax took away her hands and nudged Abi over so she could wash them. "Did Jen tell you Cass is history? That should cheer you up."

"Why would that cheer me up?"

"Oh please. You two have had a thing for each other since the day she showed up here and now you're *finally* both single. What are you going to do about it?"

"Easy. Nothing." Abi wouldn't deny her attraction to Jenna, but she was old enough and ugly enough to know that you didn't have to pursue every woman you had a bit of a crush on. By that logic, she'd be writing love letters to Cate Blanchett.

"Why the hell not? I was watching earlier. You practically combusted when you saw her."

That was another thing Abi could hardly argue about, but it didn't mean much. Her emotions were all over the place. "Can you blame me? It was like a kid starved of sweets for months suddenly being given a giant bowl of ice cream, topped with whipped cream and sprinkles."

"I can just imagine what you'd do with Jenna and a vat of

whipped cream."

Abi rolled her eyes. "It's not like that between us. We're mates and there's nothing more going on."

"For now, but if you ask me, you guys would be great together."

That was dubious. Jenna had a very definite type, and it was still sharing a bed with her. "We're hardly compatible, are we?"

"Like hell you're not. You two have just got this disease afflicting at least half the lesbian population. Everyone else can see you pick the wrong women when the right one is under your nose, but you're oblivious. *How* is anyone's guess, because you openly drool over each other. It's a real feat of bloody-mindedness."

"Get lost. Jenna doesn't see me that way. I'm not power hungry or emotionally distant enough to meet her strict criteria and I'm unwilling to give myself a charisma-bypass to correct that."

"You'll have to do a better job of hiding it if you want me to believe *that* crap, because you've barely spoken to anyone else or stopped touching all night. You know there's still a pandemic on, right?" Jax ripped a paper towel from the dispenser on the wall and was about to speak again when the door clattered on its casters and Jenna appeared.

She squinted as she studied them both, and then her expression settled into one of mild concern. "Are you alright?"

Abi nodded. "Yep. Sorry, hay fever. Be out in a sec."

"You don't have hay fever. Asthma, yes. Stupidity, occasionally. Never hay fever."

"Sudden onset."

"Well, your dad is in the bar looking for you once you've got your *hay fever* under control."

"My dad?" Abi strained to look over Jenna's shoulder. Sure enough, Stanley stood chatting with the father of one of the teenagers while swinging his keys around his index finger. Had it come to this now? Had she regressed to her childhood self, about to get a lift from her dad like all the other kids? It was one thing when he was already on his way out to the supermarket, but this felt different. *Worse* different. "Oh," she mumbled. "Don't know why he's here."

"Aww, he's come to collect you," Jax cooed, trying to hide a smile. For someone only weeks away from forty, she could be an immature jackass sometimes. "You'd better run along."

Jenna backed out, distracted when one of the other players called her over, and Abi landed a swift kick on Jax's trainer.

"Thanks for that," she hissed.

"What?"

"Embarrassing me in front of Jen."

The smile erupted now. "Why would you care what Jenna thinks?"

Abi only glared. She had no good, honest answer to that, and was now glad her dad was there to take her home.

2

# JENNA

"Sometimes I wonder why I pay a mortgage." The sight of another clump of reformed chicken made Jenna's lip curl. By Thursday evening, takeaways and supermarket meal deals had lost their already scant appeal.

Jax's nose wrinkled as she leant over the arm of her chair, peering into the plastic salad bowl. "That *does* look rough. What's it meant to be?"

"Chicken Caesar, but I think they only get away with calling it that because the lettuce has been around since the last days of Rome."

"When was the last time you had a home cooked meal?"

Jax prodded a crouton and Jenna gave up, dumping what remained of her dinner on the table. It was unlike her to leave food, but she'd make an exception because she wasn't sure that abomination qualified, and the addition of a grubby finger hadn't helped.

Slumping back into her seat, she then recalled her week so far. Monday was gym night. On Tuesday the barbershop she owned opened late and someone was sick, so she had to cover.

Last night was training. Now she was back in the clubhouse for a committee meeting.

"It must have been Sunday," she decided, before quickly raising her index finger to signal a correction. "Actually, I was doing paperwork on Sunday, so Saturday." With a theatrical sigh, Jenna let her wrist flop onto the arm of her chair. "Maybe I should just set up a bed in the changing rooms or my office and be done with it."

"You need to get a life, buddy."

"I have a life. Living has never been the problem."

She did it hard and fast, which had become an issue in and of itself. Doing was the only option. Resting was excruciating and lockdown had sent Jenna into a spiral. It had been all too easy to fall back into the same patterns over the past couple of months, now that she was free to do so, and she knew she needed to break them. The stack of self-help books on her bedside table had confirmed it.

She watched the rest of the committee file in and head towards the bar. It triggered a wave of nausea but this time she couldn't blame the salad—it was guilt. Stepping down as treasurer was necessary but the uneasy feeling persisted. Wasn't letting people down for your own sake selfish?

She was still debating when Jax derailed her train of thought.

"Do you want my advice?"

"Not really, but I expect I'm going to get it anyway."

"Hey!" Jax frowned and folded her arms tight over herself. "There are far worse people to ask about life than me. Or love, come to that..." She raised her eyebrow and then a mischievous smile.

"Why didn't you say this was really about my love life? In that case, it's a definite no. Asking you about love and romance is like asking *Cass* about love and romance..."

"Is she still trying to get you back?"

Jenna shrugged. That was a very good question. "I thought we were on solid friend ground but the other day she booked us a table at *Les Saisons*. Now I'm suspicious."

"She booked you a table at a Michelin starred restaurant? No wonder you're suspicious. What a cu—" Jax stopped mid-word, unfolded her arms, and nodded hello to the chairwoman as she passed them on her way to the toilets.

"It's lovely and I've always wanted to go but that's sort of the problem. I know how Cass operates. It's a bit like sponsoring the kit but throwing money at a situation doesn't always improve it."

"No? Works for me."

Two years ago, they would both have made the same remark, but not now. Money was no substitute for spending quality time together. Being with someone who worked sixty hour weeks, even during a pandemic and when you were struggling to hold it together, was no fun. For the first time in her life, Jenna could honestly say that money and status weren't everything, however much she liked Cass's Mercedes and desperately wanted one.

"Do you ever wonder what it'd be like to fall in love with someone?" she asked. For some reason, it'd been on her mind since Cass phoned with the dinner invitation. "I mean *really* fall in love."

Jax frowned again. Perhaps she was confused by the alien concept of 'love', given her fast and furious approach to relationships. Or, more accurately, her fast and furious approach to one-night stands. "Weren't you in love with Cass?"

"No," Jenna replied, wondering if it was a terrible thing to admit. Especially to someone who knew them both. "I feel like I *should* have been in love with her, but I wasn't. At least she didn't cheat, that's a step up from my last relationship, but something never really connected. Y'know? It's got me thinking that maybe I need to stop going after people who are good on paper and have all the right credentials, and act with my heart as well as my head for once."

"Maybe the trouble is that you don't go after anyone at all."

"What do you mean?"

"I mean exactly what I just said. Have you ever asked a woman out?"

"Of course—" Jenna shot back, but then her face scrunched and she had to right it quickly. Admitting Jax may have a point was a rare and unwanted event. "Well, I've never needed to!"

Women always made the first move. In Cass's case, it had been obvious what she wanted from the minute Jenna stepped into her office to sign contracts on her new house. What had been a straightforward conveyance to that point, suddenly required more phone calls to go over details. Then, when Jenna had moved in, she'd gone old school and sent flowers. Not just 'welcome to your new home' flowers but 'I want to see you again' flowers accompanied by an expensive bottle of Champagne.

"I'm interested," Jax began, before pausing to take a sip of her pint. "Have you ever liked someone and been disappointed that they never asked you out? Because we both know you wouldn't have done it yourself." She peered over the glass still hovering near her lips and gave Jenna a look that said *don't even argue*.

"If they'd been interested, they would've asked!"

*Shit.*

"Oh, like you would?"

Jenna grumbled quietly and rubbed her hands over her shorts. They were far too small, and she really needed to buy new ones. New boots, too, and a few bits for running. "Do we still get a club discount at that sports shop in town?" She bent over to inspect her socks. Were they even a pair or was the left one navy rather than black? "I need some new kit."

"What...?"

"Sports kit. I need some."

"I heard you, but weren't we in the middle of a conversation?"

Jenna straightened and offered Jax a smile. "I thought that was over. I'd moved on."

"Well, *I* hadn't. We were making progress until I hit a sore spot. Why won't you accept that if you want something different you might have to put yourself out there and act differently?"

"I just said the exact same thing. It was my entire point. The change of subject wasn't because I disagreed." It was because of who had come to mind, how little Jenna wanted their mutual friend to know about it, and how sure she was that she would never be brave enough to make the first move. "What more is there to say?"

"Plenty. If we're on the same page, I need you to convince Abi to shake things up as well, because she also makes horrible dating choices. It's clearly a lesbian thing. "

"That's not true, no one's ever baked for me!"

"Huh?"

"I'm talking about Abi's ex. I thought she was lovely." Annoyingly so, on occasion. She was always perky, always had her shit together, and always had Abi's undivided attention. Lucky bitch. "I particularly liked her on the weeks when she sent brownies."

"Oh. Right. Yeah, I'm sure she was lovely, and yes, her brownies were delicious, but that didn't make them right for each other. Successful relationships are about more than finding someone you fancy who has their own electric mixer and a baking book. There are deeper levels of compatibility than that."

Jenna scoffed. She knew that didn't necessarily mean they were compatible, but it must still be nice to have someone who would make an effort for you. Rather than say that, though, and risk where it might lead, she had a second shot at changing the subject. "Do we need to alert the World Health Organisation of another side effect from the Covid vaccine?"

"What do you mean?"

"I'm just wondering why you're suddenly so bothered about who either of us dates. You're the last person I'd expect to find giving out advice about love. I thought you just did lust."

Jax smiled sweetly. "I'm a romantic at heart."

"No, you're not."

"Okay. I'm not, but you two are. I'm allowed to think my friends deserve good things."

Jenna couldn't resist a little laugh because that was endearing. For Jax. "The pandemic has changed you but I'm not complaining. It's changed me too, so I'll give it some thought." She glanced at her watch, hoping the diversion had worked this time. Even if it hadn't, the meeting would start in a couple of minutes, and it now felt like the safer option.

"When did you get this?" Jax took hold of Jenna's hand and inspected the Apple Watch she'd invested in during the last lockdown.

"A few months back." She shook off Jax's grip. "I got it to track my runs."

"Since when do you run? I thought you just hit the gym for strength training and conditioning."

"I did. This isn't for fitness."

"Is someone pressuring you into it, bud?"

So much for being safe. Jenna laughed again, just enough to hide the nerves that'd resurfaced, but this time they weren't because of the meeting or even Abi. No one besides Cass knew how much she'd struggled, and she didn't plan to change that to explain the purchase of a new watch.

"It's a wellbeing thing. No headphones, just the sound of my feet on the path and the steady in and out of my breathing. I'm heading out after the meeting so I can wind down."

Jax was about to return to her pint but stopped with the glass half raised to her mouth. "If you're running to relax, why are you tracking?"

"Because—"

"You can't stand the idea of not knowing whether you're improving?"

Jenna didn't reply. It was too much for her to admit that Jax was right again and every time she opened her mouth, she only seemed to make things worse.

* * *

An hour later, Jenna stood in the car park and shook her hands out by her sides. She closed her eyes and let her head flop forward as a light breeze rippled over the playing fields, bringing with it the sound of a dog barking somewhere in the distance, and the smell of freshly cut grass. It was only now that she could hear her own breathing, shallow and thready. She emptied her lungs, paused, and took a long drag of sweet summer air.

As she slowly released it through lightly puckered lips, she cricked her head from side to side and reopened her eyes. Then, after a few gentle stretches, she fiddled with the settings on her watch and decided not to turn on the tracker. How far and how fast she travelled shouldn't matter. The journey was what counted, or some other bollocks she'd read on Instagram.

By the time she'd reached the end of the drive, the crunch of her trainers on the gravel had fallen into a steady cadence. She turned left, past the laughing and clinking of the pub garden, and then hung another left onto the road out of the village. It was the main thoroughfare back towards the town, but besides the pub, one small shop, and the football club, there wasn't much to attract traffic. It meant that kids could ride their bikes along the pavement and Jenna had to dodge a small boy as he careered towards a lamp post with legs flailing, omitting a high pitched squeal. She glanced back and laughed when he came to an abrupt stop only inches from doom, his helmet slipping forward to partially cover his eyes.

Reassured that he was fine, she carried on jogging towards the bridge marking the edge of the village. There was a footpath just before it, diverting pedestrians down a narrow dirt track parallel with the railway line. If you followed it to the very end, you'd pass the churchyard and come out at a stile leading to a patchwork of fields, and that was Jenna's target.

She'd just reached the last in a series of bungalows and was scanning the overgrown brambles ahead, trying to find a gap, when a call of "hello!" made her smile. This must be a nice place to live. An idyll where people spoke to their neighbours, as she imagined everyone did in the north of England. Unlike on her own street, where the only time anyone acknowledged your existence was because you'd obstructed their driveway or accidentally stolen their wheelie bin.

She called back a cheery "hi" and continued, but the bellow of her name in reply stopped her dead. She turned sharply, trying to work out who it had come from.

"Jenna! That's you, isn't it?"

She recognised Stanley in an instant. It was hard not to, because Abi's dad was a big man in all ways. He rested one hand on a stone wall at the end of the bungalow's long garden, and waved with the other.

"Oh, hello!" She raised a hand to shield her eyes as she walked the twenty-or-so yards back towards him. "Have you moved? I was sure you lived in town, near Abi's old flat. Didn't I pick her up from your house once?"

"This is my sister's place. We pop over once a week to keep on top of things for her, although a few small jobs have turned into quite a lot of bigger ones." Stanley motioned towards a mobility scooter parked in the open garage, adjacent to the bungalow. "We came to mow the lawns and somehow we're now getting ready to build an access ramp out into the back garden. She struggles to get around." He puffed out his cheeks and ran his hand over a thinning crop of white hair. "I'm exhausted. Once we're done, I should come in and see you for a bit of pampering. What do you reckon?"

"You can be the inaugural customer in my new shop, if you like. Full preferential treatment. How do you feel about a Turkish shave?"

Stanley laughed, which was fine because she was half joking. He wasn't exactly her typical customer. "Another shop, huh? Good for you, love." He leant forward and tapped his nose. "If you need any advice or help getting it fitted out, you know where I am. My little black book might come in handy."

"It would definitely come in handy if you're serious." Having a builder as an ally was always helpful when you were trying to negotiate with contractors. She'd already had several quotes and they varied wildly. It was hard to pick apart why, how, and which route to take.

"Of course! Just get Abi to give you my number. I haven't got any cards to hand right now." He patted his pockets as if he needed to prove the point.

"Speaking of Abi, I'm glad she finally turned up at training last night. Take it you had something to do with that?"

"No! Nothing I said did any good. I think it was Jax who wore her down in the end. That and I know she was desperate to see you again."

"To see me?!"

"Well, all of you."

Jenna's face flushed and she was grateful it was already a little pink from running. Of course he hadn't meant her specifically. "If she was so desperate, why didn't she want to come back?"

"She did, but the more sessions and matches she missed, the harder it became. Have you got time to say hello?"

"Abi's here?" Jenna's face prickled again and she glanced down at her mismatched socks, wondering how much of a state she looked. She'd assumed Stanley meant that Petra was helping.

"Yep," he replied, unhooking the latch on the gate a few feet to his right. "I expect she'll be raiding her aunt's biscuits by now."

"I bet she will," Jenna whispered under her breath, unable to resist a small smile. She'd taken Abi's comment about mowing her aunt's lawn for biscuits as a joke, rather than a serious commitment, but was unsure why. It was exactly the type of thing Abi would do because she was just as lovely as her parents.

Jenna closed the gate behind herself and followed Stanley up a stone path. It split the garden into two rectangles of perfectly manicured lawn and at the top was a small area of patio, joining the front door to the garage and driveway. It was peppered with colourful pots, in full bloom, and Stanley stopped to remove a weed from one. After throwing it into a green garden waste sack, propped against the side of the building, he wandered into the garage.

When he opened the internal door, the sound of the lawnmower was audible, but then the engine cut.

"Abi!" he yelled.

Jenna laughed as she bellowed back "what?" like a moody teenager. It was little wonder she got on so well with Jax.

"There's someone here to see you!"

"If it's Ma, tell her to get her own biscuits! I'm fed up of her scrounging mine when she hasn't lifted a finger."

A few seconds later, Abi flew through the door but then stopped abruptly, a chocolate chip cookie gripped in her teeth and a waste sack in each hand. She had on a pair of old Timberland boots and a T-shirt that declared she was Arsenal 'til she died.

Jenna followed flecks of grass up Abi's legs to a pair of cargo shorts stained with green and brown splotches. "I hope you haven't trailed that mess all through your aunt's house."

One of the bags plopped to the ground and Abi pulled the biscuit from her mouth. "I always clean up after myself, don't worry."

Seeing Abi sweaty and tanned from hard labour in the sun always reminded Jenna of the old Diet Coke adverts with the sexy gardener who sprays himself in Cola and wrings out his T-shirt to reveal six pack abs. Except in this fantasy he was replaced by a woman with the most defined arms Jenna had ever seen. She wondered briefly whether Abi would mind throwing her around a bit. Or at least downing a frosty can of Coke. She'd missed the weekly guilty pleasure of Abi turning up at training in her work gear and stripping on the side of the pitch.

Stanley jolted Jenna from her fantasy when he grabbed the bags of rubbish, carrying them down the driveway towards the wheelie bins.

"What are you doing here?" Abi asked, once she'd finished demolishing her biscuit.

"I was just out for a run when your dad saw me. Letting off some steam after the committee meeting."

"Oh, yeah. That." Abi's face screwed. "Jax tried to get me involved but I can't take on anything else right now. Need to focus on getting some work. Besides, I'm terrible with numbers." She shrugged as if long since resigned to that fact. "How come you stepped down as treasurer?"

"Also busy with work," Jenna replied quickly, compelled against all reason to justify herself. It still felt like a poor excuse, even if it was the truth. "I'm opening another shop in a few weeks. And I'm already doing the social sec role."

"Fair enough. Do you want a cookie? My aunt makes the best biscuits, but don't tell my mum that. She put a lot of effort into reading English baking books to keep up with the Jones's at all our birthday parties and, so far as she knows, she holds the crown."

Jenna laughed at Abi's endearing obsession with biscuits, and followed into a small kitchen with boxes of pills strewn across the counter. A faint whiff of antiseptic hung in the air, reminding her of her grandparents' house, and it caused her smile to falter.

"Is your aunt here?" she asked, peering around the door into the lounge. "I don't want to intrude."

"My mum's taken her shopping, but she wouldn't mind you being here. She loves visitors."

The antiseptic smell was where the comparison with Jenna's grandparents ended because they hated visitors. Impromptu ones, at least. And any they were related to. "Your mum's cute. Especially that thing about the baking." She turned away when an attempt to smile again didn't quite come off.

"Does your mum bake?"

"My mum was never any good in the kitchen."

"What about your gran? I remember you saying you spent a lot of time with her growing up."

"Gran's a great cook but she's not so big on baking." Jenna took a cookie when it was offered and examined it closely through one eye, relieved to have something else to focus on. "What's so special about your aunt's biscuits?"

"Depends which biscuits we're talking about," Abi explained as she took another cookie for herself and held it up for inspection. "With these, she manages to get just the right mix of crispy and chewy."

"I'll be the judge of that."

Abi motioned as if to say *be my guest*, and Jenna ripped the cookie in half, noting a satisfying amount of goo inside. "These are amazing," she murmured as she took a bite and a large chunk of partially melted chocolate glued itself to the roof of her mouth. "Do you think she'd give me the recipe?"

"She doesn't need to because I have it. Maybe I'll bake them for you some time."

*In those work boots? Two guilty pleasures.*

Jenna laughed and almost lodged a second mouthful of cookie in her windpipe. She spluttered and banged the middle of her chest, as Abi looked on with a mixture of concern and confusion. "Sorry," she croaked, once she could just about breathe again. "I'm not laughing at... never mind."

"Come on," Abi said with a smile as she nudged Jenna's foot with her boot. "What's so funny?"

"Nothing. Really. Seeing you has just corrected everything wrong with my evening." That wasn't the full truth but it was as much as she was willing to say.

"Don't I always make your world better?"

There was another burst of laughter, but Jenna couldn't disagree, and not only because she was busy stuffing herself with the rest of the cookie.

3

**ABI**

"Don't say a word," Abi warned as she stepped onto Ida's driveway on Sunday morning and bent to tie the laces of her Timberlands. She'd already endured the same discussion three times and it wore as thin as the tattered string holding together her boots. "I'm totally capable of helping you. I'm not an invalid."

"I didn't say anything," Stanley replied, grunting and stacking the bag of cement in his arms in front of the garage. He returned for another but paused and frowned at Abi when she strode to the back of the van and lifted the same load. "This is going to be a lot more demanding than mowing the lawns, though, and you've got a football match to play today on top of whatever we do this morning. Don't tire yourself out."

Correction, she *might* have a football match to play. Being selected for the squad didn't guarantee getting on the pitch. She'd WhatsApped Jenna on Friday evening and they'd joked that 'of course' Abi would play because the team couldn't function without her, but that was bullshit. It functioned perfectly fine without her and there was only an issue the other way round.

"If I can't carry a couple of bags of sand and cement, I've no chance of running around a football pitch."

"You're worried about this game, aren't you?" Stanley's serious expression mellowed when Abi's only reply was a withering look, and he rubbed his eyes with his thumb and forefinger. "Christ, I just had flashbacks to when you were fourteen and I asked if you had a crush on that girl from football summer camp. What was her name? Daisy, or Deirdre or something."

"Deirdre?! I have never in all my life had a crush on a Deirdre. That's your own past you're raking up. Wasn't she the woman you were with before Ma?"

"Hey, keep it down! She'll go berserk and I'm on the rare promise of a fry-up."

"Because of someone you dated almost forty years ago. Really?" Abi laughed as Stanley ducked, his eyes fixed on the net curtains in case they twitched.

"Your mother's a very passionate woman."

"Oh God, too much information." Abi screwed up her face and stuck two fingers down her throat to emphasise her disgust. Finding a well-worn copy of 'The Joy of Sex' in the bookcase next to her bed had provided enough insight into their marriage, and she didn't need any further detail.

Mercifully, Stanley dropped it and they continued working in silence until they'd unloaded all the bags. Then they sat on the back of the van and Abi shielded her eyes against the late morning sun. There was a lot to lament since she'd moved in with her parents, but she'd never regret getting to spend more time with her dad, even if he occasionally embarrassed or grossed her out.

"You know," Stanley mused. "You won't like this, but you have a tendency to go for women who are a bit like your mum."

"Oh no, don't go there."

"It's true. Strong, confident—"

"Overbearing?" Abi offered, and there were a lot of other options besides. Petra had always struggled to cope with a daughter who spent her teenage years on building sites with bricklayers called Barry. Her youngest had boyfriends and pregnancy scares for them to bond over, but she didn't know where she was with women and football. The gulf in interests was a wide one to bridge and, despite being well intentioned, Petra often misdirected her efforts.

Stanley provided the soft buffer between them and, as usual, only laughed as he unscrewed the cap on his Thermos. Even ten feet from a functional kitchen, he was never without a flask of tea. "You can't deny you like a woman who makes a fuss over you, love. That last one was also a bit of a feeder, just like your mum." When Abi grumbled, the laughter stopped and his tone became more earnest. "You're still not over her, are you?"

"I'm over *her*. I'm just not sure I'm over what she did. I don't understand why she agreed to move in and then changed her mind."

"The first lockdown pushed lots of people to move quicker than they wanted. If she wasn't ready, it was for the best. You might have to accept that you'll never understand exactly what happened."

Abi shuffled on the boards lining the floor of the van. She knew that, but it was hard not to wonder. If her ex had taken the plunge, circumstances would've been different and Abi might not have struggled so much, then ended up living in her old bedroom. Alone and wondering what she'd done wrong. Or as alone as you could ever be with Petra around.

"Suppose," she muttered finally, unsure why she was struggling to let this one go. Dwelling on failed relationships wasn't usually her style.

"Is there anyone on the horizon at the moment?"

"Can't imagine I'm going to attract the woman of my dreams

while I'm living with you. No offence." The idea of sex with Petra and Stanley at it on the other side of the wall would not be a turn on for the average thirty-something, and if it was, they had bigger problems.

"You probably won't like this either, but your mother's always thought you should go after Jax."

The comment pulled Abi from her malaise so quickly that she almost snorted because they were a match made in the depths of hell. Jax didn't get close to anyone romantically, while in that regard, Abi would confess to being exactly like her parents.

"Please, please, please keep Ma away from Jax when she picks me up for the game later," Abi begged, although she knew it was futile. Once Petra had an idea about something, neither empirical evidence nor common sense would budge her.

Stanley wrapped an arm around Abi's shoulder and gave her a quick squeeze. "No can do, sorry. There's tea and cake ready to go."

"She must be desperate to impress if she's gone into quintessential English housewife mode. She knows Jax is American, right?" The thought of Jax enduring tea with Petra was almost comical. Abi let out a delirious laugh—it was all she could do. "At least after the eighteen months we've had, I can say stranger things happen."

"If you can survive three lockdowns, your business drying up, and then a mixture of Covid and asthma trying to finish you off altogether, you can survive a bit of cake with your mum. She means well."

Released from Stanley's grip, Abi scooted away and swung her legs as she stared at the ground. "I know she does, but I'm losing count of how many times I've reminded myself of that over the past eight months. It must be into the high thousands now." She didn't want to appear ungrateful. If her parents hadn't taken her in at Christmas after her income evaporated, or looked after her when she fell ill, she didn't know where she'd be. It was just an overwhelming experience after living independently for well over a decade. "I just wish Ma could... relax. Give me a bit of space and not fuss. I know it's only because she cares, but it's too much sometimes."

"Wait until you've got kids of your own. I'll remind you of this conversation when you're ringing me up frantic because you're in A&E with a broken nose and the school's writing home about detentions or, worse still, suspensions." He raised his eyebrows and glanced sideways.

"That was one time!" Abi reminded him, and it was all a big misunderstanding. Sort of. "Besides," she continued, letting out a wistful sigh. "I'm not sure I'll ever have kids now. When you reach your thirties, you find that maintaining a long-term relationship is harder than TV would have you believe. Let alone any of the rest of it."

Stanley chuckled. "Hark at her, thirty-three and over the hill."

"I didn't say I was over the hill, did I? I'm only pointing out that even now, most people I know are still bouncing from one disaster to the next." Her mind returned to Jax, who had so many notches in her bedpost that she'd reduced it to a pile of sawdust. Then there was Jenna. Her relationships lasted longer than Jax's, but there was always some sort of drama going on. It was a pattern of heartbreak and little wonder she'd given up. "Everyone walks away so easily these days. I guess it's because they can just pick up someone else. We're all disposable commodities."

"Unlike in my day, when you got a girl pregnant and stood by that mistake in abject misery for the rest of your life. Yes, those truly were better times."

"Get lost! You love Ma. You'd have to, or you wouldn't put up with her hiding your crisps."

"Yeah, alright," he conceded. "Your mother suffered terrible homesickness, though. Especially after you were born."

Abi frowned. "What's that got to do with anything?"

"I know you think we've always had it easy, but we haven't." Stanley paused for a sip of tea, then tipped the dregs on the ground and screwed the cup back onto his Thermos. "Long term relationships take work. You have to step up, even at two o'clock in the morning with a new-born screaming the house down and a wife crying because she wants money for a flight to Spain when you're barely covering the mortgage." He smiled, as if the memory were now one that he treasured. Then he jumped down from the van. "Please don't waste time obsessing over someone who turned out not to be right for you because it was better to know that sooner rather than later. Besides, it's not *her* you miss, and we both know it."

There was a lot to unpick, and Abi's frown returned; she wasn't sure where to start with his jumble of advice. "When have I ever been afraid of hard work?"

"Never, and it's a good job because I need those bags carried around the back now. Hop to it."

\* \* \*

With the job complete, they headed home, and Abi ran upstairs to change into her team tracksuit. Then she wandered back downstairs and into the kitchen, where the smell of lard greeted her. It was good to see they'd all stuck to their family pact of helping Stanley reduce his high cholesterol.

"Brunch is ready!" Petra called in a tone so shrill that it almost shattered the windows.

Abi peered into four pans containing eight rashers of bacon, six sausages, three fried eggs, two slices of fried bread, mushrooms, tomatoes, baked beans, and what looked like it might once have been black pudding. Then she grinned as she searched for any Spanish influences, like a few slices of chorizo hidden under the rest of the meat. It was a game Petra had played with Stanley for years.

"That's sweet, Ma," she said, prodding at a rasher of bacon and then snatching away her finger when the fat popped. "But you know I can't eat all this greasy food before a match."

"Nonsense!"

It was another situation where arguing was futile, so Abi resigned herself to pulling out a chair. The kitchen had a small dining area and butted up against the wall nearest the door was a rectangular table, which Petra had already set with a wipe clean cloth. On it was a jug of fresh orange juice, a pot of tea, a rack of toast, and a neatly folded copy of the Sunday paper.

As Stanley came racing through the front door, rubbing his hands together with glee, he vocalised what Abi was thinking: "You spoil me."

"Yes, she does," Abi agreed under her breath.

"Will your friend..." Petra began, her eyes rolling up and her arm making a circular motion as she pretended to search for Jax's name. Then she clicked her fingers. "Jax! That's it. Will Jax want something to eat?"

"I don't think she'll have time. She needs to set up for the match."

"Very nice of her to collect you."

"Mhm."

"And she dates women, yes?"

"Not if she can help it. And before you say anything else, Jax is just a friend."

Petra slid a plate of fried meat in front of Abi and set another down for Stanley. "A friend, yes." She stepped away, but only as far as the cake on a wooden board next to the cooker. She lifted it onto a glass stand and stood back to survey it, then tilted her head and frowned, wiping away the trail of jam that'd dared ooze from its middle. "All the best marriages start with friendship."

"I'm sure they do, but—"

At the sound of the doorbell, Petra strode down the hallway, whipping off her apron to reveal an immaculate emerald dress. It was showtime, and Abi's stomach twisted as she braced herself for what would ensue. But when Petra returned a few moments later, she was the one who looked crestfallen, the apron limp in her hand.

"No Jax," she declared.

The relief allowed Abi's stomach to unclench, but when she looked up and saw who was standing in the doorway, it dropped into her arse. "What are *you* doing here?" she asked in a far more accusatory tone than on Thursday night. It was a whole different ball game when Petra was around and in matchmaking mode.

"That's nice." Jenna folded her arms and rested sideways against the door frame, not seeming to take it personally. "I come out of my way to pick you up, and this is how I'm greeted."

"But... Jax?"

"She had something to do. Or some*one*. It's always tough to know with her."

Abi covered her mouth to stop a laugh from escaping when Petra's jaw dropped in shock. It must be a blow to find Jax wasn't the dream daughter-in-law she'd imagined.

Petra's expression fell to a frown as she appraised Jenna, only averting her eyes momentarily to snap a lid down over her cake. Then she threw the apron onto the work surface and began preparing her own food.

Stanley offered a warm smile to make up for it and pushed out the chair next to him. "Don't hang around out there," he encouraged, beckoning Jenna over. "Pull up a pew."

"Thanks, Stanley." Jenna finally moved out of the doorway. She didn't sit, though, instead sneaking a sausage from Abi's plate. With it pressed to her lips, she looked down and smiled apologetically. "I get nervous before a match. It makes me eat. Once before a cup game, I went through an entire tray of chocolate fingers."

"Don't worry about it," Abi replied as she surveyed the mountain of food and her stomach gurgled pre-emptively. "I can't manage all of this myself, so go wild."

There were five cardboard boxes stacked behind Stanley, and Jenna pointed to them with the end of her sausage. "Are these the leaflets you messaged me about on Friday? What on earth do you plan to do with them?"

"I'll drop them through doors, of course." Abi stood, quite happy to take a break from her fry up. Unlike Jenna, stress had the opposite effect on her appetite. "I considered attaching them to carrier pigeons," she continued, flicking open the top box to reveal a glimpse of the contents. "But I decided that was a bit old fashioned, so I'll do it myself."

"Isn't putting leaflets through doors old fashioned, too? Most people stick them straight in the bin. Plus, it's terrible for the environment."

"Thank you, Greta Thunberg. Most of my customers *are* old school."

"But I thought you didn't have any customers," Jenna delivered matter-of-factly. It stung, but at least she was focusing on Abi's failures as a businesswoman, rather than on her deeper emotional issues. That was a relief after the shirt meltdown on Wednesday night. "It might be time to reach out to a different market. There are hundreds of new houses going up around the edge of town, all belonging to remote workers who've moved away from the city to enjoy their outside space. You get me?" She pulled out a leaflet and dangled it between the thumb and forefinger of her free hand, a look of pure disgust on her face. "Who designed these for you?"

"I did, and don't cover them in grease." Abi snatched the sheet and held it against her chest. She'd spent hours in front of her laptop, finding the right mix of clipart and bold typefaces.

"Why didn't you speak to Jax?" Sighing demonstratively at Abi's blank stare, Jenna sat down next to Stanley and licked the grease from her fingers. "You need to leverage your contacts. I can't believe one of your closest friends is a designer who would've given you a discount, and you still tried to do it yourself."

A discount was fine, but Abi had very little free cash to throw around. A small portion of her savings remained, but that evaporated with every fault they found with the van, and she needed the rest if she ever wanted her own place again. "I don't know." She stroked the leaflet and laid it back in the box, then returned to her seat. "I've ordered them now. What do you suggest I do instead?"

"Start by telling me what your grand plan is, then I can give you some pointers."

There wasn't so much of a grand plan as a vague half formed one. Abi had never been great at this part of things. Most of her former customers had been with her for years, and she'd gained new business through word of mouth.

"I don't have one," she admitted. "So far, all I've done is order the leaflets. I was going to drop them this week."

"I'm guessing that most of your clients come back because you do a good job." Jenna slipped her phone from her pocket, then peered over the device and waited for Abi to give an affirmative nod before her thumbs began to whizz over the screen. "Great, so we need to harness that. A Facebook page is free, and there are loads of local groups we can link you into. People will also be able to see all the great ratings you're going to get."

After a few moments more of tapping, her tongue sticking out to the side a little, she turned the phone to show a new Facebook page. She'd already shared it with all her contacts, and it had six likes. That wasn't bad in thirty seconds, and Abi was quietly impressed.

"I don't have a Facebook account," she pointed out cautiously, knowing it would win her another sigh. "How am I meant to keep it updated?"

"When you get home from the game, you're going to set one up so I can make you an admin. And later we're speaking to Jax about getting you a decent logo to go on here." Noticing Abi was about to protest, Jenna gave her a stern look. "How much did you spend on those leaflets? Just say *yes, Jenna*. This is an investment in your business, the same as the leaflets. Sometimes you have to speculate—"

"To accumulate," Abi cut in, grabbing her mug of tea and smirking over the top. "Where did you get that revolutionary insight, Harvard Business School?"

"Don't get smart with me when I'm trying to help. The logo is a no-brainer given how awful your current one is, but we need to think properly before you lay out any more money. There's no point in expending resources on marketing with no measurable outcomes."

Jenna was hot in business mode; never had the words 'measurable outcomes' been such a turn on. Her eyes sparkled when she was in full flow, revealing every hue of brown and the little flecks of green. They were the best eyes Abi had ever seen, full of warmth and fun, but she had to divert her interest to the floor under the table when Jenna leant forward again. She actually wanted a response this time.

"Um—" Abi ventured, scuffing her foot over a splash of tea.

"Um? I think what you mean, once again, is *yes, Jenna*."

"Yes, Jenna. Absolutely. Whatever you say."

"That's more like it." Something caught Jenna's eye and she stared through the open back door, her head tilting as she smiled. "Did you do your parents' garden? It's great."

"Oh, yeah," Abi replied casually. She took a sip of tea and turned her head to follow Jenna's gaze down the path through borders of roses to Stanley's raised vegetable beds. It was one of the first projects she'd tackled in her late teens. "I've been giving it the once over. Getting back in the game."

Jenna's smile was now accompanied by a little raise of her eyebrows. "On that note, we should get going in a minute."

Stanley's cutlery clattered on the side of his plate, then he pushed out his chair and rushed to the kettle. "Hang on a sec. If you're going, I'll make you each a Thermos."

"Thanks, but that really isn't necessary." Abi put down her mug, then rubbed her forehead as Jenna sniggered.

"Don't be daft." He was already grabbing the box of tea bags from the cupboard, quickly followed by two Thermos flasks from his vast collection. "It's no trouble."

Putting her dad to any trouble wasn't Abi's objection, but she couldn't say any more before Jenna jumped in.

"Two sugars please!"

"You are *so* not funny," Abi mouthed.

"Alright, calm down," Jenna mouthed back. "We've got a match to win." She grabbed Abi's fork as she stood, spearing some mushrooms and then wedging them all in her mouth. "Finish your food. We need to leave or we'll be late."

Abi glanced at the clock on the wall and let out a burst of laughter. They had loads of time and she suspected Jenna only wanted an excuse to steal her fry up. She also realised that, for the first time in her life, she hadn't even considered whether they would win.

4

## JENNA

A few paces from Cass's front door, Jenna stopped short and took a swig of her tea. Then she waved for the electronic video doorbell Cass had insisted on installing after her neighbours twigged that she was still working from home a lot and started having packages delivered there. Ever community minded, she refused to become a Royal Mail depot.

"What are we doing here?" Abi asked, her hands shoved into the pockets of her tracksuit bottoms.

She looked uncomfortable, which Jenna knew was because she'd never liked Cass, but she needed to get over it sharpish. They were here because Cass wanted to employ a gardener, and she was just the type of client Abi should be after. Personal differences didn't come into it.

"This is why we needed to leave early. I realised on the way to your place that I can get you an easy win on the work front, so take your hands out of your pockets and look like a professional gardener."

"I *am* a professional gardener."

"I know you are, so relax. This will be a piece of cake."

The door opened and Cass's lithe body filled the frame. She

was never one to slob out, even at home, and wore a loose white shirt on top of impossibly well pressed chinos. The streak of grey which usually ran through the front of her pixie cut was gone, though, and Jenna offered her a smile of recognition. "Hair looks good. Had it done?" *And by someone else?*

"Thank you. I have."

Cass returned the smile as she slipped on her running trainers from the rack next to the door. She never twigged when she might have caused offence. Not that she had on this occasion; it was a good thing if she was going elsewhere to have her hair cut. After five months, give or take a few slip ups in the early days when they were lonely, it felt like they'd finally both moved on. So did Cass's agreement to let Abi quote, because the frostiness wasn't entirely one way.

"Probably easiest if I take you around the side," Cass continued, clicking the door shut and then gesturing towards the wrought iron gate to the right of the house. When they were all on the other side, she creaked it shut and followed down the passageway. "It's good of you to come out on a Sunday. When Jen mentioned you were working again, I couldn't miss the opportunity. I've done nothing with the garden since before lockdown and it's in a terrible state."

Cass's house was on the end of a row of Victorian terraces and there was only a small patch of patio at the front, but the rear garden stretched all the way down to the railway line. The grass was lush but far too long, and poking from it were a family of gnomes with faded red hats and chipped faces.

Cass took a few steps forward and crouched beside one. "I thought these would cheer up the place. I was rather pleased with them, but they're looking neglected now. It'll be good to have them back to their former glory."

"Can't beat a gnome," Jenna whispered under her breath. *But only because they don't fight back*. She'd always hated the bloody things; they creeped her out.

Abi waded through the grass and inspected the bushes at the end of the lawn. "It won't take much to have this whole garden back to its former glory," she called up to them. "Have you ever thought about doing something more with this space? A pergola, maybe?" She ran her hand through the foliage, then bent to stroke a tabby cat sunbathing in a barren patch, but soon shot up when a branch poked her bum.

Cass frowned. "Sorry. My bushes really are in an unruly state. It's not like me to let things get so overgrown down there."

Jenna bit her lip as she made eye contact with Abi and noted she'd done the same. After telling her to be professional, they could hardly both fall apart over a bit of innuendo.

Abi wandered up the lawn. Her hands had found their way back into her pockets but she was smiling now, so she could get away with it. "Don't apologise. I'd have no work if everyone had the time to do this themselves."

"Would you like *this* work?" Cass asked with a hopeful lilt in her voice.

"Definitely. I can drop you a written quote through the door tomorrow and if it's acceptable, I'm free to start... well, whenever."

Jenna almost winced after dressing up the situation to make Abi sound a little less desperate. If she had no other work, she might be beaten down on her prices or regarded as inferior by anyone who didn't know the situation.

Thankfully, Cass took it in stride and didn't openly do either. "Great, I'm sure it'll be fine. I don't suppose you'd be able to come next Saturday? I need to be in the office most of this week, so won't be around for access to power sockets or water until then, but I'd like to get it done ASAP."

"Saturday it is."

"Perfect." Cass took a few steps towards the back door. "Come and help me with the drinks," she instructed, beckoning for Jenna to join her.

Resisting the urge to salute, Jenna left Abi to continue inspecting the tubs on the patio and followed Cass into the kitchen. She leant against the work surface and sipped her tea, already anticipating what this was really about and happy to cut to the chase rather than prolong her scolding. Every time they spoke recently, they seemed to end up in conflict. "I take it you want to ask me about the contracts?"

"Yes," Cass replied, rummaging around in the fridge. "Have you looked over them? We really need to get those signed if you want to be in by the end of the month, and given speed was one of the selling points with which I got you a discounted rate on the lease..."

She didn't finish her sentence, but Jenna got the gist. No stalling or it would make Cass look bad after she'd put together a good deal. Plus, the landlord was an old client turned friend, as everyone Cass knew seemed to be, so it was doubly important not to rock the boat. Not that Jenna intended to, it just added a layer of pressure.

"I meant to take them home to read on Friday but they're still under a pile of paperwork in my office. I'll get to them tomorrow, I promise."

"You know, for someone who's talked about opening another shop for all the time I've known her, you do seem to be dropping the ball a lot."

Jenna took a deep breath, composing herself to keep from sounding snippy. She wasn't stalling. Getting a business back up and running after a global pandemic had shut it down for months had been a big undertaking. Things were almost back to normal now, with a full book of appointments, but it had still given Jenna pause for thought. The new shop would be bigger and involve more overheads than the first, and while she wanted to progress, it was still a little scary.

"That's unfair. There's just been a lot on, and I want to get this right."

Cass shut the fridge door and set a lemon on the work surface next to Jenna, followed by three cans of artisanal lemonade. "I'm sorry you feel attacked, but can you make sure you definitely find the time tomorrow? I'm being chased and I know I'll have another call by the end of the week."

"I'm sorry if you're getting it in the neck. That was never my intention."

Considering their business concluded, Jenna set down her Thermos and took three glasses from the cupboard, knowing Cass would never serve drinks straight from the can. She poured out the lemonade while Cass ran up the stairs, presumably to use the bathroom, but she hadn't said, and Jenna didn't really care enough to ask. Now that she had what they'd come for, she just wanted to get out of there as fast as possible.

When Jenna stepped onto the patio, Abi pulled out a chair at the garden table but became distracted by a large pot full of brightly coloured flowers. Like Stanley had done, she gently ran her fingers through, as if she could instinctively feel for anything that was out of place.

"You seem really happy when you're talking gardens." Jenna took the seat opposite and smiled as Abi continued, finding and extracting more weeds than flowers the further she rooted around.

"Are you the same at work? Is trimming beards what you always wanted to do?"

Jenna considered for a second, but she wasn't sure how to answer that honestly. She loved being her own boss, but she wouldn't say that male grooming was a particular passion. "My school offered a choice between vocational courses in childcare, football coaching, and hairdressing. My grandad said I needed to be practical and go where there were most job opportunities, so I picked hairdressing and then supplemented that with a barbering course. To be fair, he was right, because no matter what happens we'll never be replaced with robots."

"My dad used to say the exact same thing," Abi replied, finally sitting down and bashing some dirt from her hands. "It's why he wanted me to be a builder, like him."

"I could see you as a builder. Put those muscles," and with that Jenna leant over, squeezing the top of Abi's arm, "to good use."

"Hey, I put them to good use landscaping." Abi flexed her bicep, which Jenna happily took as an opportunity to run her hand over it again. "My dad was excited about the idea, but I was more interested in gardens than building extensions."

"Did Stanley lose his shit like my grandad when you tried to argue about making a career of it?"

"Why did your grandad lose his shit, if you agreed with him?"

Laughing, Jenna diverted her gaze to the floor. "Well, I mean..." She looked up again. "I may not have agreed with him at the time. Where would be the fun in that?"

Abi also laughed but it stopped dead when she took a swig of her drink, her face contorting as if she'd just sucked a bag of lemons. She swallowed and went to speak again but then her mouth clamped shut. After a few moments, she murmured, "Mmm, lovely."

"Liar," Jenna whispered, laughing when Abi tried to discreetly spit the drink back into her glass.

They were still giggling when Cass returned with her iPad tucked under her arm and a glass of lemonade in hand. "Have I missed something?"

"Nope." Abi made eye contact with Jenna, then bit her bottom lip.

There was silence for a few moments as Cass set her iPad and glass on the table, then made herself comfy in a chair. It gave Jenna a chance to consider some conversation starters because she knew she'd need to be the facilitator. This was going to be odd, though, the three of them sat around exchanging pleasantries. It was a good job Abi and Jenna needed to leave for the game soon; the experience would be time limited.

"So," she began, with no idea where she was taking this. All conversations with Cass led back to work, and with Abi they usually revolved around football. Maybe they should have politely declined the drink and left, not that Cass had given them the option. "Abi, what happens in your house when England play Spain?" It was football related but she'd drawn a blank. "Do you get stuck in the middle?"

"No, I stay as far away as possible," Abi replied.

"Why, do your parents fight?"

"Worse. They flirt. Like crazy."

"Aww, that's sweet! Your parents are really lovely." It was unfathomable to still feel that sort of connection after so many years, but the thought was reassuring and heartwarming all the same. Maybe there was some hope.

They chatted about Abi's parents and how nauseating Abi found them for a few minutes but then ran out of steam. Finding herself back to square one conversation wise, Jenna drummed her fingers on the arm of her chair, trying to come up with something else. She was still thinking when Cass beat her to it.

"I was so sorry to hear you'd been ill. It must have been dreadful."

Abi shuffled in her seat and it made the hairs stand up on the backs of Jenna's arms. She was adept at detecting a change of atmosphere at twenty paces and felt the rapid grip of panic, propelling her bolt upright. Cass was probably the last person in the world Abi would want to discuss this with, and there was only one way Jenna could think of to diffuse the situation. "I hate to cut this party short, but we should probably get going." She glanced down at her watch and pretended to read the time. "I hadn't realised how late it is and I promised Jax we'd help set up the goals."

Abi pushed out her chair and stood up when Jenna did, then downed a few gulps of lemonade. "Thanks for the drink."

Cass looked just as relieved not to have to socialise and picked up her iPad, no doubt to work. "I won't hold you up." She glanced at Abi. "I'll look out for your quote tomorrow and see you next Saturday." Then she turned to Jenna. "And I'll expect to hear from you in the next couple of days, too."

Jenna waited for a few moments to see if Cass would follow that up with even a half-hearted good luck for the game, but she knew it wasn't coming. Her lack of interest in anything important to Jenna outside the realms of work had always been a sore point whilst they were together but it didn't matter anymore. Cass was Cass, and it was best to accept her as she was, which meant thanking her for the work and then focusing on what was important. They'd got the job done and secured one win. Now it really was time to go after another.

## 5

## ABI

Abi stood in the changing room and tugged on the sleeve of her shirt, which was a fraction too small. The number eleven would fit fine, of course, but it was being worn by an eighteen-year-old. Not that it was wise to bemoan that fact. All she could do was keep a neutral expression and try to hide how much it had rattled her.

"Bloody thing," she muttered, wriggling under the fabric and pulling the hem down over her shorts to stretch it. She was so focused that a tap on her shoulder made her jump, and she spun around, almost taking her eye out on a peg.

"Have you got any tape?"

Abi reached into her bag, pulling out the roll and throwing it at Jenna. "You didn't have enough time to buy your own in the months and months we had off?"

Jenna only smiled and put her foot on the bench as she wrapped tape around her sock to keep her shin guard in place. "Nope. Besides, stealing from you is a ritual. It contributes to my success."

"Yeah, I know a thing or two about those." Abi pulled on her sleeve again until the thread snapped and eased its grip on her bicep. Then she stuffed her tracksuit bottoms and T-shirt hard into her bag.

"Y'know, it's possible you'll be even luckier in that shirt. Remind me when the last time was that you scored a goal...?"

"Sod off."

"Sore."

"I'm not sore."

"Are."

"Not!"

"Ladies!" Jax yelled over the din in the changing room. "I hate to bring this meeting of minds to an end when you're on the verge of curing cancer but sit down so I can go through the team."

This was the part Abi had been dreading. She parked her bum on the bench and fumbled with the roll of tape when Jenna handed it back to her. Anything to refocus her mind on appearing unconcerned when Jax reeled off the line-up, and she wasn't in it. She knew she wouldn't be. It made total sense. She needed time after being ill, but once again, knowing something and feeling it were two different things. Just as she knew that Jenna getting her a job with Cass could be a real positive, didn't mean it felt that way. It only reminded her that Cass had a tonne more money, her own home, and a full-time job that would keep her busy the whole week.

Abi tried to zone out and forget about it while Jax explained what she was doing with the defence. Then, as they moved onto the midfield formation, her heart rate sped up and her eyes dropped to the changing room floor. She stared at a clump of mud next to Jenna's boot until Jax finished reading out the team, omitting her name. She was a sub for the first time in her Sunday league career, and the confirmation felt like someone had kicked a ball hard at her stomach.

"Let's go, Blues!" Jax shouted, before tossing the changing room keys at Abi and asking her to lock up.

Abi grabbed her hoody from a peg, wrapping it around herself and zipping it to the top. Then she checked her inhaler was in the pocket, trudged across the tiles, and stepped down onto the patio. For a few moments, she watched everyone else hit balls at the goal and tried to find some enthusiasm or encouragement. Being a team player usually came easily, but it was taking an unprecedented amount of effort.

When she finally made her way to the sideline, Jax shook Abi's shoulders and then straightened out her sleeves, as if she were about to wave off a child on their first day of school. "Make sure you keep warm. I want you on after the first twenty. Left back."

"Left *back*? Defence? But I've never played defence in my life."

"Yes, left back. I wouldn't put you there if I didn't think you could handle it. Total faith."

"Not so sure about that," Abi replied quietly. She supposed she had wished to get on the pitch. It was only a shame every opportunity came with a big *but* stapled onto it somewhere. All she could do was what she always did—put in the hard graft and pray for a bit of luck. It had to pay off at some point.

When Jax made the sub, Abi was still trying to convince herself. She swallowed hard against a wave of nausea and balled her fists. Then she focused, listening to the calls from beside her in the centre of defence and trying to work out where she should be. For the first five minutes, though, it wasn't enough. Sometimes, no amount of hard work made up for complete ineptitude. Or trembling so much that you fluffed a pass and gave away a throw.

"Are you okay?" Jenna mouthed from the halfway line.

Abi nodded, but that nod was a lie. She wasn't okay. She was failing, and everyone could see it. Just as they would see if she fell apart, because there was no toilet to run into now. She had no protection and nowhere to hide.

"Come on," she urged herself as the opposition winger lumbered down the line. She was slow, which was rare for a winger, and it meant Abi could match her for pace. That was something, at least, and might give her a chance to prove to Jax that letting her play wasn't a catastrophic mistake, if she could translate the advantage.

When the winger tried to knock the ball past her, Abi anticipated it this time and got a foot in, putting the ball out for another throw but stopping her from ending up one-on-one with the keeper. It was enough, and it won her a cheer from the sideline.

For a while she kept it up, surviving even if she didn't thrive in the position, until she saw an opportunity to break free and move higher up the pitch. One of the opposition defenders got cocky and took a run but didn't have the skill to back it up, so Abi stood off and stole the ball instead of diving in, pushing forward while they were out of position. This was her chance to show what she could really do, and she was going to take it.

Carried forward by a rush of adrenaline, she hammered down the wing, glancing to where she knew Jenna would be. They'd played together so many times that even after an eighteen month hiatus, Abi could intuit Jenna's next move.

Sure enough, Abi looked over again and saw Jenna making a run off the last defender. She hit the cross, aiming just behind the defence, but her legs were tired and she scuffed the ball slightly so that it only reached the opposition right back, not Jenna.

*Shit.*

With the score nil-nil and only a few minutes left before

half-time, Abi panicked. She'd lost possession and was now the one who'd left a massive gap.

"Fuck, fuck, fuck," she muttered as she sprinted back as fast as her legs would carry her. She gritted her teeth and committed every ounce of strength to catching up, but was still a few metres behind the winger when she received a pass that would play her in, just before the edge of the eighteen-yard box.

Through on goal, and with The Blues' heavyset centre back thumping across in a losing battle to cover, the player twisted right and Abi saw a way to stop her. She knew she had to go for it, because her lungs were burning and her calves were tightening as they prepared to cramp. If she didn't act now, she had no chance, and might even end up giving away a penalty, so she tucked her right leg under herself, lunged forward, hooked her left foot around, and aimed for the ball.

The next thing she knew, she hit the ground with a thud, and all she could hear was the faint wheeze from her own chest. She rolled over and rubbed it, relieved to find the tightness easing as she regained her breath. The very last thing she needed today was an asthma attack. But as the adrenaline faded, the repercussions dawned and flooded her stomach with familiar nausea, because the winger was also on the floor and clutching her ankle. The calm broke as the opposition yelled obscenities, and all the colour drained from Abi's face.

"Oh shit, are you alright?" she stuttered out.

The opposition manager ran across the pitch with a medical bag in hand and arrived before she got an answer. Not that Abi needed one. This wasn't the Premier League and players didn't roll around on the floor for effect—she was in pain.

"What the fuck were you doing?" yelled the opposition centre back as she towered over Abi and nudged her in the ribs with a boot. "Huh?"

"It was an accident, I didn't mean to hurt her!"

"Fuck off. No way was that unintentional!" The centre back kicked harder, this time going for Abi's leg and forcing her to roll out of the way. "You can dish it out but you can't take it. What a surprise!"

Jenna arrived, shoving the girl hard in the back so that she stumbled forward and then turned to square up. "Hey, leave her alone!"

"Get lost, Blondie. As if you're gonna do anything."

"Try me."

Abi jumped off the floor with surprising athleticism the minute Jenna was in peril, but she didn't have time to do anything because the ref came over to deliver the final blow. It was a knock-out punch which forced her eyes closed in shame, but not before she glimpsed at a red card. It was another first for her Sunday league career.

"You got what you deserved there," the centre back sneered.

Abi opened her eyes again to find the opposition manager propping up his injured player, supporting her to stand on one leg. They hobbled away without saying any more, so Abi stuck her hands on top of her head and did the same. The ref wanted to resume the game and she needed to leave the pitch.

Jax stared blankly as Abi walked towards her, but shrugged when she reached the sideline. "Well, at least she didn't score. That's good, right? You successfully defended."

"Could've gone better, though. Couldn't it?"

"Perhaps, but you'll be alright. We've still got a couple of weeks before the season starts. Time to get in some more training."

Would she be alright? Because right now, Abi didn't want to see a football pitch again in her life. Not unless it was being streamed in glorious 4K resolution to the new television in the clubhouse. "We'll see."

"That's the spirit. Sort of."

"No. I mean, we'll see if I play this season."

Jax turned to watch the game, but then twisted back and frowned. "You're joking, right?"

"I could've seriously injured her."

"It's a contact sport!"

Even so, there was contact and there was... that. They occasionally faced players who were aggressive or dangerous, and it was usually because of a lack of skill. Abi didn't want to join them. "I'm ashamed of myself. Honestly. I didn't set a good example in front of the youngsters. Maybe this is proof that I wasn't ready to come back yet."

"Don't you think you're overreacting? It wasn't entirely your fault; someone should've covered your run properly. Besides, there was no harm done. Just get back on it in a couple of weeks."

Jax threw the changing room keys at Abi, who grabbed her hoody and slunk off in their direction. Was she overreacting? It was one thing if she was struggling in her own head, but she was certain it was another when it started hurting others. She was also sure Jax wouldn't have let anyone else off that easily, and she hated getting preferential treatment.

Abi let herself into the changing room and slumped onto the bench. The wall was cool on her back, and she rested her head on the whitewashed brick. For a few minutes she sat in silence, bar the muffled shouts from outside, and counted dead flies on the ceiling. It was a comfort to find they'd missed a spot when cleaning.

Her concentration only broke when Jenna appeared in the doorway, breathless and pink. "Are you alright? It's half-time. I just wanted to check."

"You forgot your sweets, right?" Abi managed a small smile and shuffled, slipping off her boots and storing them back in her bag. She was stalling, unsure what to say. She felt like she'd been lying about, or at least concealing, how *not* alright she was for months. "I'm—"

"Struggling?"

Jenna had hit the nail on the head. She was always adept at cutting through the crap, and Abi nodded. "Right."

"If you need to talk, I'm here."

"Yeah?"

Jenna took a few steps forward and joined Abi on the bench. "Yep. And Jax is, too. We were both really worried when you were ill."

"I was pretty worried as well," Abi admitted. She felt the hard press of tears and willed them to go away. It was one thing having a little heart to heart, but she didn't want Jenna to see that. Despite what she said, she didn't seem to want to talk about it at all, which was probably Abi's fault for shutting her out for months. She'd shut *everyone* out, besides Jax and her dad, so she could hardly expect anyone to want to hear about it now.

When Jenna reached into her bag and held up two packets of sweets, Abi seized the opportunity—literally—by grabbing the Haribo Starmix from her. It was all she could think of to divert attention away from herself and regroup. "I reckon you should let me have all my favourites since it's my first game back and it's gone so badly. Only fair."

"What's fair is you getting your own sweets."

Jenna's palm slid up Abi's quad as she tried to snatch the packet and almost fell forward. It added arousal to an already jumbled mix of emotions, and Abi sprung off the bench. Usually she enjoyed sparring with Jenna, but right now, she was on a knife's edge. "I'll bring my own sweets when you buy your own tape."

"It's hardly the same thing!"

Jenna stood and strained for the bag. Then she jumped, and Abi had to slide her foot out of the way to keep from being studded. As she did, she turned so that her back was to Jenna, and rummaged around for a gummy ring.

"You can have one of these," she offered, holding it over her shoulder.

Jenna stuffed the gummy ring into her mouth and then wrapped both arms around Abi, grabbing the bag so that they were both holding it. The move put them in a stalemate. Neither could go anywhere because Jenna now hugged Abi from behind, and if she let go with either hand, she'd lose the sweets.

With Jenna pressed tight against her, and the scent of her perfume at close range, Abi's chest constricted. The arousal was still there, but so too were the tears, poised to break. What the fuck was happening to her? It was as if her body couldn't quite decide how to react and was generating random responses.

"Let go," Jenna instructed.

"Don't you need to get back on the pitch? Jax might sub you."

"As if! She won't take me off when I just scored a goal."

Somehow, the excitement of that revelation and the relief of feeling a definite emotion caused Abi to let down her guard, and she loosened her grip enough for Jenna to snatch away the sweets. Abi wiped a tear from under her eye and had just about raised a smile by the time she turned around.

"Look at that, I got my sweets back *and* made you smile. Double win." Jenna held out a cola bottle for Abi to take in consolation. "Are you going to come into the bar after the game?" When Abi hesitated, Jenna gently kicked her foot. "Come on. It's either that or go home to watch TV with your parents. Plus, we're laying on food. *Free* food. I'll give you a lift after."

Abi sighed. Then she nodded. Then she felt sick again. She wouldn't bother asking what the worst was that could happen because with her luck, the universe would probably give her food poisoning.

6
---

# JENNA

"I thought you were sick of this place?" Jax asked as she leant forward on the bar, eagerly watching as the last of three pints were drawn from the tap.

Jenna hovered her phone over the payment machine and waited for the ding. "I am." But the alternative was heading to dinner with her grandparents earlier than necessary and that held absolutely no appeal. "Do you know where Abi is?"

The barmaid slid over the drinks and they both took one, but the third glass sat untouched. Jenna scanned the clubhouse for its owner because she'd been a long time sweeping out the changing rooms. It was a self-imposed penance for her behaviour on the pitch, but Abi was taking it way too seriously.

Jax shrugged. "Last I saw, she was helping prep the food."

"Wait with the drinks. I'll be back."

Dodging in and out of tables packed with opposition players, all waiting to eat, Jenna made her way to the kitchen. "Have you been tampering with my rota?" She held the door open with her foot and folded her arms. "I'm certain you're not on food duty until somewhere around mid-season."

Suspended mid-action with steam billowing into her face,

Abi was crouched in front of the oven. She let out a long "umm", which Jenna knew was because she didn't have a leg to stand on. Finally, the heat must have permeated her oven gloves because she leapt up and slid a tray of sausages onto the work surface, then slammed the door shut with her foot.

Craning to peer over Jenna's shoulder, Abi tried and failed to look like she hadn't been completely busted. It was written all over her guilty little face. "I'm just trying to be helpful."

"No, you aren't." After following Abi's line of sight to the gobby opposition centre back, Jenna let the kitchen door swing shut. "You're trying to make up for earlier while conveniently hiding from that girl."

Abi's eyes darted around the kitchen. "Err."

"Err. *Yes, I am, Jenna.* You've bested me again."

"It made sense for me to do the food since I came off at half-time. The player on your rota needed to change and it would've delayed us eating."

There were stainless steel catering fryers lining the work surface and they hissed with fat when Abi opened one. She asked Jenna to pass her a serving tray and pointed to a low cupboard on the far side of the room, then lifted the fryer baskets one by one, setting them on hooks to let them drain.

"We could've waited," Jenna replied, not allowing herself to become distracted. Once she'd dislodged a tray from the cupboard, she set it down next to Abi and went to continue arguing, but was interrupted by a loud gurgle from her stomach and placed a hand on it. "Traitor."

Abi laughed and began tipping the baskets of chips into the tray. "You can continue telling me off in a second but for now, help me carry the food out. I don't think I can handle you hungry."

She would get no argument, and not least because she was smiling again. Seeing Abi so on edge since she came back had knocked Jenna a little off kilter too. Even being awarded player of the match hadn't felt the same as it usually did, and she'd missed rubbing it in Abi's face while they were getting changed.

She was considering whether she could still get in a jibe about it when, once again, she was sidetracked by a far greater issue. Abi had already laid out paper plates and condiments on a table in the bar area, but there was something missing.

"Where's the ketchup?" Jenna asked, setting down the tray of sausages.

"We don't have any."

"Why in the world don't we have ketchup when there's everything else under the sun?" Including hot sauce, which was an outlier when it came to condiments for chips.

"Because everything else had been bought in bulk to cover all the friendlies, but whoever did the shopping under budgeted ketchup—the only sauce anyone ever wants—so we're out."

"Why not just buy more, though? If you're down on the rota for food, it's your responsibility to make sure we have everything we need."

"She said she didn't know how to get reimbursed now she can't go to you, so she didn't bother."

"Are you kidding me?"

"I know." Abi held up her hands, then licked some grease from her thumb. "The minute she told me, I knew what a lack of ketchup was going to do to you. It's not my fault, though, so don't shoot the messenger. Do you need me to go to the village shop?"

This was typical. The rest of the team were perfectly happy to turn up every week and reap the benefits, but Jenna suspected they had no idea of the work that went in behind the scenes.

Lost in vengeful thoughts, she hadn't noticed that Abi was still staring at her and waiting for a response. "Jenna? Shop?"

With a shake of her head, Jenna mumbled a quick "no, it's okay." Then she smiled again. "Thanks, though."

"Were you having visions of dancing ketchup bottles?"

"No, I was wondering if I should tell the committee I've changed my mind." It was unlikely anyone else would volunteer and they couldn't go without a treasurer.

"Because there was no ketchup? That's a bit extreme. I thought you didn't have time?"

"I don't."

"Then I'm sure we'll cope. Don't take this the wrong way, but the club isn't going to crumble because you're no longer our treasurer. You're not *that* important."

"Excuse me?"

Jenna knew she wasn't *that* important, but before she had the chance to reply properly, Abi added, "You know we don't just want you around because you pick up after everyone, right?"

"You're a hypocrite." Jenna dropped the proverbial mic there and turned on her heel, now also wanting to retreat to the safety of the kitchen. If they were going to have an argument, they were doing it in private.

"Excuse *me*?" Abi followed, pushing through the door and then heading straight for the sink. She turned on the tap, flooding the bowl with hot water, and squirted in a generous dollop of washing up liquid.

Waiting to make her point until Abi was wrist deep in suds, Jenna gestured up and down the scene. "Just look at what you're doing."

Stopping with a sponge in one hand and a bread knife in the other, Abi glanced from one to the other. "Washing up?"

"Yes. Making yourself useful because you're worried you've let people down. Isn't that sort of the same thing?"

Abi shrugged. "Maybe you're right. The only difference is that I genuinely have something to make up for, and you don't. I feel really bad about what I did today."

Jenna inclined her head, disarmed by Abi's vulnerability and the sad look on her face. "Are you sure you don't want to talk?"

There was a long pause while Abi scrubbed hard at something in the bowl, and when the silence between them stretched on to a second cooking implement, Jenna worried an answer wasn't coming. It made the hairs stand up on the backs of her arms again but this time it was accompanied by a slightly sick feeling that was only partially due to hunger. She hated seeing Abi like this.

"Abi? C'mon, I'm not a mind reader. Talk to me."

Abi dried her hands on a tea towel, then turned around and placed them on her hips. "Do you really want to hear about it?"

"Of course I do. Why would I keep asking if I didn't?"

She shrugged. "I'm just getting mixed messages, because whenever I'm not doing great or it comes up, you shut down the subject. It makes me feel like you don't actually want to know."

Jenna glanced down at her own feet. She hadn't imagined for a second that she might be the problem, and she was half wishing she hadn't asked now. So much for thinking that dinner with her grandparents would lead to the most gut wrenching conversation of the day. "I'm sorry. I thought I was doing the right thing." She looked up and flashed Abi a smile.

Abi's frown suggested that it hadn't come off. "I feel like I've upset you and I'm not sure how."

"You haven't," Jenna lied. She *was* upset. It stung worse than having to suffer bland chips; she hated getting things wrong. "Anyway, this isn't about me. It's about you." She walked to the sink and picked up the tea towel Abi had discarded.

"It's kind of about both of us. It's fine if you'd rather not go over how shitty Covid was. I get it wasn't easy for anyone, not just me, and not wanting to talk about it would be understandable. I won't be pissed at you."

Jenna made another attempt to smile but she still couldn't

pull it off. She knew Abi wasn't pissed at her, she was pissed at herself because she understood how much it hurt when someone dismissed your feelings or tried to brush difficult stuff under the carpet. It was exactly the reason she'd be spending as little time as humanly possible at her grandparents' house later that evening.

Her hands dropped to her sides. Then she let out a little sigh at herself for making things even worse by being a defensive arsehole, and began drying a knife from the draining board. "I really am sorry."

Abi settled in alongside and resumed the washing up. "It's fine. To be fair, I should've said something sooner. It was just hard in the moment, and I kept thinking, you know what, I guess we're only teammates and we haven't seen each other for a while. Maybe she's just being polite."

Only teammates? For some reason that cut Jenna deeper than anything else. She thought they were friends, and she didn't have many of those. "Right." She stared intently at the knife as she dried away every drop of water. "Okay."

Abi held out a spatula and Jenna finally set down the knife, showing the same attention to detail with the new implement.

"Are we okay?" Abi asked, nudging their shoulders together.

"Yep." Another lie, but Jenna didn't know what else to say. She didn't even want chips anymore, which was when she knew things were bad.

"You seem kind of miserable, though. Do you want to maybe go for a drink tomorrow night so I can cheer you up?"

"Yeah?" Jenna almost winced at the amount of enthusiasm she'd conveyed in only one word. She hated herself in this needy state, but it didn't stop her from asking if they were inviting the rest of the team and secretly hoping that the answer was no.

"We can if you want, but I was hoping we could catch up properly."

This time, the smile that crept across Jenna's lips was genuine. "Just the two of us, then? Sounds good." She had to bite her lip, sure she looked like a lunatic right now. First, she was getting bent out of shape over ketchup. Now she was ridiculously overexcited about a simple drink. It was a good job no one could see inside her head, or they'd think she was completely loopy. "So, are you going to tell me how things have been the past few months? For real."

"For real? They're getting better, I think. I know I'm lucky because I had my parents to back me up, and I recovered. A lot of people had it worse. I just need to move on. Embrace *new normal*, whatever the fuck that is."

Jenna laughed. "Don't ask me, but I'm glad things are improving. And I meant it when I said I'd help. Starting with cheering us both up tomorrow night."

# 7

## ABI

Abi made her way down the high street and stopped in front of Jenna's barbershop, where they'd arranged to meet. They'd never spent much time alone outside of football before, and she had second thoughts as she imagined them sat in stony, awkward silence when expected to be social of their own accord. Or discussing the weather. It didn't help that she'd done nothing for months besides be ill, and they'd already covered that topic of conversation. Sort of.

Deciding it was too late to back out now, and that she didn't want to anyway, she gave the door a shove. The lights were off because the shop was closed, but it swung open and jangled a little bell suspended over the frame.

"Is that you?" echoed from somewhere deep inside the building.

"Yep!" was all the reply Abi managed before the potent scent of wood and musk almost knocked her over.

She steadied herself on a Chesterfield sofa which sat under a mirror covering almost the entire right-hand wall. Above were industrial light fittings and through the archway to her left was a bigger space with a rough wooden counter at the back. She hadn't been in before, but it was as she imagined: upmarket and most likely overpriced. Not the type of barbershop Stanley frequented, with a blaring radio and the odour of kebab grease permeating from next door.

Wandering through and leaning against one of the barber chairs to ground herself, Abi took a deep breath and tried to relax. It was only Jenna, and it was only a casual drink.

"Won't be a sec!" Jenna yelled. "I'm just digging out some... dammit!"

A loud thwack reverberated down the corridor at the back of the room and Abi took a few paces along it to find Jenna crawling around the office, shovelling pages into a manilla folder. "Need a hand?"

"Yes please."

Abi manoeuvred herself onto the floor with all the dexterity of an arthritic eighty-year-old. She may have only played a quarter of the match yesterday, but it had damn near killed her. "You alright?"

"Mhm."

"Sure?"

"Yeah. A bit tired, that's all."

Now Abi knew something was up, because 'tired' was her first excuse for all incidences of emotional turmoil. It was right up there with when Petra said, "it's fine", and she didn't buy it for one second. "Liar. Let's not do yesterday again, huh?"

Jenna sighed. "No, okay. I'm just in trouble with my solicitor turned girlfriend turned ex but still solicitor. Otherwise known as The Boss."

Abi handed over the few sheets she'd collected. "Sounds complicated. And kind of kinky." She smiled when her comment, and her ill-fated attempts to get back up using a chair on wheels, won her a laugh.

"You're an idiot."

"Ouch. That hurt almost as much as this." Abi rolled up the leg of her shorts to show off the graze which ran to her arse cheek, but she had no real desire to go over it again and carefully let down the fabric when Jenna's face screwed. "If you're done being rude, would you like to vent? I reckon I probably owe you something in return by now, given the number of times you've helped me out."

Jenna looked genuinely startled, gawping as she stepped away and tucked the folder into a tote bag on her chair. "What have I done, besides causing an argument?"

"How about giving me business advice, driving me to the game, and getting me a job?"

"Oh, yeah. All that helping in order to be useful. Point taken. In that case, I'd like a pony, a Rolls Royce, and a year of skivvying. Also," Jenna added, pointing to her feet. "Lick these immediately."

"We'll stick to venting for now." However enticing it was to lick any part of Jenna's body. "So, what's up?"

Jenna picked up her tote and strode across the room to flick off the light switch, plunging them into near darkness because the office had no windows. It had nothing at all, in fact, besides a desk, chair, computer, and filing cabinet, but Abi didn't have much time to consider Jenna's stark work environment. She was too bewildered and fumbling towards the door as it inched shut.

When Abi finally escaped, Jenna was fiddling with the answering machine on the reception desk. "Tell me how you're feeling now."

"That was a quick deflection."

"Thank you. They're one of my special skills."

Abi waited for Jenna to say something more, but she only exited the building, locked up, and led them towards the fancy wine bar on the far side of the street. It was a surprise because

Abi had only ever seen her chugging pints in the clubhouse. *Il Mondo* was more of a Petra haunt.

Jenna broke the deadlock when they reached the door, turning around with a quick "shit" and jogging back in the opposite direction. "I forgot some stuff for Jax's birthday party," she called over her shoulder. "Wait there. I'll be back in a second."

Abi ignored the instruction and followed. When she reached the shop, she had a tote bag thrust at her stomach and clutched it there. "How come I'm not invited to Jax's party?"

"You are."

"I'm not."

Jenna stuck out her tongue and jiggled her key in the lock. "Yes, you definitely are. I sent the emails myself. We couldn't put it in the WhatsApp group. She would've seen it, and the whole thing is a surprise."

"Ah. Right."

"Let me guess, the only technophobic millennial in the country hasn't checked her email in a while?"

Chewing her top lip, Abi followed Jenna into the foyer. "Might not have looked at my personal one, no."

Jenna laughed. "You look all sweet and wounded. Did you honestly think I wouldn't have invited you?"

She pinched Abi's chin and smiled as she gave it a quick tug from side to side, then she rushed off in search of whatever she'd forgotten. It was only the briefest of touches but felt surprisingly intimate, and Abi was relieved Jenna was now rooting through a stack of boxes on the counter. It meant she couldn't see the incriminating shade of red that had just painted all over her face.

"So," Jenna asked while she stacked the boxes on top of one another. "Are you free next Friday?"

Abi laughed at the ridiculous notion that she might have

other plans. Or at least, other plans that didn't involve eating crisps on the sofa with her dad. "I might squeeze it into my hectic social calendar, yeah."

"And we'll be so grateful that you've made time for us little people. I can use the opportunity to start on the next phase of my duties and set you up with someone."

"At football? But I already know everyone." And they were straight, coupled, or Jax.

"Untrue. There must be someone. How about the new under eighteens manager? She's nice. And single."

"Oh, so she's good enough for me, but you wouldn't date her yourself?" Which presumably meant she wasn't wealthy, power-hungry, or stuck up. Those were all good signs.

"I just mean, I've only met one of your exes, but she was kind of... a good girl. Y'know? She used to send you off to football with brownies for the team, and so I figured that was your type."

It was hard for Abi to know what her type was any more, because nothing had ever worked out with the women she dated. Stanley was right about her most recent ex, and that relationship epitomised her previous experiences. They were a bit like her van—comfortable enough for short journeys but not built for anything long haul. "I don't want to think about types. If there's a connection and it feels right, I'll give it a shot."

"That's a very healthy attitude. Jax would be proud."

"Jax? What has Jax got to do with this?"

Slinging the tote bag over her shoulder, Jenna dipped in her hand and pulled out her keys. Then she picked up the stack of boxes and thrust them at Abi, knocking her back a few paces. "Promise you won't get mad, but she said you always go for the wrong women and I should help you fix it."

Abi's mouth hung open. She could guess how Jax wanted Jenna to 'fix it' but hadn't expected her to be so brazen. "I don't suppose she said that it was a lesbian affliction, too?"

"She said something about lesbians, yeah. How did you know?"

Abi rolled her eyes and followed Jenna towards the door. Apparently, there was one thing worse than talking about the weather, and Jax should be careful if she wanted to make it to her next birthday.

* * *

An hour later they were sat in *Il Mondo*, filling party bags with cheap tat. It was an odd thing to do in the town's most upmarket establishment, but Jenna didn't seem to care about that, spreading boxes of rubbers, sweets, and other crap across two tables and the floor.

One barmaid served the smattering of customers, enjoying a few post-work drinks in chrome-plated surroundings. She'd taken an interest in their endeavour while cleaning glasses. Eventually, she caught Abi's eye and mouthed, "what are you doing?"

Jenna kicked Abi under the table. "Stop flirting with her."

"I'm not flirting."

"Like hell you're not! Go over there and ask her out or something if you're being more open-minded. You can show her your war wound."

"Get lost," Abi protested, lobbing a lolly at Jenna's head. "She looks straight as hell." And bored. It was the only reason she'd paid them any attention.

"How in the world can you tell that? I bet you'd say I was straight if you didn't know me, too. Just because we're both blonde and kind of femme. It's such a crock!"

Abi scoffed and reached into a box on the floor beside her, rummaging for a tube of sweets. "I would never say *you* were straight. Being gorgeous has got nothing to do with it. You've got major lesbian energy." Still focused on the task in hand, Abi couldn't locate any more Smarties and had to strain, sliding down her seat. It wasn't until she found what she needed and straightened up that she realised Jenna was staring at her with a mischievous look on her face. "What?"

"You think I'm gorgeous?" She nudged Abi more gently with her foot this time.

"No. I—" Abi stuttered, with no hope of controlling the heat scorching down her face and rapidly burning her chest too. "I meant—"

"No, no, you can't take it back now. It's out there and you'll have to live with it."

"I didn't—"

"You didn't what? Mean it when you said I was gorgeous? So, are you saying I'm ugly?"

"Well, no... You're not ugly at all... You're beautiful." Abi rubbed both hands along her face, stretching her cheeks and showing the pink under her eyes. "I think I'm having an out-of-body experience. Is it time to go home yet?"

"Home alone or with her? Then again, maybe you'd prefer to go home with me...? Who knows?"

"I should've known this drink was only an excuse to torture me."

"Yes, you should know by now that torturing you is my soul pleasure in life." The mischievous smile remained fixed on Jenna's face and her eyes glinted as they darted to meet Abi's. "That's the second time I've turned you all red this evening."

"What?" Startled, Abi looked up from the party bag she'd resumed filling, horrified to feel her face bloom again. Had Jenna caught her out in the shop? If so, she needed to leave immediately because her crush was getting out of hand and alcohol wasn't helping. Maybe going after the barmaid wasn't such a bad idea after all because Abi clearly needed to do something about her haywire hormones. She also needed happy hour to end—pronto.

"Make that three," Jenna teased. "Are you sure you're not ill?"

"Fuck off."

"Menopausal?"

"You're impossible," Abi grumbled, kicking Jenna's foot under the table.

"And you're getting so pouty these days," Jenna countered, nudging back. She slid her foot over Abi's and gently tapped it, trying to needle her, and when she got no response, did it again. Then again. Then again, until the barmaid came over with a tray and asked if they had any empties. When she'd gone, Jenna giggled and almost knocked over her drink. "Did you see that?"

"See what?" Instinctively drawn in, Abi leant her elbows on the table, her voice barely registering past a whisper.

"We clearly had no empties. It was an excuse to come over."

"Fuck off."

"Is that your stock reply to everything now?"

If Jenna was going to keep on about the barmaid, the answer was yes. "Have a sensible conversation with me and you can have a different response."

"If you insist. I'll pick the topic."

"That's very convenient."

There was a long pause while Jenna scanned the bar. When her gaze settled back on Abi, she reached into the tote, pulling out her phone.

"What are you doing?"

"Texting Cass back to confirm next Saturday. Well done for yesterday, by the way. I know you've never liked her but this is business."

"Hang on, I never said I don't like her! She's..." The search for descriptive words—positive descriptive words, at least—was tough and Abi's eyes shot up to a broken ceiling light. Wherever she turned, peril seemed to lie ahead. "Think they need to replace a bulb."

"Mhm. You're almost as good at avoiding tough conversations as I am."

"A-ha! So you admit there's something going on."

With an airy sigh, Jenna sat straighter and set down her phone. "You won't drop this, will you?"

"Nope." And not only because the diversion suited Abi. Whatever was happening in Jenna's life, it was clearly stressful, and her desire to help was genuine. "You don't have to tell me if you really don't want, but I'm happy to listen."

After a few moments of distractedly drumming her fingers on her phone, Jenna submitted. "Fine, I guess this sharing thing goes both ways, but it's not very exciting. We've clashed a little over the new premises I'm taking on, that's all. She's a great solicitor and being really helpful, it's just…"

"Just what?"

Jenna's lips vibrated. "I don't know. Mixing business and pleasure. Terrible idea." Her face scrunched and for a minute Abi thought she was going to shut down again, but she carried on this time. "I always planned to open another shop, but then the virus hit and obviously we had to shut for ages. Things were tight, so I shelved it."

"Makes sense."

"Right. Then a few weeks ago, she contacted me to say one of her clients has a building in the perfect location, which of course it is, but—"

"You still aren't ready?"

The admission seemed a difficult one for Jenna to make, and she shrugged slightly, her mouth curling into a tight-lipped smile. "No, I'm not sure I am. This is a larger space than my other shop so the lease is a bit more expensive, even with Cass negotiating a good deal. It's a big step."

"So why didn't you just say no?"

Jenna picked up her drink, swilling dregs of bright orange liquid around the glass. "I did at first. Then I got swept along. Plus it really is something I want to do... eventually."

"Hard to imagine you getting swept along with anything."

After a few moments of consideration, Jenna shrugged again. "I could still pull out, I suppose, but I know I'll be letting people down." There was another pause while she drained the last of her cocktail. "I only told my grandparents the split is permanent last night, even though it's been that way for months, so I'm already in the doghouse. Whatever happens, I'm for it."

Abi tilted her head, partly with sympathy but also out of confusion. Jenna always seemed so confident and straightforward, and Abi couldn't imagine her doing anything she didn't want. "You're for it if you pull out, or because you've split up with the rich lawyer lady, or because you didn't tell them?"

"All three. She can do no wrong in their eyes, so if she thinks the new place is a good idea, they'll keep supporting it. And when they also find out that I was the one who dumped her—" Jenna pulled her finger across her throat in a slicing motion and her face contorted into a pained expression. "Any ideas?"

Despite wanting to help, Abi didn't have a single one, except to push a full cocktail in front of Jenna. Maybe happy hour wasn't such a bad thing after all. "Sorry, I'm out of my depth. Have you tried getting drunk and running away from your problems?"

"Every day." The joke made Jenna laugh, and she raised the glass in a quick 'cheers' before taking a sip. "It'll work out," she concluded, setting her drink back down. "But dinner with my grandparents last night was stressful, so I'm glad tonight I've got some company that's... easy."

"I don't mind you calling me easy. In this context."

The comment troubled Jenna, even though Abi had meant it

light-heartedly, and she squinted. "You know what I mean. We always have fun together. I really did miss you."

"Yeah. I do know what you mean, and I missed you too." This time when Abi nudged Jenna's foot, it was an offer of comfort. "For what it's worth, I have total faith that you can make this work if you decide to go ahead. Take a bit of your own advice and see this as an opportunity."

A smile lingered until a ding sounded from Jenna's phone, and she jumped. "Jax this time. She's working on your logos."

"Thanks for asking her about that. I guess it does make sense if she's happy to design me one. I'll give her some money. Can you ask how much she'd usually charge?"

"Yes, boss. Anything more I can do for you? I don't recall agreeing to be your secretary, on top of everything else."

Abi was about to object but was still stuck on the first part of Jenna's reply. "I quite like the sound of that."

"What, me calling you The Boss? I bet you do. We can work on your non-existent love life, but in the meantime, you'll have to sort yourself out." When Abi floundered, blushing and fidgeting with another party bag, Jenna grinned as if she'd got the response she wanted. "What? I'm not ashamed. Women let you down, but you know what doesn't? Your vibrator."

Unsure how to reply, Abi only sat and counted the crap in her party bag for a moment. She wasn't ashamed, but discussing sex toys with Jenna was about the last thing she needed. Not least because it opened her mind to hundreds more fantasies when it required no help in that department. "I have enough sex toys, thank you very much."

"No such thing."

"Pretty sure there is. Especially when your sex drive is AWOL because you're ill. My body has had bigger things to worry about, trying to get better and remember how to breathe. You know, trivial stuff."

"And has your sex drive returned now you're better?"

"Um, yeah. It's definitely back." *And it's another thing you've helped with.*

"Then are you sure you don't want some recommendations? Because I'm advising you on everything else."

"I'm very sure," Abi replied, despite the opposite being true. She'd love to continue this conversation, or perhaps get a live demonstration, so she pinged a limp red balloon at Jenna by way of distraction. It hit her shoulder before landing on the table. "I notice you somehow twisted the conversation again. How in the world do you do that?"

Jenna tossed her phone onto the table and grabbed the balloon, blowing it up and then slowly deflating it. For a few moments, she looked Abi dead in the eye, and then it was as if she stared right past her into the distance. The shift in mood caused Abi to frown, but as quickly as it came, it passed, and Jenna smiled again.

"I told you," she answered finally, making a farting noise with the last of the air. "It's my special skill, but I'm working on some new ones."

## 8

## JENNA

"Monday night drinking is not the one," Jenna grumbled to herself on Tuesday morning as she approached Cass's front door. It opened before she'd knocked, and Jenna stumbled back a few paces, shielding her eyes against the sun. Was it always this bright?

"Are you ill?" Cass asked bluntly, before taking a sip from the mug in her hand.

"Self-inflicted."

There was a nod that said *I knew it* and then Cass stood aside to let Jenna pass.

"Are you okay?" conveyed no more warmth and so Jenna dismissed the question quickly. She didn't want to get into deep and meaningful conversations with a raging hangover. In fact, she didn't want to get into deep and meaningful conversations at all.

"I've got the contracts." Wafting the manilla folder behind herself as Cass followed her into the kitchen, Jenna winced when it almost went flying again. "Is there anything else you need from me?" She set it down safely on the worktop and finally turned to make eye contact.

Cass's demeanour had softened somewhat in the intervening fifteen seconds. Workday hangovers weren't the norm, so she'd likely read between the lines and remembered what time of year it was. "Thank you. No, I think that's it now. Do you want to go in for another look around this morning? It was hard to get a proper feel for the place when the shop fitters were there quoting."

"Definitely. Sounds good."

Jenna had woken with a renewed determination to make the new shop work, in addition to the hangover. It might mean deviating from her tried and tested business plan, but Abi was right. Had Jenna not forty-eight hours ago told her to embrace change and see it as an opportunity?

*Shit. Abi.*

Jenna raised a hand to her forehead as she recalled her behaviour the previous evening. What she remembered of it, anyway. She'd had way too much to drink and led them down a path of flirting and innuendo. Unwelcome flirting and innuendo, if the embarrassed look on Abi's face for most of the evening was anything to go by.

Pushing the thought out of her mind for now, she turned her attention to the steaming cafetière and mug ready and waiting for her on the kitchen table. Cass was very particular about her blend and the aroma smelt like salvation.

"I wonder," Cass ventured cautiously. "Do you think we might invite along a builder I know to look at the place and give you one final quote? He's not specifically a shop fitter but he can do this type of work and he's a client of mine. His company flips quite a few houses so it could mean more conveyancing work for the firm if I can keep him sweet. There would be no obligation, but it makes good sense for both of us if I make the introduction."

This was Cass all over and Jenna smiled as she poured her coffee. "I don't see why not."

"Good. I'll give him a call now."

She set off down the hallway, mobile phone already pressed to her ear, and Jenna laughed. She took a seat and hitched up her knee, then cupped the mug in her hands and blew over the top. "Hello old friend," she whispered, before taking a delicate sip. The only other thing needed to complete her hangover recovery kit was something sweet and chocolatey, and the thought returned her to Abi.

With a sigh, she set her coffee down on the table and pulled the phone from her pocket. She clearly wasn't going to stop worrying until she'd made contact and confirmed whether they were even still speaking. How the night ended she wasn't entirely sure. All she knew was that the boxes of party bags were not in her house so must have been returned to the shop, and that her car was not on the driveway, so she had probably done the right thing and called a taxi. Hopefully, she'd find it again in the town centre car park.

Keeping her message breezy, she went with: "I need cookies. So hungover!"

It could often take Abi hours to reply so Jenna was surprised to see a message flash up almost immediately. Perhaps she hadn't been so offended after all.

"I still owe you some home baked ones. Maybe for your next hangover?"

"Saturday, then!" Jenna replied, now wondering how Friday night would go. She'd enjoyed the opportunity to banter with Abi off the leash, now they were both single, and she'd quite like to do some more of it.

"Done. If it helps, I'm working with my dad today and I want to die."

"All that effort to stay alive and now you want to die?"

"Figure of speech."

"What are you working on?"

This time, there was no instant reply. Jenna peered down at the screen, impatiently waiting, and tapped it against her palm again. When still nothing came through, she gave up and slid the device back into her pocket. Abi was probably just caught up with some work if she was helping her dad today.

"It's done," Cass called from the hallway as she strode along it. She appeared in the doorway and ran a hand through her crop of hair. "He's going to meet us outside at eleven."

Her smile gave her an air of smug satisfaction, which wasn't a surprise because she loved putting together a deal. There was something about being in the thick of things, wheeling and dealing, which really turned her on. They shared that. In fact, it was something they'd quickly bonded over, so Jenna didn't begrudge her a moment to revel. Or have any qualms about asking for a counter favour.

"I'm wondering if you can do something for me in return."

Cass's hands came to land on her slim hips. "That depends upon what it is."

"I need someone to make sure Jax turns up at the club on Friday night for her birthday party. On time." She'd been told there was a social and that attendance was not optional, but Jenna wanted a guarantee in place.

"Me?"

"Yes, you. You're our only mutual acquaintance who won't already be at the party. Although, you could still stay and join in. You *are* invited."

Cass's lip twitched as if she were holding back her genuine response. She wasn't really one for slumming it in football clubhouses, however recently they'd been given a refurb. "I don't want to butt in if it's going to be all football people. This is your thing."

Jenna nodded. She wasn't going to argue when they already had so many other opportunities to disagree. "Well, the offer still stands if you change your mind, but will you help me out with Jax?"

Cass took a moment to consider. "I suppose I do need some website updates. Maybe I'll call her later and mix a bit of business with pleasure."

*Not for the first time, hey?*

Jenna thanked Cass and escaped to find more hangover cures while she continued her journey into town. She'd already walked an hour to Cass's, hoping the fresh air and exercise would help, and making it any further would require sustenance.

Having put the idea of baked goods into her own head, her next stop was at a corner shop, where she bought a bag of triple chocolate chip cookies. Two had been consumed before she made it to Starbucks to order another Americano with an extra shot. She was finishing the dregs when she pushed open her office door and confirmed the location of all those party bags. They were on her desk, neatly stored away in boxes. Even drunk, she had excellent organisational skills.

After throwing her empty cup in the recycling bin, she lugged the boxes of party bags to the corner of the room. Then she finally had the space to sit down and pull out the floorplan for the new shop before they met the builder. She'd already sketched out where she wanted everything, and the styling would of course be on brand, but something didn't feel right, and she was running out of time. Perhaps she was still hung up on the higher costs. The bigger risk. It went without saying that she'd run the numbers before agreeing to the lease, and with the extra capacity it was workable, but extra capacity also meant more appointments to fill and more wages to pay. She stared at the number of barbering stations and her heart thumped from a mixture of coffee, sugar, sleep deprivation, and worry.

A gentle buzz against her leg caused it to happen again and she jumped, fumbling to pull the phone from her pocket. Scrolling through the messages, she was quietly impressed when Abi had the technical skills to send photos, however blurry. She turned the phone on its side and tried to work out what they were of, but still had to ask for clarification.

When "Stud walls!!!" came back, she smiled at the number of exclamation marks. It might be obvious to Abi, but Jenna had no clue what a stud wall looked like, and she replied with a series of question marks.

"We're working on a barn conversion. Splitting the upstairs into bedrooms. It's currently one big space."

Abi sent another picture, this time a clearer wide angle shot of a series of wooden structures marking out the boundary of each room, and a light went off in Jenna's head. She looked from her phone to the plans she'd been worrying over. What if she did the same in the new shop, splitting the room up into smaller ones? She could offer more services or, better still, rent treatment rooms to freelance therapists.

"You're a genius!" she sent back.

"Are you taking the piss?"

"No, for real! For once, I'm being deadly serious with you!"

"Okay. In that case you're welcome. What are FRIENDS for?"

Jenna frowned at the screen. Why had Abi screamed friends?

It was perfectly possible she'd accidentally hit the caps button, and Jenna was about to type back another jibe about Abi being useless with technology until she realised the reason and her face fell even further. Her palm came to land on her forehead as she recalled telling Abi, in depth, about how she wished they were closer and how much her friendship meant.

"You remember that, huh?"

"I don't remember much but I remember that."

Jenna let out a strangled noise as she continued to curse herself for getting so drunk. Then she rolled back the chair and stood up. She'd have time to think of a reply in the car—presuming she could find it—with the assistance of her remaining cookies. For now, though, she had business to attend to and that took (convenient) priority.

\* \* \*

It soon became clear that walking along the street with a bag of cookies was a misstep, because the town Jenna had selected for her new shop was far more upmarket than she was used to. There were people sat outside small independent coffee shops, feeding puppaccinos to cockapoos with quirky bandanas. There were remote workers with their MacBooks, making use of the free Wi-Fi. There was an estate agent showing off the front of a converted church to an immaculately groomed couple. These were the kind of people Jenna wanted to attract. Or, at least, they would be once she'd wiped the crumbs from her chin.

When she reached the building, positioned between a florist and a delicatessen, she crumpled the cookie bag, chucked it in a bin, and raised a hand to shield her eyes as she peered through the floor to ceiling windows. Her signature old style barbering chairs would go in the front. Behind them would be a central reception desk. Then, beyond that, she was now imagining that the corridor would be extended and lead to a series of private treatment rooms. It was a genius idea and she owed Abi a pint. Or maybe a Coke, because the idea of any more alcohol was causing her stomach to lurch.

She was about to pull out her phone and make the offer, hoping to gloss over any talk about her drunken overshare, when someone tapped her on the shoulder and she spun around.

"Stanley?" Jenna's frown morphed into a smile at the sight of his friendly face next to Cass's more sullen features.

"Do you two know each other?" Cass asked, pointing from one to the other.

"This is Abi's dad! You're not the builder, are you?"

"The very one," Stanley replied, with outstretched arms. He had a clipboard in one hand and a tape measure in the other. "I wondered whether it was you we were meeting. How are you, love?"

"I'm a bit delicate thanks to your daughter." When Cass's features tightened even further, Jenna looked away. She felt a bit like she'd been caught out but didn't know why or what for. "Shall we go inside?"

"I didn't realise who you were," Cass muttered as she unlocked the door and pushed it open. "I'm sorry."

It was tough to tell what she was sorry about. Was it the mention of Abi twice in almost as many days, or disappointment that she'd just introduced Jenna to someone who she already knew? Whatever the answer, Cass swiftly returned to business mode. She stepped over the threshold and dangled the keys, as if to make the point that she still held some power, because they'd been entrusted to her by her client.

Jenna followed her in and then turned to face Stanley again, trying not to let whatever was going on with Cass dampen her excitement. "Thanks for coming to take a look. I've had a few quotes already but they've been all over the place and in any case, I think I want to change the brief so they're probably redundant now. This is a bit off-piste, but can we split up this space into smaller rooms?"

"Wait," Cass interjected before Stanley could reply. "That

hasn't been agreed. You'd need permission before making any structural changes."

"I know, but if the owner says yes?"

Stanley walked to the back of the room and poked his head down the existing corridor, where he would have found a small kitchen, a toilet, and a room full of old networking cables. Then, when he returned, he glanced up at the beams. "You can, but it'd be a shame given how bright and airy this room is at the moment. Those big windows in the front are the main source of light, and if you create additional rooms, they'll have none. You've also got very high ceilings here, and I'm looking at this lovely floor..."

He swept his foot over the original oak boards and Jenna's heart sank. It'd seemed like the answer to her prayers but no one else was sharing her positivity. "Oh."

"You sound disappointed."

"I am a bit. I walked in here with this vision for a buzzing multi-treatment hub, but it sounds like that's not going to happen."

"I didn't say you couldn't do it, only that I think it's unwise to put up walls. In my opinion, your best bet would be to use screens if you want to break up this space. Then, if you need a fully private room, you could convert that old office at the back. It'll also be a cheaper way of doing it, I expect. And quicker."

This was the kind of problem-solving Jenna needed, and her smile returned. "I'll take your advice." Especially if it was going to cost less and still achieve the same outcome. She supposed there was no reason, on reflection, why the space she rented out should be in private rooms. It may even be preferable to take this route, because there'd be more interaction. "Is what you've just suggested something you can do?"

Stanley shrugged. "I definitely have contractors with the skills. We need to go over the details but in theory, it's a yes."

Jenna turned to Cass, who'd remained uncharacteristically quiet throughout their exchange. She wanted to know if there would be any problem implementing Stanley's suggestion, but before she got a chance to ask, Cass announced that she needed to take a very important call, sweeping past them both and out through the front door.

Stanley watched Cass pace in front of the window. "Looks intense."

"Best to leave her to it. I'm guessing she's redundant in most of this, anyway." Which was probably part of why she'd just made a show of taking a *very important call*.

"How has she come to be making referrals? Are you a client of hers, too? I'm not complaining if it brings me more work, but it does seem like a bit of an odd thing for a solicitor to be doing."

Jenna laughed. "Yeah, it is, but Cass isn't just my solicitor. She's also my ex-girlfriend. And the owner of this place is a friend of hers, so..."

Stanley nodded. "I get the picture. I've found that in business, it's generally who you know and not what you know. Or, at least, the two things have equal importance. That's why I'm going to say the same thing as I did the other day. Even if you don't go with my quote, I'm happy to give you a bit of advice."

That was all very well and good, but if Stanley could come up with the solution, and a quote that was workable, Jenna would love to hire someone she could trust. "That's really kind but I have no intention of taking advantage."

"You wouldn't be, but fair enough."

They went over the whole building, discussing everything from sink placement and electric sockets to wall coverings and additional lighting. By the time they'd finished, Cass had returned, now smiling and running a hand through her hair.

"How are we getting on in here?" she asked, inhaling deeply as if she'd been outside negotiating world peace.

"I think we're just about done."

Cass looked down at her watch. "Then shall we get going? I've a mountain of paperwork."

After making one final sweep of the room, Jenna followed Cass and Stanley back out onto the street, more confident than ever that things were finally moving in the right direction. Even her hangover was subsiding, and she was eager to get back to the office to start making more plans. There was only one thing standing in her way, because Stanley was waving and walking towards the car park, also eager to go and quote another job, but Cass was making less decisive movements in that direction. Given she was the one who had hurried them along, she was now stalling and didn't seem to want to leave.

"Everything alright?" Jenna asked, hoping they weren't about to get into any conversations that might kill her buzz. "You rush off if you need to. I'm just going to grab a coffee and some lunch, then head back to the shop."

She returned her attention to the plethora of cafes she'd walked past on the way in. It could be dangerous working here, especially when you had a sweet tooth, and she decided it was time for something savoury.

Before Cass could say much more than "okay", Jenna thanked her and plumped for the closest place. She pulled up a chair outside and picked up a menu. Then she set it back down again and couldn't resist reaching for her phone instead.

"Did you know your dad was quoting my shop fit??" she asked Abi.

It made her smile to see that, once again, the reply was almost instantaneous. "No! What?"

Jenna relayed how Stanley had ended up being introduced by Cass, and then followed up with, "If I hire him, will I be hiring you too?" *And will you come to work in those boots?*

"Sorry FRIEND, I'm hoping to have my own work on. But my dad will do a great job if you hire him!"

"You sound more confident today. Willing to admit I'm right?"

"I dropped in Cass's quote first thing and she's already accepted it, even though I added on a bit extra."

"Was that for the pain of having to work for someone you don't like?"

"I told you I don't not like her! We're just different people. Besides, aren't you the one who said I need to go after clients with more money?"

Jenna laughed and picked up the menu again because a waitress was making a beeline for her table, and she needed to choose something. She ordered a BLT baguette and another coffee, then returned to her conversation with Abi.

"You didn't seem keen."

"I wasn't. I just wanted things to go back to how they were but I guess that can't happen, so…"

"Want my advice?"

"Do I have a choice?"

Jenna tapped through to her pictures and found a quote she'd screenshotted from Instagram. It said, "Stop worrying about what could go wrong and get excited about what could go right". Then she sent it to Abi with the caption, "You always have a choice. I'm making a leap of faith too. Will tell you all about it on Friday."

9

## ABI

*PING!*

Abi's head snapped up and she grumbled as she scanned the living room for the source. It was Friday evening, and she was having a well-earned rest before heading to Jax's party. Or at least she would be if it weren't for...

*PING!*

"Is that yours?" Stanley mumbled over a bag of crisps. When it went off again, the surprise of a third message landing on Abi's phone was enough to break his hour-long staring contest with the television. That normally only happened when he ran out of snacks.

"Yeah." Abi strained as she fumbled along the sofa cushion under her back in a half-hearted attempt to find the device she knew wasn't there. The pinging wasn't that close. She gave up and for a few moments the only noise came from a crinkling crisp packet and an advert for a car buying service, but then...

*PING!*

"You're popular for a change."

She rolled off the sofa and crawled over the carpet, collecting a stray crisp on the way and lobbing it at Stanley's head. He flinched but then settled again, grabbing another packet from the side table next to his recliner chair.

"It'll just be Jenna." They'd been messaging each other all week and Abi had seldom been far from her phone, waiting for them to pick up conversation again. "She's reminding me to book the taxi. And to take a shower because she knows I smell." The phone pinged one last time. "Oh, and she's thanking me for sorting the pass the parcel at such late notice."

"Pass the parcel?" Stanley laughed and shook his head. "How old is Jax, again?"

"Don't. It's her fortieth next week, but Jenna says Jax missed out on the traditional British kids party experience, and she wants to remedy that."

"I've got a lot of time for Jenna. She has her head screwed on."

"Yeah, Jenna's great." *Really great.*

Abi tried to push quite how excited she was about them spending another evening together to the back of her mind, and messaged to confirm she'd ordered them a taxi. Then she contemplated changing. She agreed with Jenna that she needed a shower, as much to wake herself up as anything else, but before she got any further, Stanley muted the television.

"What?" she asked cautiously as he turned and eye-balled her, still on all fours next to the sideboard.

"You know *what*. Come on, you've been avoiding the subject all week. Have you decided whether you're playing this season?"

That was the last thing on Abi's mind, and she didn't want to get into it. "Does football matter that much?"

"Yes, it does. You were desperate to go back, but I heard you tell your mother you might not be able to make the first game of the season, and I know it wasn't just to stop her going."

"I started building my website and I need the weekends to finish. It's important." Rather than inevitably have to explain to

Jenna about the lack of funds, Abi's plan was to build her own website and eliminate the need. It hadn't gone well so far, though, despite the 'idiot proof' creation software.

"You can bugger up your website any time. It won't hurt to take a day off for football."

"Rude!" Abi exclaimed, before slowly climbing to her feet. "I know you mean well with the football stuff, but I can make this decision for myself."

Stanley was about to continue arguing the case when the door clattered. He clawed for the empty crisp packets, springing from his chair like a drug dealer about to experience a police raid, then jogged to the kitchen and disappeared to hide any incriminating evidence.

"How was your day?" Petra shouted over the muffled sound of her rustling bags. "Have you finished your leaflets?"

"Okay," Abi called back. "I've only got half a box left now." She chuckled a little when she heard her dad rush into the hallway to take Petra's shopping and then her features scrunched to find it went silent. She knew they were kissing. "Cut it out!" she yelled when, moments later, they were still at it. "Disgusted first-born in earshot!"

"Shut up, you!" Stanley shouted back. "Or I'll tell your mother your secret." Abi darted towards the door, desperate not to have Petra involved in the discussion about quitting football, until he added, "How is that girl you took down last week?" and she relaxed again. As secrets went, it wasn't the worst.

Petra wandered in and sat next to where Abi had just plopped down on the sofa. "What's this?" She put a hand on Abi's forehead as if the news meant she may have a temperature. It was impossible to even look at her the wrong way these days without it being a sign of illness.

"Nothing. Dad's just teasing because I got sent off last Sunday."

*Lucky Number*

"I wondered why you were so quiet after the game!"

"It's not a big deal," Abi lied. It still felt like a huge deal, but she was trying to forget about it and move on.

"You don't look well." Petra tutted and tried to reach for Abi's forehead again but had her hand batted away. "This wouldn't have happened if you'd let us watch."

"How do you figure that?!" Incredulous, Abi slumped further into the sofa cushion.

"Because I always bring you good luck."

That was highly questionable. The last game Petra attended was the league cup semi-final, and they lost 7-2. Not much luck had followed her that day.

"You think, do you?"

"Yes, always. You'll see. Your first game of the season will be better." Sitting a little taller, Petra gave a quick nod to show the discussion was over, but Abi had other ideas.

"I thought you were away that weekend, tormenting your other child?"

"Just an excuse for a dirty weekend in Brighton," Stanley piped up as he appeared in the doorway.

"Please no!" Abi dropped her phone on the carpet, grabbed a cushion, and buried her face in it. She really didn't need to know any more about their plans.

Stanley laughed until Petra pulled the cushion away and threw it at him. "Be quiet. We will be back in time for the game."

"I already said I might not make it to that and even if I do, I'm a grown woman," Abi pleaded.

"Is this it now? Am I banned from your games?" Petra's was another accent which had mingled and become more English over the years but, like Jax, her roots often betrayed her during a confrontation. "Are you ashamed of me?" she asked, her eyes so wide that she looked possessed. "Your own mother? The woman who raised you, and loves you, and—" She finally paused mid-rant, folding her arms and awaiting a suitable response.

"Of course I'm not ashamed of you!" Shame had nothing to do with it, and that was the truth. Usually there would be no problem if they wanted to catch the odd match throughout the season, but not when football was the only place Abi had to escape. It was enough to give her pause for thought about quitting altogether.

"What is it then?" Petra pressed. "Hm?"

Abi ran her palms down her face and took a deep breath, then squeezed her mum's hand. "I just need a bit of space from time to time. I am so, so grateful to you and Dad for taking care of me. You're absolute heroes. But I'm thirty-three and I want to act like it again."

"You're never too old to need your parents."

"I know," Abi replied quickly to make sure Petra couldn't get back into a flow, but after that, it was a struggle to find the right words because none would help. When she really couldn't think of anything else to say, she went for the old fail safe: "Do you want a cup of tea?"

Abi grabbed her phone from the floor and made for the kitchen door. Once safely on the other side, she tapped out another message to Jenna, asking if they could leave any sooner. Then she sent a GIF of a drowning dog to emphasise the severity of her situation.

"I'm already making tea," Stanley assured her as he wandered in behind. "You get ready, love."

"Thanks, Dad."

Before she got the chance to leave, Petra also padded across the kitchen into Stanley's arms, grumbling about how tired she was. He kissed the top of her head, but just as Petra's eyelids drooped, they shot open again. "Have you eaten all those crisps?"

Reaching behind himself while providing a human barrier, he brushed the empty packets towards the sink. "Absolutely not."

"Your cholesterol!"

Abi ignored the desperate plea for help in her dad's eyes and left them to it, bounding up the stairs to change. She hadn't given herself long in the end, and by the time she'd showered, styled her hair, and found clean clothes, the taxi was only a few minutes away.

Heading back down the stairs at breakneck speed, she came to an abrupt stop short of the front door because Stanley blocked her way. They'd already discussed work and football, though. What the hell else could there be?

He answered her question when he stepped aside and slid open the top drawer of the hallway cabinet. "I forgot to say that this turned up earlier. I opened the box by mistake but presume it's yours." Stanley held out a small rectangular package wrapped in tissue paper stamped with a picture of a purple dildo. Then his face turned almost the same colour as he added, "Unless it's your mother's and I'm in for a surprise on this Brighton trip."

The last part sent Abi over the edge. She almost died right there and then, snatching the package and tucking it inside the flannel shirt she'd decided to wear loose over a tee. "Shit," she muttered under her breath. Memories of ordering a new vibrator when she got home from *Il Mondo* hurtled back, and she cringed. "Sorry Dad. It's, um... a birthday present. For Jax."

She waited for him to disappear so she could hide it somewhere for later, but he only held open the door for her and didn't budge. It was hard to know whether to laugh or cry, but she couldn't consider it for long because the taxi was outside, blaring its horn. All she could do was mumble a quick "goodbye" and jog down the path with the box still tucked inside her shirt.

Jenna turned and smiled from the front passenger seat. "Hey."

At least from there she couldn't see the beads of sweat forming on Abi's upper lip. The squirm as the taxi pulled off was far more conspicuous, though. What was Abi supposed to do now? She was heading off to the football club with a vibrator. For a moment, she wondered if she was in some awful sitcom. If not, she could write one.

"Hey," she echoed.

Jenna turned to grin, but then her face fell. "Are you alright?"

"Yeah, don't worry. I'm not ill or anything, I—" On second thoughts, Abi was feeling a bit ill right now, but at least the shock had woken her up.

## 10

## JENNA

Jenna stood in front of Abi in the football club car park, tapping her foot with worry. She'd expected another night of teasing, based on what she'd endured at training on Wednesday, and right now she'd prefer that over Abi acting weird. "So, what's the problem?"

Opening her shirt and glancing over her shoulder, Abi whispered, "This." Then she shielded the package she'd just flashed and stepped back because the side door to the clubhouse had sprung open and startled her.

"Right... and what is it?"

"It's a vibrator!"

Jenna burst out laughing, a hand landing on Abi's shoulder as she tried to steady herself. It was partly with relief that there was nothing wrong. She wasn't in the mood for any more angst after spending most of the week wrestling numbers. Tonight was all about fun, and she intended to have some, even if it would now be at Abi's expense. "Did you bring that along as some sort of chat up prop? Because if so, you need more help than I can give."

"Of course I didn't! I forgot all about it because I was so

drunk when we went out on Monday and then my dad took the delivery earlier. He gave it to me just as I was leaving."

"Decided you could use a little help after all, huh? How in the world didn't you remember, though? You must have seen the order email come thr—" Jenna stopped dead and let out another shot of laughter. "Oh, no. Well, let that be a lesson to check your emails."

"Or it could be a lesson not to get drunk with you."

"No, it's not that. I promise."

Abi huffed and held out her hand. "Do you have a key to the changing rooms so I can hide it until later?"

"You want me to go into the changing rooms with you to hide a vibrator?" Jenna asked, adding air quotes to the last bit. "Are you sure this isn't your terrible attempt at seduction?"

"Would you just shut up and help me?"

After repositioning the package under her shirt, Abi marched to the concrete patio outside the changing rooms. Then she waited for Jenna to open the door and pull on the light cord before creeping inside. A shower area ran along the back of the room, and Abi peeped around the wall, trying to find a hiding place.

As she inspected every crevice, Jenna scoffed. "Does it matter where you put it? We'll get it again before we go and no one else will come in here before then. For goodness' sake, anyone would think you had Class A drugs or something. It's only a vibrator."

"It isn't *only* a vibrator. Have you any idea how much this thing cost me? The answer is more than I can reasonably afford, and if someone steals it, I'll cry." Abi finally plumped for a spot in the corner of the shower area, under an old towel someone had discarded.

"That's *really* inconspicuous."

"You're the one who said no one will see it. Just make sure we don't forget it's here."

"Oh, I'll remember it's here, and that's the most important thing. I wonder how many drinks it'll take to keep me quiet."

"How about cutting me some slack? If it's not you, it's my dad bugging me about football or my mum trying to set me up with Jax."

"Jax?!" Jenna exclaimed, before barrelling into more laughter. Now she was two up on Abi, who clearly regretted that slipping out because she groaned and trudged out of the changing rooms.

Jenna had just about composed herself by the time she'd crossed the patio and entered the clubhouse, where the bar staff had strung celebration banners in a variety of lurid colours. They'd also laid out finger foods and the boxes of party bags and games she'd dropped off earlier in the day. It looked like a children's birthday party circa 1996, exactly as planned, although the crude 'pin the tits on the barmaid' was admittedly less on theme.

"What in the depths of all hell were you thinking?" Abi frowned at the poster of a bikini-clad woman, cut out and stuck on another poster of a pub. It had done nothing to improve her mood.

Jenna shrugged. "As you know, I was very drunk on Monday night. It was not a time to be on eBay."

"I don't care how drunk you were. You've still gone down in my estimations."

"Coming from the person who arrived at a kids party with a vibrator." Jenna giggled as she took a pair of paper boobs from a pile on the table, unable to resist another jibe. She could tell Abi wasn't *really* upset, she was just playing along, and eventually she'd break.

"I hate you."

*There we go.*

"No, you don't." Jenna squinted and stuck the boobs on the

picture, making sure they landed on the barmaid's head. "See, it's very simple."

"That wasn't my point," Abi replied, before pursing her lips in a vain attempt to conceal a smile.

"Your point will have to wait, I'm afraid." People had been arriving for a while, but there was still no sign of Jax. It was the only problem blighting what had been a very entertaining evening so far, and Jenna wanted to get on with enjoying herself. "Where the fuck is the guest of honour? All that effort and she can't even show up on time. Your girlfriend is going to end up in my bad books." She smirked with the satisfaction of getting in a shot about that, too.

Abi rolled her eyes and shuffled forward, giving Jenna's trainer a gentle nudge with her foot. "Would you like me to find her?"

"Hmm," Jenna pondered as a way to stall. "In a minute. You're not getting out of being teased *that* easily." She straightened Abi's shirt, still in disarray from hiding her vibrator box. "You look great, by the way. Is this new?"

"Sort of. I got it a couple of summers ago but haven't had any opportunities to wear it."

"You look like a little lumberjack." It was only a shame she'd decided against wearing her work boots, because that would've really completed the look.

"You look nice, too," Abi replied quietly, her eyes darting down to the lace-trimmed black camisole Jenna had decided to wear in an attempt to smarten up her jeans. Unfortunately, her tan lines were awful and it only highlighted that she looked like a drumstick lolly.

"I look ridiculous," she replied.

"You look great. You always look great."

Abi's sheepish smile was as cute as her outfit and Jenna struggled to return herself to the original point. She'd love to spend the whole evening flirting, especially now that she knew it hadn't scared Abi off on Monday night, but they were still missing Jax. "Thank you. I appreciate you lying. Would you mind checking outside for me while I make sure the cake has arrived?"

"Cake, you say? Leave it with me. I'll make sure I find her."

"My hero."

Jenna pulled her phone from the back pocket of her jeans and was about to message Cass about her tardiness when she saw the silver Mercedes that she so coveted rolling down the driveway. Jax was finally here, and Abi was already jogging across the car park to greet her, which meant it was time to prep the rest of the guests. There was no point trying to hide them, that would be ridiculous, but until the cake came out, they needed to stick with the story about this being a social.

Having set the expectation, Jenna dashed into the kitchen, where she lifted the lid on a big white box containing a football field in buttercream, with twenty-two perfectly crafted chocolate players. The bakery had done a great job.

Once she'd confirmed they'd also delivered the decorations she'd ordered, she rushed back out into the bar area, expecting to find Jax inside, but she was still having what looked like an intense talk with Abi in the middle of the car park.

Jenna waved, but neither were paying any attention. She was about to go out and cajole them along, but that would look suspicious. Instead, a piece of mischief struck her and she ducked through the back door. She laid a trap for later, then returned to the bar again, but still Abi and Jax were in the car park. What were they talking about that was more important than the party?

The only thing for it now was a drink, so Jenna headed to the bar and ordered herself a double rum and Coke. Then she stood by the side door, trying a few more times to catch Abi's attention and failing miserably. She was halfway through her drink before the pair of them finally sauntered into the clubhouse, still deep in conversation.

"I hope we're not keeping you from each other?" she asked. Her choice of greeting had the desired effect of making Abi's shoulders roll forward, rightly anticipating more teasing. Curiously, though, Jax's did the same.

"I'm sorry it's ju—" Jax got out before Abi blathered over her about shutting up and needing a drink.

Jenna frowned, wondering what on earth was going on between them. Surely Petra's matchmaking hadn't worked, because they were about the least compatible couple in the history of dating, but there was something amiss.

They exchanged complicit looks, before Jax deftly changed the subject. "Yes to a drink! And it's my birthday next week," she noted, elbowing Abi gently. "Not that anyone's remembered, so I guess they're on you."

Abi and Jax made their way through the groups of guests, chatting and joking, until they reached the far end of the bar next to the pool table. Jenna followed, absently stirring a straw around her drink. She still couldn't work out why Jax looked like she'd been caught out.

"I take it you don't want one?" Abi asked, nodding down at the glass in Jenna's hand.

Jenna took out the straw and downed the remaining half of her drink, then set the empty glass on the bar. "Wrong."

Abi's eyes widened. "Fair enough. You were serious about another hangover. Noted."

Jax laughed. "Another hangover?"

"Yeah. We went out on Monday night and both got twatted. It wasn't intentional it just sort of... happened."

This time, Jenna couldn't quite discern the nature of the looks Abi and Jax exchanged, but whatever the cause, it resulted in a sudden compulsion to have Abi alone again. She didn't know where it had sprung up from, but the feeling very definitely verged on jealousy. "Hey, can I fill you in on the big leap of faith I told you about on Tuesday?" she asked, sidling up to Abi as she turned to face the bar and tried to flag down the barmaid. "I'll be nice."

"Promise?"

Jenna nodded. "Meet me outside as soon as I've done the cake reveal."

She headed back into the kitchen and rooted around in a bag to find the number candles she'd ordered in extra-large size. Then she added as many sparklers as the cake would hold, lit them all, and stepped back to keep from burning off her eyebrows. Perhaps it was overkill, but there was no time to worry about that now, because she needed to carry the cake through before the sparklers burned out.

A few of the other players had already been primed to start up a chorus of happy birthday as soon as she appeared, and when Jenna kicked open the door, they began a steady warble which became louder as everyone else got the message and joined in.

Jax shoved Abi on the shoulder and then whispered something in her ear. It made Jenna's heart thump and she had to quickly right her smile when it faltered.

*There's that jealousy again.*

"Happy birthday!" Jenna shouted when she reached them, setting the cake down on a table and taking a step back again because she was beginning to sweat.

"Holy smoke!" Jax also backed off, her hands pressed to her cheeks. "This is amazing. Thank you so much."

"You're welcome. Now blow it all out before someone calls the fire service."

"I don't mind if you want to get me a firewoman for my birthday."

The comment was Jax all over, and Jenna laughed. Then she caught Abi practically salivating over the cake, which was a relief because Jenna knew how to deal with that kind of competition. "If you can find a knife, you can have the first piece," she said, giving Abi's shoulder a quick rub. "Bring me some outside?"

Abi didn't need telling twice. She was off like a shot, and Jenna made her way out of the bar through the back door. There was a bench under the window, and she sat on it to wait.

A few minutes later, Abi emerged. In one hand was her pint and another rum and Coke, pinched precariously between her thumb and forefinger, and in the other was a paper plate stacked high with green frosted sponge cake.

"Have you left any for anyone else?" Jenna asked as Abi set the plate between them on the bench. She stuck her finger into the buttercream and then licked it off slowly.

"Oh, I'm sorry. Did you want some too?" Abi sat opposite, set their drinks on the floor, and pulled the plate towards herself. Then she took the top slice, using her free hand to catch the crumbs. "So, what's this leap of faith? I'm intrigued."

Jenna wiped her finger on her jeans. Then she held up her phone and scrolled through pictures of the new shop. "I'm going to divide this room up," and with that she skipped through a few shots to give a better view, "so I can rent out space. Then I'm going to convert the back room so there's also a private area for a massage therapist or something. It'll generate extra revenue."

"Sounds like a great idea."

"I hope so. I ran the numbers this week, using your dad's quote, and it'll cost a little bit more than I'd originally planned to get everything set up, but hopefully be worth it in the long run." With full occupancy she'd more than cover the rent before she even started, which was a great position to be in.

"Well, you have to speculate to accumulate."

Jenna playfully slapped Abi's stomach with the back of her hand. "Alright, smart arse. What do you think, seriously?"

"If anyone can do it, you can. Total faith. You'll be fleecing hipsters in no time."

"Hey, I don't fleece anyone!"

Jenna whacked harder this time, and Abi rubbed her stomach. "Alright, I take that back. Please don't hit me again."

"I was asking because I value your opinion, but now I'm questioning why."

"I'm also questioning why, to be honest. Isn't this more of a Cass thing?"

Frowning, Jenna turned the phone over in her palm. "I know you think it's weird that I still spend time with Cass but—" When Abi went to interrupt, Jenna shushed her. "She's basically a good person when you get to know her."

"You *really* don't have to explain yourself to me."

"I know I don't have to, but I want you to know there's nothing romantic between me and Cass anymore. We're just friends."

For a few seconds, Abi stared silently. Then she got a mischievous glint in her eye. "All caps friends?"

Jenna tried to glare rather than laugh, whilst pulling the plate back towards herself. "You need to watch out, or that expensive vibrator of yours might find a new owner, and so will the rest of this cake."

"I'm only teasing you. For the record, I was just feeling insecure on Sunday and having a wobble. I worried that maybe I'd mucked up our friendship by not getting back to you for so long. It's actually pretty sweet that you cared so much. I appreciated the effort."

"Did I say I cared...?"

"Afraid so. It all came out when you were drunk."

Jenna tried and failed to keep from blushing. She knew she

cared, and she was beginning to realise quite how much.

## 11

## ABI

One devastating hangover was enough for at least the next decade, so when everyone else was downing shots and trying to eke out the fun before last orders, Abi broke away and headed outside to finish her pint in peace. She sat on the wall and stared out over the playing fields, listening to the crickets chirping somewhere in the darkness whilst waiting for her taxi to arrive. Her moment of peace didn't last long, though, before the door swung open and allowed the party noise to escape.

"Are you okay, bud?" Jax asked, poking her head through the frame.

"Yeah, just taking a break. Have you enjoyed your evening?"

"It's been spectacular, but I'm still waiting on that firewoman. Jenna said something about getting you in the uniform but that's probably more for her benefit than mine." When Abi reached to pick up a handful of dried mud from the ground and hurled it at her, Jax laughed and shielded herself with the door. "Touched a nerve?"

Abi only shook her head. "Don't start again. I had enough of it in the car park earlier. You know there's nothing going on between us, we've just been helping each other with work stuff."

That wasn't entirely true, but Jax didn't need to know the details. It would only encourage her.

"Uhuh. That's why she's been glued to your side all evening. Business."

"No, she's been glued to my side tonight because I've been helping her with your birthday party. I hope you've shown your gratitude."

Jax considered for a second. "Nah, I'll let you do that."

Before Abi could hurl any more mud at her, she darted back inside, and all was peaceful again. Abi took a sip of her pint, before setting it on the wall next to her. Once again, though, she was quickly interrupted. The door swung open and this time Jenna appeared. It was a good job Jax wasn't there to gloat, or glimpse the big smile that Abi was desperately trying to hide.

Jenna walked over and straddled the wall next to Abi, dangling one leg off the edge. "I wondered where you'd disappeared to. How did you get on at pass the parcel earlier?"

The question was innocuous enough, but Abi gathered from Jenna's tone that it was leading somewhere. "Not well. I didn't even win a sweet. Why?"

"Oh, no reason. Just thought you'd be good with small packages."

Twigging, Abi rolled her eyes for the umpteenth time that night. "Yeah, hilarious. Am I ever going to live that down?"

Jenna laughed. "I'm sorry. It's too much to resist. Just like teasing you over Jax..."

"I'm not interested in Jax."

"Sure?"

This time, the bravado faded away, and Jenna sounded worried more than teasing. It made Abi smile again because she was starting to think Jax was right. Either that or it was just wishful thinking, aided by about half a dozen pints of lager.

"It's only my mum desperate to set me up with someone," Abi qualified.

"Relatable. My grandparents are the same. They think I need someone to look after me, which I guess is only natural. They got together when they were seventeen and have barely spent a day apart. I wondered how they'd be with my sexuality, given how old school they are, but it didn't bother them at all. So long as I find *someone*."

Abi turned to hook one of her legs over the wall and face Jenna. "My parents are fine with it, too. I'm not sure they have much choice."

"I can't imagine you with a guy."

"I had a boyfriend once," Abi recalled, wondering if it really counted given they'd never so much as kissed or even held hands. "I was only twelve at the time and he was less a boyfriend, more a boy who was a friend. We played football together every evening and people just assumed. To be fair, he turned out to be gay, too."

"Shocker. Are you still friends?"

"Nah. He was bullied out of the school team and stopped playing, then I was also chucked out, so we drifted. I wish I'd done more to stand up for him but I don't think I really considered it too much at that age. We have it so easy when you think about it. Any woman can turn up here and play, but if you're a gay, bisexual, or trans man, it's a different story. Football culture sucks sometimes."

"Yep. Although it isn't fine for us to play everywhere. My last team were horrible."

"Is that why you ended up here? I always wondered why you wanted to drop a league."

"Winning isn't everything."

"Mhm."

"I'm serious! Yeah, we were top of the league, but it got to the point where I dreaded football every week because the atmosphere was so crappy. Back-stabbing, bitchiness... it was like being on the set of Mean Girls. The kicker was when they bullied out a trans player who only wanted to train with us and meet new people. They were total arseholes."

Still buoyed by booze and interested to know where the line between them was drawn, Abi hooked her hand around the back of Jenna's knee and gently stroked it with her thumb. "That's really shit." Her heart thumped when Jenna took hold of her wrist. She thought she'd gone too far, but Jenna just wanted to play with the ring on her thumb. She held Abi's hand in her lap and spun the two bands, whilst absently staring at them. "You know if anyone upsets you here, I'll kill them."

Jenna laughed. "Wouldn't that just make you part of the problem? Besides, I can't really see you killing anyone."

Abi flexed the bicep of her free arm. "It's the sentiment that counts."

Jenna squeezed Abi's muscle. It finally broke her fascination with the ring, and she let her hands drop into her own lap. "Yeah, I know. This is exactly why I love The Blues."

"We are pretty awesome, but I still don't understand why you came *here*. You could've gone to another team in the higher league. You're easily good enough."

"Just a feeling, I guess. My first training session I remember you inviting me in to play pool, buying me a drink, and thinking how nice you were. I knew we'd end up friends with the caps lock on and that was more important to me than anything else."

Abi had to stifle a laugh. She *was* nice, but that wasn't why she'd bought Jenna a drink. Or invited her in to play pool. It was a mixture of thinking she was smoking hot, and Jax putting every player on the team under order to secure Jenna by any means possible. "I'm glad my plan worked."

"Me too. I was considering quitting altogether at that point, and you guys saved me from making a big mistake. Years on the school team trying to be taken seriously, years in the county youth system... what a waste. I'm glad I didn't give up."

The thought of a little blonde girl with pigtails, running rings around all the boys, made Abi smile. "I bet you were a real pain in the arse to play against, even then."

"You better believe it. I was always football mad and idolised Kelly Smith. I wanted to be an England goal scorer, just like her. In hindsight, she was also my first crush."

"Kelly Smith?! I can't imagine you with a footballer."

"What the fuck does that mean?" Jenna shoved Abi hard on the shoulder, so that she had to put out a hand to steady herself on the wall.

"I don't know, it's just... can you really see the likes of Cass on a football pitch? For a start, her cigarette might go out."

"I've dated footballers before! In fact, my first girlfriend was on the county team with me, and I was crazy about her."

"When you were how old?"

"Fifteen."

"Right, and since then?" When Jenna glared, Abi laughed. Then she yawned and stretched her arms high above her head. "I should grab my little package because my cab will be here soon."

"I've got a ride coming, too, so I'll let you into the changing rooms."

Abi reached behind herself to grab her pint. She would've downed what remained, but Jenna stole it before she could get the glass near her lips.

"Hey!" Abi protested.

Jenna only shrugged and set the empty glass back down on the wall. Then she got up and pulled a set of keys from her pocket. She unlocked the changing room door, threw it open, and leant against the frame to let Abi pass.

Jogging across the changing room, Abi rounded the wall into the showers and then crouched to grab the old towel. She lifted it up, then froze. "What the fuck?" she shouted. "Where is it?"

Flapping the towel to make sure the box wasn't tangled in it somewhere, Abi straightened up and stepped back around the wall to find Jenna spluttering. If this was her idea of a joke, though, it wasn't at all funny.

Jenna disappeared into the away team changing room and came back waving the box in the air. "Looking for this?"

As Abi made her first stride across the tiles, Jenna darted through the door and swung it shut.

"Fuck's sake," Abi muttered, rattling the handle. For a second, she thought Jenna had locked it and her heart pounded, but then she realised that in her haste she wasn't pushing hard enough.

She finally spilled out onto the patio. "Where are you? This is not funny!"

"Yes, it is!" came back in reply from somewhere near the goal mouth.

Abi jogged across the patio and down the ledge onto the grass, taking care of her step as she tried to avoid any divots, but she had no chance. She couldn't see a thing until the white of the goal post came into view. "Where are you now, you little shit?"

This time Jenna's voice came from behind, somewhere near the car park. "This must be a great vibrator!"

Abi sprinted over the grass, but when she reached the drive, tiptoed across the gravel and then stood deadly still. One window was ajar, and a little chatter floated out from the bar, but the car park itself was quiet.

A slight crunch came from behind a car, and Abi spun around to find Jenna darting towards the back of the clubhouse. When Abi gave chase, she squealed.

"No, no, no," Jenna pleaded, struggling to breathe for laughter as she reached a dead end. Someone had left a stack of cardboard boxes that needed breaking down for recycling and it blocked the way. "You know I always win." A small security light illuminated Jenna, inching backwards with her hands in the air and the vibrator clutched in one of them. But then she gasped and pointed behind Abi. "Shit, look at that!"

Abi turned before she knew what was happening and Jenna flew past her, but this time she was close and soon caught up. She reached for the back of Jenna's top just as she passed the entrance to the clubhouse.

Jenna shrieked again, putting out a hand to steady herself on the wall. Then she backed up against it, still spluttering with laughter.

"You're not winning this time. Hand it over." Abi strained to reach but Jenna stood on tiptoes, and Abi fell forward, placing a palm on the wall beside Jenna's head. It was either that or face-plant the brick.

"Can't," Jenna whispered next to Abi's ear, her breath warm against Abi's neck. She lingered there and as their torsos pressed together, Abi's arm dropped away. Her legs were close to buckling, too, and not only from the exertion of running when she was already exhausted.

Abi was trying to steady herself when Jenna's reply registered.

*Can't?*

She looked at Jenna's hand and realised it was empty. She must have put the box down or dropped it, but a desire to be close to Jenna once again overtook Abi's desire for her vibrator. The scent of jasmine and orange-blossom gave Abi a head rush and drew her forward, dancing closer to Jenna's lips.

The small amount of light from the clubhouse twinkled in the brown eyes trained on Abi's mouth. Did Jenna want this too, or was Abi still being blinded by alcohol and hope? She felt like she was back on the football pitch, forced to make a split-second decision that could get someone hurt. Only this time, it would be her.

She was still considering, suspended in a state of arousal and self-doubt, when Jenna answered for her.

It took a moment to register the kiss that had just pushed her back a step. When she did, their eyes locked and this time Abi didn't hesitate. Jenna's hands wrapped around her neck, then ran through her hair as Abi pinned Jenna to the wall and kissed her hard.

There was no room for doubt anymore, Abi was only thinking about how good this felt—raw, passionate, and spontaneous. Her whole body pounded with excitement and the sound of blood thundered in her ears, punctuated by their grunts and the scrape of Jenna's belt catching on the brick. They were both breathless as Abi's hand slipped down and clawed back up Jenna's leg, then under her T-shirt, raking over the soft skin on her side.

When Jenna took a handful of Abi's hair and tilted back her head, latching onto her neck, Abi dug her nails into Jenna's back and drew them closer together, finally losing contact with the wall. Before she even realised that she was doing it, she was grinding their hips together, her hand sliding onto Jenna's butt, but then the warm feeling of Jenna's mouth sucking up to her jaw ceased.

At first, Abi thought she really had gone too far this time. She pulled back, scrambling for excuses, before realising that Jenna was reacting to headlights dazzling her as they came down the drive. Jenna squinted and raised her arm to shield her eyes. Then, with her heart pounding, Abi restored the distance between them and straightened out her clothes, while Jenna grabbed the package from the floor.

"Here you go," Jenna offered, her voice rasping a little.

She cleared her throat and looked down at the gravel, then got into the car. The silver Mercedes with the blacked-out windows. It was Cass, and she'd been followed in by a taxi.

## 12

# JENNA

"Are you okay?" Cass asked as she cut the engine and caused the cabin to light up like The Starship Enterprise.

"Huh?" Jenna had been staring towards the clubhouse, but her head jolted around at the realisation Cass was trying to engage her in conversation. Until that moment, she'd still been backed up against the wall. In spirit, at least.

"I was asking if you're okay."

"Um, yeah. Sorry." Jenna shot Cass a smile for reassurance. She was clearly concerned as to the state in which she'd found her ex-girlfriend, but she needn't have worried. Despite expecting to struggle tonight, and Jax pulling her aside on various occasions to check in, Jenna had enjoyed herself. "To be honest I didn't think about it."

She felt a pang of guilt at that admission but didn't have the energy to dwell. There had been a lot going on with the party and the shop, and it had been a useful distraction.

"Did everything go off without a hitch?"

There was a pause while Jenna watched Abi's cab perform a three point turn and head back out of the car park. "All but Jax turning up late. I thought you were only going for one drink with her earlier?"

"We got... waylaid."

The way Cass said 'waylaid' aroused suspicion. "Oh yeah?" Jenna asked with a slight lilt which acknowledged she understood what had happened. That was why Jax looked like she'd been caught out earlier, not because there was anything going on with Abi. It also explained why Cass had texted and offered to pick them both up tonight. There was always something in it for her. "And is that all going off without a hitch, too?"

Cass laughed and took her phone from its cradle on the dashboard. Hopefully, she was sending Jax a message to hurry up and finish her drink so they could leave. "Do you know what's odd?"

"No. What?"

"That it doesn't feel at all odd to talk with you about this. I suppose that says it all."

"I suppose it does," Jenna agreed. And the fact that she felt no jealousy whatsoever also spoke volumes. She'd been sceptical when Cass had asked whether they could remain friends, because she'd never done it before. They'd felt like just friends for so long, though, that it had come quite naturally. It was the thought of Abi with Jax that had sent Jenna into a territorial tailspin.

Cass returned her phone to its spot on the dashboard and then looked over. "Can I confess something?"

"Depends what it is. Anything serious and I think you need a Catholic priest."

"Amusing, but I'm being serious. I'm not sure if you realised, but when I asked to be friends, it was because I hoped we'd get back together."

*No shit.*

"Is that why you booked us a table at *Les Saisons*? I have to admit it worried me a bit. It's a romantic place..."

Cass shook her head. "No. I'm over it now. I can honestly say that when you find someone else, I'll be pleased for you."

That was good to know, but Jenna still wasn't quite sure she was ready to let slip about the kiss with Abi. Not least because she had no idea what it meant. There had always been a bit of a vibe—enough so that Cass had been envious of the way they were with each other in the early days—but it had never been allowed to progress past a casual flirtation. And as much as Cass said she would be happy when Jenna met someone else, it still felt odd given the history.

"So, what was the fancy restaurant about?"

"I just wanted you to have something to look forward to. The anniversary..." Cass trailed off and jabbed at her phone to check for a message, even though it hadn't lit up. They were slipping back into difficult territory that she always struggled to navigate. "I know the reservation is a few days after, but *Les Saisons* is very popular."

"That's really sweet, thank you. I'm sorry things have been a big fraught between us lately but I appreciate the gesture. Hopefully now things are more sorted, it'll be a bit easier." With the air cleared, and her question answered, Jenna moved onto another. "So, what is this thing with you and Jax?"

Cass laughed. "Don't worry, just a little fun. Jax's reputation precedes her."

That was another relief. Jax was incredible and one of Jenna's best friends, but her track record with women was... colourful. She didn't do anything long term and Jenna would hate to see Cass get her heart broken. "I shouldn't dust off my wedding outfit just yet then?"

"No. I'm not ready to get into another relationship, but it's nice to have some fun."

"I bet." Fun was definitely a nice thing to have, and Jenna's mind was once again cast back against that wall.

A smile played out across her lips at just the wrong moment because Cass caught it. "What's that look for?" she asked, her eyebrow lifting.

"I'm considering having a little fun of my own. I think… maybe." She'd sounded less sure as she went on and shook her head slightly. "I don't know actually whether it would be just fun in the way you and Jax mean it."

"Maybe something a bit more than that?"

Was it? Right now, Jenna didn't know. She was currently high from their kiss and desperate to find out, but part of her was also scared. Just because she'd managed to keep a friendship with Cass, didn't mean she'd be able to with Abi when everything went tits up—and it *would* go tits up. Relationships always did. Besides, Abi might not want anything more to happen between them.

Before she could dwell, or answer, one of the back doors popped open and Jax flung herself inside. "There you are! Where did you disappear to?"

Thankfully, Cass started the engine again and plunged them into darkness because Jenna knew she'd blushed. She bit her lip to keep from grinning and incriminating herself. "I was just getting some fresh air and contemplating something." They pulled off and Jenna hooked her hand on the headrest as she peered back at Jax. "I can't believe I'm going to say this, but you may have been right the other night."

"Tell me more. I love to hear how I'm right."

"It was the thing about being more proactive in my love life. Not relying on women to ask me out. It's funny how I'm so capable of being assertive in my work life but when it comes to asking a woman out on a date I lose my shit and think of every excuse under the sun why I shouldn't."

Jax's grin was wide, smug, and annoying. "It's scary, isn't it?"

"What, admitting you have a point? Terrifying."

They all laughed now, and Jenna turned to face forward as they rolled down the driveway. Then she pulled the phone from her pocket. Her eyes blurred over the screen and she rubbed them, trying to sober up a bit. She'd always been able to hold her drink and usually hid it well but that didn't mean she wasn't thoroughly pissed again. "I'm considering giving it a go, but I need some tips. Shall I text?"

"Coward! Do it in person. What's the worst that can happen? If she says no, at least you have an answer and can move on."

"I'm not sure that is the worst that can happen." Famine, fire, and flood all felt like viable catastrophes right now.

"If this was work, what would you do? Not take a risk because it might all go wrong, or dive in and throw everything at it because of how great the rewards are if it all goes right?"

Jenna laughed as she recalled the quote she'd sent to Abi. Was the universe conspiring to bring that back around and bite her in the arse? Not that she believed in divine intervention. You got from life what you were prepared to work for. Or step outside of your comfort zone for. Whatever the circumstances you were dealt, there was always something you could control, and in this case, she knew that meant making a move.

"How do I throw everything at it, though? She may not even be interested." Although Abi had certainly *seemed* interested. She'd hung on Jenna's every word. She'd been in constant contact all week. And then of course there was the most compelling evidence—that kiss. Jenna had experienced her fair share of drunken fumbles, and they'd never felt like that before.

"You don't have to actually throw anything. Just ask her out!"

"I tend to agree," Cass added. "The only way to find out for definite is to ask this woman out on a date. Then you can move on with your life, either way."

"That is definitely the sensible approach," Jenna muttered, sure it was easier said than done.

"Does she like football?" Jax asked, shuffling around and producing some rectangles of card from her back pocket.

Jenna hooked her arm around the headrest again and frowned at Jax. "She happens to, yes. Why?"

"Because I've just been given two tickets to the opening of that new footgolf centre next Saturday, but I can't make it because it's during the day and I've agreed to help with a friendly for one of the youth teams. You can have them and invite her. Easy."

She held out the tickets and Jenna took them, before turning to face forward again. "Thanks."

"You're welcome. Now we've resolved that, where are we heading? Rather than going home shall we continue this party at one of our houses? It is my birthday, after all…"

"Mine is closest," Cass replied before Jenna could mount any objection. Not that she really wanted to go home alone.

"Fine," she agreed with a short sigh. "But if I have to listen to you two having sex, we're going to fall out. Birthday or not."

13
===

## ABI

"Are you alright, love?" Stanley asked, frowning into a bowl of bran flakes. It wasn't just the cereal troubling him, it was also disappointment that he hadn't managed to get a rise out of Abi, despite numerous attempts to tease her for buying Jax a vibrator when there was supposedly nothing between them.

"Yeah, just tired." There it was. That excuse to explain away emotional turmoil.

Arousal had cooled to disappointment as she'd climbed into the taxi last night. Alone, besides her little package, while Jenna was most likely kissing Cass up against another wall somewhere. It was a genuine struggle not to hate her, and to add insult to injury, they were about to spend the day together.

Submitting to her fate, Abi scraped most of her bran flakes into the bin and loaded her bowl into the dishwasher. Then she grabbed her keys from the hallway cabinet, slumped into her van, and continued to ruminate as she drove across town. This was why you should never listen to Jax or get your hopes up. Especially when your life was in a perpetual crap loop.

Five minutes later the silver Mercedes came into view. Abi parallel parked in front of it, got out, and wedged herself between the bumper of Cass's car and the back doors of her van, inching them open far enough to grab her tools. It was tempting to be far less careful, but she wasn't a thug, and she wasn't *that* jealous.

Taking a deep breath, Abi steeled herself to knock on the door. But before she could do that, the side gate swung open, and Cass appeared, waving cheerily as she walked across the front of the house. "Can I help you with anything?"

"I'm all set. Thanks."

Abi locked the van and carried her tools through to the rear garden. It was untouched from the previous weekend, but the grass had grown another few inches, almost engulfing the gnomes entirely.

"Are you sure you can you deal with this in a day?" Cass asked as she stared out across her unloved garden.

"Yes, although I don't want to take all the length off this lawn in one go. Not when it's so hot."

"Sounds like the sort of thing I'd say to one of my customers," Jenna quipped from behind.

At the sound of her voice, Abi's entire body tensed, and she jumped back to avoid being impaled on the fork she'd just dropped. "Oh, hi," she muttered as she bent to pick it up.

"I'm heading home, but will you call in and see me after you've met Jax later?"

"I'm not sure what time we'll finish. It might be late. You know how Jax is when you're buying her a beer."

"Tomorrow then?"

"Can I let you know?" All Abi wanted was to be as far away from Jenna and Cass as humanly possible. She'd calm down, she knew she would, but right now it was excruciating.

With a quick nod, Jenna frowned and rounded the building towards the gate. Then Cass followed, pulling a set of keys from her pocket.

Once they were gone, Abi took a deep breath and tried to focus on the task at hand. The quicker she got on with it, the faster she could get out of there, so she started prising the matted grass away from a gnome. She was about to move onto a second one when the gate creaked and disturbed her again.

"Sorry, forgot something."

Abi turned to find Jenna back in the garden, grabbing a sweater from a chair on the patio. She offered a small, sheepish smile and then ran off, and Abi knew what it was: regret and awkwardness.

She propped herself on the shovel, her eyes closed against the sun. Would nothing ever go right? If she'd ruined their friendship on top of everything else, she wasn't sure she'd cope.

When she opened her eyes again, a gnome sneered up at her and she took the shovel, unceremoniously obliterating its smarmy little face. The spade ricocheted back and hit another, and it also sprayed shards into the grass.

Abi froze. What the fuck had she done? A wave of guilt almost brought up the few bran flakes she'd managed at breakfast. They may only be old gnomes, but that was most definitely not the point.

"I need to get a grip." She chucked her spade into the grass and stood with her hands on her hips as she surveyed the mess. How was she going to explain this to Cass?

She was still considering a few moments later when the phone vibrated in her pocket. Fumbling to pull it out, she jabbed at the accept button. "What?"

A raucous laugh buzzed through the speaker. "What the hell's up with you, buddy?"

It was Jax, and Abi rubbed a hand over her brow. "Sorry. Bad moment. I've... er... never mind. What do you want?" That had come out shorter than she intended, but given Jax was as blunt as Abi's shovel, she wouldn't notice.

"Can you do four later? Something's come up and I need to move things around."

"Sure."

"I'll let Jenna know, too. Since she's your business manager these days."

"No!"

"No?"

"I just mean, I don't need Jenna." Abi gawped again at her own destruction. She didn't want to see Jenna right now, not until she'd figured out what to do.

"Okay, but can I invite her anyway? She might need our support."

"If Jenna still has a hangover, maybe what she needs is to stay in bed."

"You know what? I get you've had it tough, but Jenna's really tried to help. I thought you'd have shown her a bit more compassion."

"Over a hangover?" Unquestionably, Jenna had helped a lot. That was part of why Abi felt so guilty for smashing the gnomes, but it was hardly the end of the world.

"No, because of the reason she has a hangover. You know how much she struggles this time of the year, what with her mum's anniversary. She got so drunk last night that I messaged Cass to pick us up. Granted, it only led to us all doing more drinking at her kitchen table, but…"

Confusion turned to another wave of nausea, which drained every drop of blood from Abi's face and sent it into her work boots. Jax had also been there last night? "What do you mean, her mum's anniversary?"

"Shit," came quietly down the line. Then a huff. "It's probably not my place to go into the details if she hasn't said. But Jenna's mum got ill around this time of year, then she passed away, and the circumstances are… tough. Okay? So, can you just let me invite her? She always has a crappy couple of weeks and I want to make sure she's alright."

Abi nodded imperceptibly, then shook her head when she realised Jax couldn't see. "Of course," she mumbled. "I'll see you at four."

Jax hung up and Abi stuffed the phone back into her pocket. Then she jogged to the van. She'd made yet another huge mistake and needed help from the one person she hoped wouldn't judge her too harshly. Or at least as harshly as she was already judging herself.

\* \* \*

Not twenty minutes since she'd left the kitchen, Abi returned to find Stanley with his head in the fridge. He took a step back, his face written with guilt, and slid the bacon packet onto the shelf. "I was just—"

"I won't tell Ma," Abi replied before he finished his sentence. Then she hung her head in shame. "I've done something."

"That's good."

"No, it's something bad."

"Oh."

"Yes. Oh. I smashed my client's gnomes."

Stanley laughed. Not just a little titter, but a full belly laugh that had him clutching onto the work surface as tears rolled down his cheeks. All the while, Abi stared. Unamused. She folded her arms and glared at him, hoping for a little more support.

"Sorry, love," he managed, pulling a cotton hanky from his pocket and dabbing his face. "I know I shouldn't laugh."

"No, you shouldn't. This is serious. I behaved like an animal."

He let out another burst and then his shoulders shook as he tried to hold back. "Barbaric. We should have you caged."

"It's not funny!" She snatched the kitchen towel from its hook next to the sink and thwacked him with it out of sheer frustration. "Jenna got me a job working for her ex and I've made a complete and utter mess of it. Everything I touch turns to shit."

"I think that's a bit OTT."

"Is it? First, I take out a girl at football. Then a bunch of garden ornaments. Maybe I've got more of Ma's personality than I thought."

"I don't think you can blame your mother for this, she's never smashed any gnomes. Whatever possessed you?"

What had possessed Abi to take a shovel to two innocent gnomes? She knew the answer, and it was a simple one. Jealousy. Insecurity. Frustration. "Jenna."

"Ah." After offering a quick nod, Stanley grabbed a couple of mugs from the cupboard. As always, tea would be the answer, and the kettle already chugged close to boiling. "Should've known this would involve her somewhere down the line."

"Should you?"

"Of course. I can see how fond of her you are."

"Can you?" With a quick shake of her head, Abi tried to clear her squint. "If you knew I liked Jenna, why did you keep teasing me about Jax and that bloody... present?"

"For fun."

"Oh terrific. Is there anyone who doesn't enjoy a regular laugh at my expense?" She took over the tea making duties because it beat being made fun of, grabbing an extra mug from the cupboard and setting it next to Stanley's. By the time she'd dropped in tea bags, poured the water, and added a glug of milk to each, he'd finally straightened himself out and looked ready for a serious conversation.

"I think you need to fill me in." He leant back against the

counter as Abi handed him his mug. It was the big one, with 'World's Greatest Dad' in faded lettering on the side.

"I kissed Jenna last night," she admitted, praying he was going to live up to the title and not tease her again. "If I tell you everything, do you promise not to think any worse of me than you already do?"

"I don't think ill of you now but go on."

Abi let rip with the whole sorry tale. The vibrator. Jax sticking her oar in. The kiss. Cass coming in on her trusty steed, which masqueraded as a Mercedes. Finding Jenna at Cass's house. Then, learning from Jax that there had been a catastrophic misunderstanding. Stanley took it all in and kept a neutral expression until the kicker—Jenna's mum was dead, and Abi had been too preoccupied to find out that key detail until after the fact.

"And so, I'm a fucking dickhead," Abi concluded. She could summarise in no other way. "I jumped to conclusions when I should have spoken to her first, and I blew it. I don't deserve her after this."

"Wow," he responded after a long pause, raising a hand to his forehead and rubbing the deep furrows. "I hate to say it, love, but it sounds like that was the problem all along."

"What do you mean?"

Stanley took another few moments, all the while regarding his daughter with a fond smile. "Do you remember when you were twelve? You'd been playing for that boys' team, but they chucked you out because you were too old?" His voice trembled when he said, 'too old', as if the memory had evoked all his past rage on the subject. He'd fought for months to get them to reconsider. "Even the school team wouldn't have you anymore, although you were better than most of the lads."

Abi nodded. "Yeah."

"After that, it was a struggle to get you to school. You'd never been much cop at it."

"Is there a point to this, or are you just trying to make me feel even shittier?"

"We were at our wits' end with you," he continued, not missing a beat. "Detentions, suspensions, acting up. And then I took you to work with me, because your mother was about ready to throttle you, and something clicked."

"Mhm. We had great fun."

Stanley paused and smiled again. "Yeah, we did. Because you found what you were good at. Being outside. Working with your hands. Using your body and doing a decent day of hard graft." He took a step forward and placed a reassuring hand on Abi's shoulder. "I get why the last few months have been so tough. You've lost the things that make you feel like you, on top of being dumped with no proper explanation." He gave it a little shake. "It's shot your confidence to pieces, love. But for what it's worth, I think Jax is right. There's absolutely no reason you shouldn't go after Jenna, so stop making excuses, and next time you doubt yourself, you know what you do?"

"Put down the shovel and step away from the gnomes?"

It made them both laugh, and Stanley backed up against the counter. "Well, yes. But I was going to say, remember that this is only a rough patch. It will get better, and you have just as much to offer as Jenna. Or that Cass woman. She's not the only one with connections." He tapped the side of his nose. "Who's the one getting Jenna's shop fit done pretty much at cost?"

Abi nodded and swiped away a tear whilst simultaneously trying not to laugh again. "You're doing it at cost?"

Stanley shrugged. "Like I said, I could see how fond of her you were."

Abi took a deep breath. Then she blew it out through her mouth, trying to compose herself, but it was no good. The floodgates had already opened, and a year of grief manifested in a wave of tears and snot.

"Come on, let it all out," Stanley encouraged, taking a fresh hanky from his pocket and throwing it at her. He did sensitive, but only to a point.

Abi pressed the soft cotton to her eyes and closed them tight as she sobbed over it all. Not just the day, or the weekend, but all of it. The abandonment and confusion she'd felt when her ex called off their relationship. The fear she'd felt lying in a hospital bed and hearing the word 'ventilator', even if she didn't need one herself. The sense of failure when she packed up all her stuff and handed over the keys to the flat she'd called home for seven years. That bloody tropical fish she hadn't kept alive.

"I think I need to go and sort out this mess with Cass," Abi decided once she'd calmed down enough to speak. For a start, her tools were still in the garden.

After taking another few moments to clean up her face, she listened to Stanley's pep talk about being humble and honest but not beating herself up, and then returned to her van. She made the same journey across town, found Cass's Mercedes in the same spot as earlier, and performed the same parking manoeuvre. Then she rapped her knuckles against the front door and stepped back, shoving her hands into the pockets of her shorts. She looked down at the step but when the door opened, peered up and tried to look sorry. Which she was. Not that it was easy to admit.

"Hi," she began. "Can we talk?"

For a few seconds, Cass only stared. First at Abi's work boots as they scuffed over the path, and then at the shards of terracotta in the palm of her own hand. They were all that remained of her gnomes. "I have a security camera on the patio and it streams through to my phone. Jenna triggered it when she went back for the sweater I lent her, and I saw the whole thing."

"I'm sorry. I was out of line."

"That's an understatement."

"I know. I—" Abi let out a short sharp sigh, frustrated by herself and the ridiculous situation which was all her own making. She was so level-headed and would never have imagined turning into a homicidal maniac, rampaging with a shovel. "Look, I know I haven't made a good account of myself. What I did was unprofessional."

"What you did was criminal."

"That too." Abi's hands slipped back out of her pockets and wrung together. "I'd like to put it right with you, though, if you'll let me. I'll finish your garden. For free, of course." She couldn't really afford to work for free, but she'd do pretty much anything to atone. And not just because of Jenna. She may have lost sight of who she was for a while, but she knew she wasn't this person. "I've had a rough time and I know that isn't an excuse, but I need you to know this is out of character. If you can trust me enough to complete the job, I won't let you down again."

For what seemed an eternity, Cass continued to glower, but then she gave a brief nod. "Okay. I'll let you finish. However," she added, raising a finger and then pointing it at the gnome debris. "I also want these replaced."

"You got it. Whatever you want." Abi had the notion that she might soften Cass with a smile but losing those garden ornaments had hit her hard. She wasn't having a bar of it and the look of haughty contempt remained in place.

Abi was about to give up and return to the garden via the side gate when Cass did something wholly unexpected. "Would you like to come in for a drink before you finish the garden?"

Startled, Abi wasn't sure how to respond. She peered past Cass to make sure there were no bear traps or police officers waiting to nab her. Perhaps Cass would go for a more subtle approach and intended to lace Abi's drink with poison. Being a solicitor, she probably knew all the tricks to make a murder look like an accident.

Cass stepped aside, allowing Abi to pass down a tiled hallway and into the kitchen.

"Your home is lovely," Abi noted, hoping to make some more peace. It wasn't a lie. Or unexpected. Cass's house was immaculate, but... sterile. There were no pictures of family and friends on the walls, and even the decoration was sparse. It was the least inviting invitation Abi had ever received.

"Thank you." Cass went straight to a box of sachets next to the Aga. "Is herbal tea okay? I'm afraid it's all I ever drink."

Despite hating herbal tea and preferring the builder's kind, Abi nodded. Then she scanned the kitchen walls for any signs of life, but none existed. They were all blocks of plain light grey.

Cass filled a stylish chrome kettle and set it on its stand. Then she prised the lid from a battered old biscuit barrel. It was about the only thing that didn't fit in with her chic minimalist décor. "Would you like one?" she offered, giving it a little shake in front of Abi.

Perhaps they were going to find something in common after all, besides Jenna. Inside was everything from ginger nuts to garibaldis, and Abi puzzled over the right selection. She was partial to a chocolate digestive, but there were both the plain and milk versions, and she couldn't decide.

Cass smiled for the first time and gave the barrel another wiggle. "You can take both."

"Are you sure?"

She laughed now. "Yes, I think I can spare you two biscuits. You'll want them if you're tackling this mess." Cass nodded towards the garden, where Abi's shovel was still visible in the grass through the open back door. Then she set down the tin and turned to take the kettle, which had just boiled. "You and Jenna are close, aren't you?"

Abi's heart leapt. She wasn't sure what Cass meant by 'close' and now questioned how much she'd seen in the car park. "I guess," she said cautiously, stacking her biscuits on the counter. "Why?"

"No reason. I can just see how much she values your opinion. And credit where it's due, the idea of splitting up the new shop into smaller rooms is very good."

"It wasn't my idea, though. It was Jenna's. This is all on her."

"Even so, I was a little concerned about her until that point. She was stalling but she wouldn't say what was wrong. Perhaps I'd not been supportive enough, given everything that's happened... personally. But you were."

Was that Cass's real worry? The thought softened Abi. She took the mug of herbal tea, cupping it in her palms and blowing over the top. She'd judged Cass harshly, but with no real foundation. It all came from a place of jealousy and insecurity.

Abi offered a smile, then nodded towards the garden. "I should crack on if I'm getting this finished today."

"Okay." Cass returned Abi's smile and then busied herself again, wiping the splashes of water from the worktop. It seemed like that was the end of it and so Abi grabbed her biscuits from the counter and made for the door, but as she reached it, Cass stopped her. "Hey, Abi?"

She turned back, her heart in her mouth. She knew that had been too easy. "Yes?"

"I won't tell Jenna what happened today. She's got enough to deal with, and it wouldn't serve any purpose. However, I will say one last thing to *you*, even though I know I'm overstepping the mark. Jenna cares a lot about you, and she cares just as much about what you think of her. So if you want to work out this thing between you, whatever it is, remember that. And if you make her feel like it's safe to let you in, don't hurt her. Otherwise, you'll be joining those gnomes."

## 14

## JENNA

Jax lifted a pint of orange juice from the bar. She'd settled on a stool, looking no worse for wear after a night of excess, if you discounted the fact that she was wearing sunglasses indoors. "Hey, hey! It's Barbie and Ken!"

"It's what and what, now?" Jenna looked around the clubhouse and tried to figure out who Ken was meant to be. She was certain she'd arrived alone.

"I think she's talking about you and me." Abi entered via the side door and sheepishly raised her hand. "Hi."

"Oh. Hi. Um."

*Really cool.*

Abi was still in her work gear and Jenna dragged her gaze from the floor, up over Abi's Timberlands until she reached a white T-shirt with the sleeves removed to show off her incredible arms. The arms that had, less than twenty-four hours ago, pinned Jenna to the wall outside.

"Are you... okay?" Abi asked, pulling out a stool next to Jax.

"Yes, I'm..." Jenna shook her head. She felt like she'd been caught out turning puppies into coats, and she needed to get a grip. "I just need to run and check the kitchen was left tidy last night."

Once safely on the other side of the kitchen door, she closed her eyes for a moment and tried to pull herself together. This was Abi, her friend with the caps lock on. Who was now her friend with the caps lock on who she desperately wanted to ask out, despite zero experience in that area and the small complication of a third wheel.

She glanced around the room, satisfied that it was clean, except for the cake box still sat on the far work surface. With any luck, it would contain leftovers; a sure-fire way to diffuse any awkwardness. She jogged over and flipped open the top to find the tattered remains of her football cake, which now looked like the pitch around mid-season after it'd been rained on and churned for weeks. Not that Abi would care.

When Jenna returned, Jax had an iPad in hand and flipped open the cover. "Shall we go over these logos?"

"Yes!" Work Jenna could definitely handle this. She was confident and assertive, unlike the bumbling wreck who still wanted to hide out in the kitchen.

Jenna set the cake down on the bar next to Jax's satchel and waited as she tapped through to a grid of images, all with a running theme—Abi. Gone was the crude clip art of a gardening fork, and in its place was a burly woman in overalls wielding a shovel.

Abi tilted her head. "They're great, but they're very... me focused."

"That's because you *are* your business. You're what people buy into."

Jenna took the iPad from Jax and pinched to zoom in. "I couldn't agree more." She pointed to the one she liked best, feeling far more at ease. "You really need to play on this. It's your brand. And if you wanted to, you could totally expand by hiring more women."

"Expand?" Abi frowned, then flagged down the barmaid when she appeared carrying a box of crisps from the storeroom. "Let's stick to one thing at a time. You really think these logos are a good idea? And do you want a drink?"

"I think they're a great idea. I wouldn't have suggested them to Jax if I didn't. And yes please, I'll have a Coke."

"You suggested them?" Abi ordered their drinks and then turned back to face Jenna, folding her arms.

"Are you going to keep repeating things I've already told you?"

Jax snatched back her iPad. "I'm so glad to know you were on the same page before I spent hours designing these."

Abi shrugged. "I'm sorry. This really isn't my area of expertise so I'll take your advice. Can I get a copy of whichever one you think is best for my website? They all look the same to me. Not that you haven't done a great job."

"The same?!" Jax looked mortally wounded and pointed at the handle of the shovel. "This one is green." She shook her head and set the iPad down on the bar. "I'm going to forgive you, though, since you're technically a paying customer."

"Great. So you'll send me what I need?"

"I can just put the logo on your website, don't worry. Jenna briefed me on that, too."

"Actually, I've started building my own." When they both stared at her blankly, Abi shrugged again. "What? I want to save money. I'm happy to pay for the logo but for now I'm just going with this free site builder. I can get it redone properly when I'm back on my feet and earning again."

Jenna and Jax exchanged glances, then Jenna patted Abi's shoulder. "Okay. Maybe we should just have a backup."

She shuffled angrily. "Rude."

"Don't start pouting again. I'm only being realistic."

"No, what you're being is rude."

"Realistic," Jenna repeated.

Before they could get into a stride, Jax slipped off her stool and pulled a packet of cigarettes from her pocket. "I can't handle this with a hangover. You two have it out while I smoke and then give me your answer."

She headed for the back door and Jenna took her place, shuffling onto the stool Jax had vacated. "How did you get on with Cass earlier?"

Abi's eyes shot up to the ceiling. "Er—"

"Er?" Jenna repeated again.

"I know your game. You're changing the subject."

"We're done with that. You can build your website, but if it's a disaster, we're getting Jax to do it. I'll force her into a massive discount if necessary."

"No, you won't," Abi replied firmly, her eyes dropping to meet Jenna's.

Before Jenna could reply, the door sprang open and Jax appeared again, cursing that she couldn't find her lighter. She tapped her pockets and looked around herself, becoming increasingly agitated. Paying no mind to either of them, she stood between the two stools and leant over the bar, as if she might find it lurking in a fridge or slop tray.

"Have you seen it?" Jax asked, but Jenna wasn't listening.

She was too thirsty, both figuratively and literally, and unable to take her eyes from Abi. So much for work talk being safe and comfortable ground because the sudden intensity of their exchange had just thumped Jenna back against that wall again. Fumbling for her drink, she almost knocked over the glass and Abi laughed as Jenna sprung up to grab it, spilling Coke on her hand.

Abi reached over the bar and grabbed a thick roll of blue

tissue. She tore off a few squares and nudged Jax out of the way, dabbing the liquid from Jenna's palm.

Jax put her hands on her hips. "Do I even exist?"

"Did you hear something?" Abi replied without looking up. She balled the tissue and then wandered off, rounding the bar and heading towards the kitchen.

Jax frowned as she plonked herself back on a stool and tapped the footrest with agitation. "Why do you look like someone's just given you a lobotomy?"

Jenna shook her head and then cleared her throat. She really didn't want Jax to know that it was Abi she had a crush on. "No reason."

Jax didn't look at all convinced but chose not to press. "Have you asked that woman out on a date yet?"

Jenna shrugged and took a sip of her Coke, trying for nonchalant but unsure if it had come off. Right now, she was pretty sure you'd need to be both blind and deaf not to notice the chemistry. "Not yet, but I'm working up to it."

"Okay, but don't take too long. You've only got a week."

"I'm pretty sure I can find the courage in an entire week!" If only Jax knew that it was her presence causing the bloody issue. Asking Abi out was scary enough, without an audience. They'd kissed, they were flirting, there was tension. So why did this still feel like a big leap?

"Good." Jax leant in and lowered her voice. "Look, there's something I should probably mention to you, before anything's said about it. I'm sorry, but I accidentally let slip to Abi about your mum earlier."

"You did what?" All the colour drained from Jenna's face. She hadn't expected that, and it had plunged her desire into a bucket of ice water. She was still gawping when Abi returned from the kitchen.

"Right," Abi said, drying her hands on her shorts. "Are we all done with this logo? What's everyone doing now? Do you fancy maybe getting dinner?"

The three of them having dinner together was a big no because Jenna now had two difficult conversations to broach with Abi. She had no idea how she'd cover them together. It would have to go something along the lines of, "Hey, my mum died and it sort of ruined my life. Oh, and by the way, do you fancy a game of footgolf next Saturday because I fancy you like crazy and really want you to bang me up against the clubhouse wall again some time."

Jenna sighed. She might need time to come up with something a little less brutal than that. First, though, she needed a sure-fire plan to keep Jax away. As luck would have it, she had the perfect idea.

Abi and Jax were already talking about the best pizza joints in town and Jenna cut through a heated debate about sourdough bases. "Actually, I was wondering if you wanted to come to my place. I've got popcorn and romcoms ready to go, plus we can have a chat."

At the mere mention of romcoms, Jax screwed her face. "Ugh."

"Is that a no?"

Of course it was. She hated romcoms, and had hopefully taken the hint that she wasn't welcome.

Jax's head inclined and she studied Jenna's face. "No, I think I'm all set," she said cautiously. "I'm going to give everything a miss and get an early night. Try to kill this hangover." Then she mouthed, "Are we okay?"

Jenna nodded. They were, it had just been a surprise. Jax knew how private she was when it came to her family. Especially her mum. But Jenna was also sure, however much of a pain in the arse she was sometimes, that Jax wouldn't have said anything unless there was a good reason.

Abi had missed the entire exchange because she was busy peeking in the cake box. "I'm up for romcoms. I need to get changed first, though. I'll swing home and then come to your place."

Jenna got up and pulled the box wide open. "If you want some, just take it. I might have some too, given I was expecting hangover cookies..."

Abi picked up the largest slice of cake. "Sorry. I planned to make them this afternoon but Cass's place took longer than I expected."

"You can make it up to me by letting me jump in your van. I got a taxi up here."

"You got a taxi? Why?"

Pinching a sliver of icing, Jenna shrugged. "I had a *lot* to drink last night. Wasn't sure I was safe."

"You had that much, huh?"

Abi sounded a little disappointed, and Jenna caught her eye as she huffed slightly and took a big bite of cake. Her pouting was kind of cute.

"Yes, I did. But don't worry," she reassured Abi, nudging her boot. "I remember everything that happened this time."

## 15
## ABI

Abi parked on the kerb and then stalked up the driveway. Her dad's car wasn't on it so she knew he was out, but that wasn't her biggest concern. A far greater threat to her tentatively positive mood could well lay in wait on the other side of the front door.

Jenna hung back and studied Abi with a look of curiosity and, perhaps, confusion. "I still can't figure it out. Are you embarrassed of me or them?"

Abi's head snapped around, her hand on the key as she shoved it into the lock. "Why would you think I'm embarrassed of anyone?"

"I don't know. Something about the number of times you told me I didn't need to come in if I didn't want to." Prodding Abi's side, Jenna wore a devilish smile. Then she glanced up. "Or the panic-stricken look on your face when we pulled into the street." She patted Abi's T-shirt, which clung to the sweat pooling at the base of her back. "Or the fact you're so stressed that you're sweating right now. I don't understand what the problem is, though. I've met them tonnes of times."

"I—" Abi started. She searched for a good explanation for all the evidence, but came up blank. Submitting, she went for her fail safe and logical reason. "Maybe I'm a little embarrassed by my mum. I mean, that's just common sense. She is likely to—"

"Get me to help set you up with Jax?"

Rolling her eyes, Abi let out a long sigh and pushed open the front door. She knew Jenna wouldn't let that drop. "Look." She turned to stop Jenna from going any further. "There's something you need to know about my mum."

"What's that?"

"You probably already noticed this, but she's crazy."

A burst of laughter shot out of Jenna, and she shook her head. "You can't say that about your mum."

"I agree. It's not a nice thing to say, but in her case, it's accurate. For a start, she thinks she's our lucky charm. I mean, have you ever heard anything more ridiculo—"

"Woah, hang on!" Hooking her finger into the waistband of Abi's shorts, Jenna tugged her back from continuing through to the kitchen. "That's crazy, is it? Says she, who was in tears because she lost her lucky shirt?"

Confounded again, Abi tried to walk forward with Jenna still pulling her back. She made it a few inches towards the kitchen, with Jenna giggling behind her. "That's... different."

"Oh yeah?"

"Yes."

"How?"

"I don't know. I'm still deciding."

With another burst of laughter, Jenna let go, allowing Abi to hurtle forward a few paces. She stopped in the kitchen doorway and peered around for any signs of life, but the place was empty. Perhaps she'd lucked out.

Jenna pulled out a chair and sat, hitching up her knee and resting her chin on top. "While you're deciding, tell me more about this Jax thing."

"Do I have to?"

"Yes. Why is your mum so obsessed with setting you guys up?"

That was an excellent question, but Abi didn't have an answer. "I don't know," she replied with a dismissive waft of her hand. "She has it in her head that we'd make a good match. Which is absurd."

"She didn't try the same after I came over?"

"Nope."

Jenna nodded. "Oh, I see. Didn't think I was good enough for her little girl?"

Abi snorted as she opened the fridge to find them some cans. The notion of Jenna not being good enough for anyone was ridiculous. "She just has fixed ideas about things and if you get in the way, she doesn't like it."

"Noted. Any potential girlfriends have to pass the mum test. I'll keep that in mind."

"I'm not really sure I want you setting me up with a tonne of people."

"Who said anything about a tonne of people? You need someone special."

"Yeah?" The hopeful lilt in Abi's voice was new. So was her desire to continue this conversation. Unfortunately, though, she wouldn't get a chance because the front door clattered. How two people made so much noise, she couldn't fathom, but her parents filled the house with sound—rustling bags, quips back and forth, doors slamming, laughter.

"We got takeaway," Petra yelled. "There's enough if you want some. My big strong girl has been working all da—" She stopped dead on entering the kitchen, a brown paper bag of what was presumably food in one hand and a bottle of wine in the other. "Oh, hello. I didn't know we had company."

The last thing Abi wanted was to get stuck at home all night and she replied quickly. "We're watching a film at Jenna's. I just came back to change."

"Tuesday is the anniversary of when my mum passed, so Abi's looking after me," Jenna added.

Given how long she'd kept it hidden, she relayed the information as if it were the most casual thing in the world, and Abi stared at her for a moment, wondering where so much honesty had come from. Not that she would knock it, when that one fact changed Petra's entire demeanour. She placed the bottle of wine down on the counter and then the bag after it, pulling Jenna into a hug. Whether she wanted one or not.

"Oh, my darling. I am so sorry to hear that. Has it been long?"

"Quite a while, yeah."

"It never gets easier, though, does it? My Abi will take care of you." Petra stepped back but held onto the tops of Jenna's arms. "Will you eat with us first? There is Chinese and pizza." With a little wiggle of her shoulders, Petra broke away and began pulling tubs from the bag.

"You have both?"

"I hate Chinese," Abi got in again.

Jenna mouthed "me too". Then she took a step back as Stanley blundered in with more shopping bags from the car. It looked like they'd done yet another supermarket run, but God only knew why. The cupboards were bursting with enough food to survive the apocalypse. "I'd love to stay. Thank you, that's very kind."

"Are you sure?" Abi asked, trying not to convey too much of her internal horror. "Really sure? I thought you wanted popcorn and a chat."

"Yes, I'm really sure. We can still talk later, but my hangover would love some pizza first."

There were other ways to get her pizza that didn't involve an evening of Stanley shovelling egg fried rice into his mouth while Petra narrated the television. Abi still felt the need to repent, though. "Fine, if that's what you want."

"You'll go far with that attitude. Why don't you tell your parents about your new logo? The one Jax designed for you."

At the mention of her name, Petra's ears pricked up. She turned from the boxes of food she'd begun setting out on the counter. "Jax has made you a new logo? That's very kind of her."

"It's not that kind, I'm paying her," Abi pointed out. Then she glared at Jenna, shaking her head as she noted the look of amusement which implied that she knew exactly what she was doing. "Jax is a graphic designer, Ma. She works for a big IT and marketing company in the business park. It's her job."

"Oh, then she must do well for herself!"

"Yeah, she does, but..." There was no point arguing, so Abi didn't bother. Instead, she opened the cupboard and pulled out a stack of plates. Saturday was the only night when Petra permitted them to have their meal in the living room rather than at the kitchen table, but there was no chance they'd get away with eating pizza from the box.

"Can I help with anything?" Jenna offered.

"No, I think you've done enough."

"So rude to your friend!" Petra chastised, raising her hands and then clasping Abi's cheeks to smoosh them. "And so dirty. Look at you!" She took them away and gestured up and down Abi's grass-stained work clothes. "Get changed. Quickly. You're not sitting on my sofas like this, and with company."

Abi rolled her eyes as Jenna sniggered into the back of her hand. This was just perfect. Then she set down the plates and trudged towards the hallway, but as she did, Jenna jumped out of her chair.

"You can show me your room."

"I don't think so."

Jenna tugged on Abi's arm. "Come on, I want to see all your posters and then we can talk about which Spice Girls album is the definitive. I have a lot of opinions."

"Great," Abi muttered as Jenna followed her up the stairs. When they were on the landing and out of earshot, she turned and folded her arms. It had all been going so well half an hour ago. "You're a pain in my arse."

"Me?" Jenna clutched her chest with mock indignation.

"Yes, you. Don't pretend not to know exactly what you're doing."

"You mean being friendly towards your parents, politely accepting their kind invitation for dinner, and not running away as soon as they get home? Yeah, I'm a real bitch."

It was tough to argue with that, however much Abi wanted to try. Especially when Jenna was enjoying herself.

Abi heaved a great sigh and opened her bedroom door, unsure what about the experience had caused so much excitement to rise in Jenna's eyes. She looked around the place like she'd never seen a thirty-three-year-old try to cram everything they owned into one small room before. Most of Abi's stuff sat in boxes in the garage, but there were some things she didn't want to risk, like her memory box full of old football trophies and certificates, or her collection of football shirts.

Jenna made a beeline for the box marked 'footy shirts'. "Are you just obsessed with shirts? You know they don't have magical powers, right? If you put your mum in one of these, she won't turn into Tobin Heath." Flipping open the top, she delved inside and held up an old Arsenal strip from the first season of the Women's Super League.

"My mum's actually pretty awesome at football." Abi pulled off her T-shirt and threw it at Jenna. Then she unzipped her shorts and wriggled them to the floor. They got changed in front of each other all the time and she'd thought nothing of it until she realised Jenna was biting her lip again and had gone all pink. "What?"

"Nothing," Jenna murmured, taking a second to let her eyes rake over Abi's body as she stood in only a black sports bra and briefs. Then she cleared her throat. "Have you been working out?"

"That's a terrible line."

"I know. Sorry. But have you?"

Abi nodded. She'd spent weeks prepping for her first training session, doing a couch to 5k running course, and trying to get in some sort of shape. It was part of why she'd been so annoyed to still struggle. "Work usually keeps me fit, but I thought I should put in some effort given I've had none." Grabbing out a fresh T-shirt and shorts from her chest of drawers, she hopped in and relaxed while Jenna continued to rifle through her boxes. "Do you always go into people's bedrooms and rummage through their stuff?"

"No, but—" Halted by her own gasp, Jenna pulled out an old white England shirt and held it up. "Oh my gosh, this has Smith on the back. You were a Kelly Smith fan, too?"

"Who wasn't? She's a legend."

"I used to idolise her. She's literally the reason I became a striker."

"Yeah, you said."

Jenna continued to study the shirt as if it might contain hidden wonders. "This is so cool. I didn't get any of the official kit when I was a kid because we couldn't afford it. I had to make do with knock-offs from the market."

When Jenna put it on over her T-shirt, Abi folded her arms again to keep from fidgeting. She never let people wear her shirts and it was taking all her effort not to yank it back. This was something only Jenna would get away with.

"Be careful with it," Abi urged, wincing to see the fabric

stretch over Jenna's chest. Abi had owned that since she was a kid, and it was too small for an adult woman's curves. Not that Jenna had many of them, but even so. "Just... don't damage it."

Jenna stood in front of the mirror on the wardrobe and then turned to look over her shoulder, so she could see the name on the back. "Maybe Jax would let me wear this for the first game of the season."

"And why would you want to do that? It's just a shirt, remember? It doesn't have magical powers and it won't turn you into Kelly Smith." Abi smirked as Jenna spun around and glared.

"Yeah, yeah. I'm only messing about. I don't believe for one second that a shirt can be lucky. Luck is bullshit."

"How do you figure that luck is bullshit? I'd say we're both pretty lucky, in different ways."

Jenna considered for a second, placing her hands on her hips. "I think we're talking about two separate things. There's a big difference between believing something inanimate can bring you good luck, and knowing you're lucky. One is a load of mumbo-jumbo and the other is about gratitude. Of course I'm grateful for all the ways I'm lucky, but I also know that if I'm successful at work or on the football pitch, it's because I worked hard. Not because of some magical talisman."

She'd become more indignant as she went on, and Abi found it endearing. She smiled, despite the fact that they were meant to be arguing, and then shrugged. "Tell me something that makes you feel lucky, then."

"I feel very lucky and grateful that your parents offered to share their meal with me."

As she said it, the house shook on its foundations because Petra was shrieking from downstairs about how their food would get cold. It caused Abi to jump, and she yelled back that they were on their way as she tried to help Jenna out of the shirt.

"You won't mind taking that shirt off and coming downstairs with me, then. Given you don't hold any store in such objects."

Laughing, Jenna tugged the shirt over her head. Then she laid it on the end of the bed and neatly folded it. "There. Happy?" she asked, standing back and presenting the shirt like she was a game show model.

Petra was shouting again, and Abi's shoulders hunched as she shuddered for effect. She'd be happy when they left but sensed that wouldn't happen soon. "I'm delirious," she muttered.

Jenna grabbed Abi's shoulders and turned her to face the door. "That'll just be hunger. My big strong girl has been working *so* hard," she mocked, before laughing again and marching them back down the stairs.

## 16

## JENNA

A couple of hours later, they were all sprawled out in the living room. Abi and Jenna still hadn't made it to her house for films, and Jenna was running out of time. She'd stalled all evening and eventually she'd have to make a decision. She could either have a proper conversation with Abi, or abandon the idea altogether.

When Abi shuffled to dislodge a leg from under herself, Jenna peered over from the opposite end of the sofa and smiled, her eyes still half shut. Then she sat straighter, cricking her neck from side to side. "Thank you for dinner. I had a great evening."

"You slept for most of it," Stanley pointed out.

"Exactly. Which is a great evening."

He laughed and turned off the television, then clicked on the lamp next to his recliner. "You're welcome any time."

Petra had also fallen asleep, lightly snoring on the other sofa with a blanket covering her legs, and Abi nodded to alert them all. Then she whispered, "I'll drop you home. Give me a sec."

Jenna looked down at her watch. She briefly considered walking home but it was gone ten and on a Saturday night that probably wasn't a safe option, given it would mean passing through town. The only thing for it was to accept Abi's lift.

Whilst Abi ran upstairs and Stanley exited to the kitchen, Jenna pulled out her phone to check for messages, finding one from Jax. "Are we definitely okay? I'm truly sorry about the Abi thing. If you want to go and lay flowers at any point tomorrow, let me know. I'd like to come."

She tapped back a reply, reassuring Jax that they were fine and suggesting a time to meet. Then she slipped the phone back into her pocket, stretched, and wandered out into the hallway, just as Abi came running back down the stairs with her keys in hand.

"Right, shall we go?"

Jenna took a deep breath. There was no more stalling. She'd have to talk to Abi properly in the van because that was the end of the road. Perhaps it was good that they'd be confined, with no escape. It'd stop her from wimping out.

She followed Abi down the drive. Then, after sliding into the passenger seat, clicked on her seatbelt and tried to work out how to start this.

"You and your dad are close, huh?"

"Yeah, he's great. We've always understood each other. Well, mostly. I'll never know how he can mix Chinese with pizza crusts and dip."

Jenna's laugh sounded forced, even though it was genuine, and she hoped Abi couldn't make the distinction. "Not so much with your mum?"

"You picked up on that, did you?" Abi set both hands firmly on the steering wheel as she reversed off the driveway. "Listen, I'm sorry if I was insensitive earlier, having a bit of a moan about her. I should've thought."

"It's fine, you don't need to apologise for that."

"Kinda feels like I do. I'm also sorry Jax had to tell me what happened with your mum—or at least the gist—if you didn't want me to know. It was... well, it's a long story. But I'm sorry all the same."

Shaking her head, Jenna ran her hand over a rough piece of plastic on the door. "You don't need to apologise for that, either. It's not like I deliberately hid it from you, it's just..." She trailed off, let out a quiet huff, then shuffled. "Okay, maybe I hid it from you a little."

"How come?"

"Honestly?" There was a long pause and Jenna was back to wondering how to explain. "I guess I just didn't want you to see me or treat me any differently." Shrugging and glancing over, she tried to judge Abi's reaction. It was tough in the dark, though. "Things between us are always so... easy. Y'know? Even when everything else is shit or stressful, I go to football, have a laugh with you, and forget about it all. I missed that during lockdown. *Really* missed it."

"And you thought if I knew your mum had died, things would change?"

They'd just reached the end of the road, and Jenna joined Abi in looking left and right. Once the van had pulled out of the T-junction, she was still no closer to a bearable answer. The truth was that yes, she worried every single time someone found out about her childhood or what had happened to her mum, but it was beyond a binary response.

"It's complicated."

"How so?"

"Because..." Jenna gripped the door handle and stared from the side window. "Okay, fuck it. I'm going to try to explain but just bear with me."

Abi left one hand on the wheel and, after changing gear, placed the other over Jenna's as it fidgeted on her leg. It took her by surprise and she almost pulled away, but then she turned her hand over and clasped Abi's fingers.

"You know I spent a lot of my childhood living with my grandparents?" Jenna asked rhetorically, taking her other hand from the door and spinning the ring on Abi's thumb. "Well, I was there because my mum wasn't always able to look after me. Then, when I was sixteen and waiting for my exam results, she got sick and passed away. I was already not doing very well at school because there was a lot of upheaval even before then, and everything came crashing down. My grandparents blamed her for me not getting good results, and they were already ashamed of her, so it just made everything worse. Now they deal with it by not talking about what happened. And every year I'm reminded of that awful time, compounded by the fact that they act like she never existed." She looked up from her lap, once again trying to gauge Abi's reaction. "Does any of that make sense?"

When Abi heard the crack in Jenna's voice, she let go of her hand, hit the indicator, and pulled the van up on the path, next to a street lamp. Shutting off the engine and undoing her seatbelt, Abi crossed her legs over so they were facing each other, her knee hitting the gear stick.

Abi continued to squirm, smacking her head on the roof of the van. How did she always seem to find a way of lightening the mood, without really meaning to?

"That looks uncomfortable," Jenna pointed out.

"It is, but I'll suck it up because I feel like this needs my full attention." Which was ironic because right now Abi was distracted by the awkward position in which she found herself. She'd managed to hitch up one knee, but didn't seem to know what to do with the other. In the end, she shuffled to face forward again and let out a short burst of laughter as she accepted defeat. "Okay, well you have my full attention." She paused for a beat before adding, "Do you mind if I ask what your mum did that was so terrible? It all made sense except for why your grandparents are ashamed. Why couldn't she look after you?"

Squirming, Jenna looked down at the floor. She knew that was going to be the next question and hated how she reacted at the thought of answering it. Her grandparents may be ashamed but that didn't mean *she* was. "My mum was a drug addict. She died of a drug overdose. That's what she did to disgrace them, and why they got lumbered with me so much of the time." She winced at her decision to include that last bit because she could hear how much judgement it carried. The truth was, though, it reflected how she felt. She wasn't going to sugar-coat the situation.

"That's a lot for you to deal with during an already difficult transition."

"All my grandad cared about was making sure I went back to college, so that I got some sort of qualification. I'm pretty sure he was saying, don't embarrass us like your mother did. Make better choices. Or—" Jenna came to an abrupt stop, realising how far they'd strayed into previously unknown and dark territory. She shook her head and sniffed, hoping Abi got the gist, because she couldn't finish that sentence herself.

"Or they'd cut you out, too?" Abi whispered.

"That's the upshot, yeah," Jenna muttered, wiping her nose on the back of her hand.

"I'm so sorry. I can see why that's tough to share with people, but I'm really glad you told me. For what it's worth, I don't see you any differently. You're still the most incredible person I've ever had the misfortune to be teased by."

Jenna laughed and a tear ran down her face. Once again, she was impressed by Abi's ability to ease her discomfort. "Thanks. I think."

Abi twisted and leant over to wipe Jenna's face with her thumb. "Are you going to be alright at home alone tonight?"

Jenna nodded. "Yes. I just need a good night's sleep." She yawned at the thought of it, then laughed again at how that always seemed to happen. "I'm meeting Jax tomorrow to lay some flowers."

"Then let's get you home." Abi shot Jenna a warm smile as she restarted the van. Then she pulled off the kerb and drove on in silence until Jenna had to remind Abi how to get through the maze of streets on her estate. A few minutes of calm instructions, and they pulled up in front of the neat little terraced house. Jenna's car was on the drive and Abi stopped behind.

"You okay?" Jenna asked as Abi turned off the engine to plunge them back into silence. It persisted because Abi only nodded. After a few moments, Jenna spoke again because the atmosphere verged on awkward, but she only ended up rambling over Abi. They both laughed until Jenna cut through it. "Alright, you go."

"I was only going to ask if *you're* okay. And make sure you know that if you want to talk about your mum, I'm here to listen. Same goes if you just need some company. I'm at Ida's all day tomorrow and then again next weekend, helping my dad with the rapidly expanding list of renovation works on her house and garden, but I can always take time out for you."

Jenna tried not to sound too disappointed when she replied, "You're busy all next weekend, too?"

Her mind returned to the footgolf tickets. Maybe it was for the best that they couldn't go. Abi should take some time to let everything sink in because despite what she said about being supportive, she might change her mind tomorrow when she realised what it entailed. They weren't the same people. Abi had Petra and Stanley. She'd grown up with her mum baking birthday cakes and her dad teaching her to build stuff, not sitting on the front step wondering if her mum would show that week.

Jenna's mind was about to race onto the ultimate conclusion, when Abi interrupted her thoughts. "I have to help my dad for part of the day at least, but I can make time. Is there something you wanted to do?"

Jenna shook her head. "Nah. Don't worry about it."

"No! Come on."

Abi gently shoved Jenna's leg, then let her hand linger. Once again, Jenna put her hand over Abi's and held it there. Then she reminded herself of the quote and Jax's words. Despite how unutterably exposed she felt right now, she wanted to go on a date with Abi. Possibly more so than ever.

"I was going to ask if you wanted to go to the opening of the new footgolf centre with me next Saturday. No big deal, y'know? Just…"

Before she could say any more, Abi replied with, "Sounds good."

"Really?"

"Of course. I love footgolf."

"Great. So… shall I text you the details?"

Abi turned over her hand and gave Jenna's a squeeze, and then slipped it out. "No need." She wriggled as she reached into her pocket and pulled out her phone. "I'll put it in my calendar now."

"You're using a digital calendar?"

"Yep." Abi squinted as the screen added to the light from the street lamp. "I'm trying to embrace change. It already contains three quote appointments, which came through from Facebook —thank you very much—and another from my leaflet drop. I'll accept an apology for writing those off later."

"Well done. Things are on the up, then?"

"I hope so." Abi tapped through the apps on her phone, and then peered over the screen expectantly. "What time?"

"Meet me there at noon?"

"Sold. Shall we get some lunch after?"

Trust Abi to think about food. Jenna laughed again and reassured her that there was a buffet lunch at the launch. "It's all you can eat," she added, knowing that would seal the deal. Then she pulled out her phone and fired off a quick message to let Jax know that the deed was done. She'd have time to brag about it in person the following day but for now, she was just thankful to be getting out of the van. A lot had happened in twenty-four hours and the only wall on her mind now was the one turning her limbs heavy from exhaustion. Everything but sleep could wait.

\* \* \*

Sleep was so needed that it continued until a blaring jingle propelled Jenna bolt upright.

"What the fuck?" she mumbled as panic shot through her entire body. Her heart just about resisted the urge to explode when she realised that she must have fallen asleep while scrolling, because her phone lay on the pillow next to the dent where her head had been. Usually, she kept it out of the bedroom, but she'd indulged in a little distraction therapy.

It took a few more moments for her to make the connection that if it was ringing, she should answer. Grabbing the phone, fumbling for the little green icon, and then pressing it to a mass of knotted hair, she squinted at the alarm clock on her bedside table.

*Fuck.*

"Are you on your way, buddy?"

It was Jax, and Jenna's mind raced as she tried to come up with an excuse for why she absolutely was not on her way. In the end, she couldn't. "No, I'm sorry. I overslept. I'm coming now, though."

Jax laughed. "You and Abi have another big night?"

In a manner of speaking, they had, but Jenna didn't want to get into that. "No, we actually just ended up getting a little food with her parents. I was tired, though. Apparently."

"No worries. I'll wander to the village shop. Do you need me to get you some flowers to save time?"

"That would be great, thank you. Can you also pick up three chocolate bars? I'll explain later."

Jenna thanked Jax and ended the call, then lobbed her phone onto the bedside table, threw off the duvet, and rubbed her eyes. It was noon and she never slept like this. Usually, she didn't even need an alarm. Her body woke itself at around seven without fail.

She was still in a daze after dressing, cleaning her teeth, downing a glass of water, and then flopping into the driver seat of her car. This next activity could kill her if she was half asleep, though, so she slowed down and took a moment to get her shit together.

Rubbing her fists into her eyes again, she tried to clear them, and the groggy headache lurking just behind. At least there was no hangover today, unless you counted the emotional one. Abi hadn't been in touch since last night and Jenna tried to reassure herself that it meant nothing. Just because they'd spoken regularly for well over a week and she'd been silent for half a day, only meant she was busy. Didn't it?

She stared at the Thermos flask Stanley had given her the weekend before, which was still in her cup holder, and tried to push the doubt from her mind. Then she started the engine and headed out of town towards the small church graveyard, along the road from the football club. She had to pass Abi's aunt's bungalow and she slowed down as she did so, noting that Stanley's estate car was on the driveway. It probably meant they were working there again, just as Abi had said, and she once again reassured herself.

When Jenna pulled up on the kerb in front of the church, Jax was leant against the gate with a small potted plant and a white carrier bag. She wore her shades again and peered over the top as Jenna got out of the car.

"Everything okay, buddy?" Jax asked, holding out the bag. "I didn't know which bars you wanted so I got a selection."

Jenna took the bag and pulled it open to find there were at least a dozen, and all different. "Snickers were my mum's favourite. Good work."

"Great. Do they have a purpose in all of this, or were you just hungry?"

"They have a purpose," Jenna replied as she nudged Jax off the gate and opened it for her to pass. "Whenever my mum came to visit me at my gran's, she always brought us each a chocolate bar. We'd sit and eat them together."

"So you carry on the tradition? That's really sweet, bud." Jax chuckled as she sauntered down the stone path which led to the main entrance of the church. On either side of them were old gravestones with inscriptions that were so weathered, some were no longer legible. "Where are we heading?"

The front of the church was bathed in midday sun, a picture perfect slice of English country life, but way too hot to enjoy for long. Jenna stopped to squint up at the stained glass. "Round the back. Thankfully it'll be a bit cooler there."

"Good job, or all this chocolate will become fondue."

Jax stopped to let Jenna pass her and they peeled off along a narrow sandy track to the left of the front door. It wove a path through more headstones, until they came out in a spot shaded by a large oak tree. There were neat rows of commemorative plaques, and a few wooden benches.

"This is it," Jenna said as she found the small memorial stone marking where her mum's ashes were interned. No one was actually buried in the grounds anymore because the graveyard was full, but her grandparents were regular members of the congregation and had been granted permission to lay their daughter's ashes to rest. A final shot at redemption.

"It's a beautiful spot." Jax crouched down to rub some moss from the stone, and then placed her pot plant in front of it. "They didn't have any flowers, but I figured this would last longer in any case." She craned to look over her shoulder. "Do we give her a chocolate bar, too?"

It was sweet of Jax to take this so seriously, and Jenna smiled. She may not have heaps of friends but the ones she did have were pretty awesome. "Why don't you have it for her?"

Jax grunted as she hauled herself back up. Then she followed Jenna to one of the benches and read the little brass plaque, telling her who it was dedicated to. "I wonder if anyone will get me a bench. For my services to the village football club."

"I'll get you a bench."

"Thanks, bud."

They both sat, and Jenna set the bag of chocolate bars between them. She rummaged around, pulled out a Double Decker, and ripped open the packet. Until that moment, she hadn't realised how hungry she was.

Whilst she munched through half the bar in one go, Jax nibbled more cautiously on the Snickers. "This might be inappropriate given what we're here for, but I'm desperate to know what happened with that woman you were asking out."

Jenna covered her mouth when she laughed, trying not to dribble chocolate. "There's nothing to know, yet. We're not going out until next Saturday."

"How did you ask her? I'm impressed. I have to say, I thought you'd chicken out."

"Hey! Of course I didn't chicken out. I just asked her if she wanted to come to the footgolf centre opening with me." Jenna shrugged and pulled down the Double Decker wrapper, preparing to tuck into the other half. "It wasn't such a big deal in the end." Especially after what they'd talked about first. By that stage, asking for a date seemed relatively easy.

"You did tell her it was a date, though? She knows you intended the invite... romantically?"

Jenna paused with the chocolate bar raised to her mouth. "I'm sure she will have assumed it's a date." Wouldn't she? Although now she thought about it, Jenna was questioning whether that was clear. She'd been preoccupied at the time.

Jax caught Jenna's eye and gave her a look which conveyed exactly what she was thinking. "If you say so."

"Oh shit..." Jenna's hand dropped away. Then she let out a little huff. "What do I do now?"

"I guess it depends how bothered you are about this needing to officially be a date. You could just go along and see what the vibe is. How well do you know her?"

"Pretty well." And without clarification, it would just be them hanging out again. Flirting like crazy, most likely, but with no clear directive that taking it further was on the agenda. "She's actually the person who came to mind when you asked if there was anyone I wished had asked me out."

Jax smirked and continued to nibble her Snickers. "What convinced you to go for it now?"

"Timing, I guess. For one thing, we've never both been single before, but I also meant it when I said the pandemic and the split from Cass has changed my perspective."

"Doing it differently? Another point for me."

Jenna rolled her eyes. "Yeah, yeah. I never denied that you were right, which is why I need you to help me figure out how to approach this. We kissed the other night so do you think maybe she'll realise that I want to date her without me saying something?"

Jax's hand shot out and gripped Jenna's wrist. "Hold up.

You've already kissed this woman? That's new information. Tell me everything."

This wasn't a gossip column, but Jenna was kind of excited to talk about it a bit. Even though she still had no intention of revealing the object of her desire and dilemma was Abi. "There's not much to tell, yet. We've known each other a few years, we're friends, and I've always found her attractive. We reconnected after lockdown and I've been surprised how quickly that attraction has grown, now that we're both single and able to just be with each other. Then, as you know, we kissed."

"But she hasn't asked you out?"

Jenna scrunched her face. "No, but I don't think that means a lot, does it? I wouldn't have asked anyone out a month ago, so why should I expect she's any better at it or any less scared? It's a big thing moving from a friendship to something more."

"I know. I've done it often."

The comment earned Jax a whack on the stomach. "I know you have, but I'm being serious. I'm going to find an excuse and call in on the way home," Jenna decided with an affirmative nod. "Subtly make sure she knows I want it to be a date."

Jax rubbed her stomach and scooted away. "I may regret asking this, but why are you finding excuses and being subtle? Can't you just be direct?"

"No."

Jenna had no intention of qualifying her response because it would mean admitting that she was back to being shit scared. She remembered the Thermos flask in her car and knew it gave her the perfect excuse. All she had to do now was decide what to say.

## 17

## ABI

"Ma will go berserk if she comes back from the shops and finds you like this," Abi warned Stanley as he sprawled in his deckchair. It had become a permanent fixture in the middle of Ida's lawn.

"It's such a struggle in this heat. I'm an old man."

"Come on, get up. There's still time to get some of this dug today. It's only one-thirty." She kicked at his trainer, and he slid his foot out of the way. They'd taken a break for lunch, after finishing the access ramp, and had planned to move on to the patio. So far, though, they'd only made it as far as marking out the area.

"Why don't you do that, and I'll supervise?" he said after a long, lazy pause.

Grumbling, Abi grabbed his shovel. It had come out of the van but lay idle, propped against the wall of the house. "I'm pretty sure that you need to open your eyes in order to call it supervising."

"There are no gnomes today so I'm sure you can manage."

She ignored his attempt to bait her and dug into the hard ground with a satisfying thwack, but still he didn't stir.

An hour later, a slight chill ran from the sweat pooling at the base of Abi's spine, all the way up her back. She shivered and patted it, realising she'd focused so intently that she'd already taken most of the grass off, exposing the dry earth below. She rested on the spade and exhaled loudly, wiping the back of her arm across her brow.

"Can I tempt you to help now?" she asked, with no response.

It was only when the side gate clattered that Stanley's eyes shot open. He sat bolt upright and looked around himself, his hands gripping the arms of the chair. "Who's that? Your mother's not back yet, is she?"

Abi laughed at him and pulled off one of her gloves, flinging it at his bare chest. No one else would come around the side. "Feeling a little guilty there?"

Jenna stopped, Stanley's Thermos in hand, and looked from him to Abi. "Sorry. Would have knocked, but I heard you guys chatting, so..." She held it out. "I found this Thermos from the other Sunday, still rattling around in my car. Thought I should bring it back."

Laughing again because Stanley had already closed his eyes, Abi strode across the shallow hole to take the Thermos. "Thanks. He didn't need it, he's got loads, but—" When Jenna didn't let go, Abi gently tugged. "Er, hello. Release? Are you okay?"

"Mhm," Jenna mumbled. She finally gave up the Thermos and glanced at where Stanley snoozed, before leaning in to whisper, "You're all work-sweaty."

"You like that?" Abi grinned and also glanced sideways at Stanley, this time hoping he'd returned to his nap. "Shouldn't you be at... you know?"

"I was. That's where I've just been, and it isn't far from here, so..." Jenna gestured to the Thermos in Abi's hand and then thumbed over her shoulder towards the gate. "Anyway, I just came to return that on the way home. I guess I'll get off now."

Abi made a few noises as she searched for words. She didn't want Jenna to go yet. "Um, do you want a drink?" was all she could come up with. "Beer? Wine? Tea? Soft drink?" Stopping short of reeling off the entire contents of her aunt's fridge, Abi rolled her eyes at herself.

"Sure, I could go a quick... anything."

Abi led Jenna into the kitchen, set the Thermos on the work surface, and opened the fridge. She was just about to start listing items when she acknowledged how nervous she was, took a deep breath, and stopped herself again. This was Jenna. Just because they were in an odd place right now, didn't mean Abi needed to freak out. She should talk and clear the air.

"Is a Coke okay?" she asked, grabbing two cans from the shelf. When Jenna confirmed, Abi smiled, hoping it was the first of many things they'd agree over. "Shall we take them out the front?"

She swung the fridge door shut and handed Jenna her drink, then opened the internal door leading to the garage. The garage was open where they'd been back and forth collecting supplies, and Abi made her way to the area of patio in front of the bungalow. It was bathed in sunlight and Abi squinted, fiddling with the tab of her drink as condensation ran down her wrist. "How did it go with Jax?"

"It was nice," Jenna replied, already sipping from her own can. "If you can ever have a nice time at a graveyard, but you know what I mean." She reached into the pocket of her shorts and produced a bar of Dairy Milk. "Oh, and I brought you this."

Abi laughed as the chocolate squished inside the wrapper when she tried to grasp it. "Thanks. Maybe I'll put it in the fridge for later."

"I know it's a bit warm, but it's a tradition. I always take chocolate to my mum. Jax bought twelve of them. She's actually been a really good friend today. Sometimes it's hard to imagine she's going to turn forty this week but then she'll say something vaguely mature and I'll be like, yep, there it is. She's an adult after all."

Abi laughed. "I've always liked that about her to be honest."

"Me too. We had a pretty deep conversation just now. She helped me figure some things out. Including, deciding who I should set you up with."

"Is that right?"

"Yes." Jenna nodded slowly and took a step forward.

Abi swallowed hard. This was her chance to make sure they were on the same page, and she knew she needed to take it. "So, if I asked you on a date, you might be open to it?"

"Me?" Jenna's expression turned serious, her eyes searching Abi's face. "I meant your mum was right and I should've been trying harder to set you up with Jax!"

Abi flushed and made a few noises that weren't quite words, but she couldn't backtrack fast enough. Then Jenna's lip twitched and gave her away.

"You're for it," Abi warned, narrowing her eyes. She set her can on the window ledge and tickled Jenna so that she doubled over and pushed Abi away, squealing and spilling Coke all over the patio. It wasn't long before she wriggled free, her hair flying in all directions so that she had to smooth it back into place. She pointed as Abi inched forward again, hunched over slightly and struggling to hold back a laugh.

"Don't even think about trying that again," Jenna warned, flicking her wrist and spraying droplets of Coke. Then she set the can on the ground. "I'm all sticky."

Abi took another step towards her. Instead of tickling, this time she got in low and hoisted Jenna over a shoulder in a fireman's lift, so that she yelped. "If you want me to put you down, maybe you should think carefully about what you say next."

Waving her legs in the air, Jenna giggled. "Not sure I should. I quite like this." Her body slid slowly over Abi's until her feet hit the ground, but they didn't part. "Spoilsport."

Jenna blew a ribbon of hair from her forehead and another burst of giggles escaped before she took a firm grasp of Abi's face and kissed her squarely.

When a jumble of words fell out of Abi's mouth, Jenna's eyebrows raised in question. "Are you alright there?"

Abi nodded and blew out a long breath. "Yes, I just need a moment."

"I have that effect."

With a smile to signal her agreement, Abi closed the distance between them again. She wound her arm around Jenna's back to pull them even closer, then stroked the hair from Jenna's eyes and gently caressed her cheek. Abi moved slowly, taking everything in; the smell of her, the softness of her skin, and how damn good this was about to feel.

"Are you sure this is okay?" she whispered, still acutely aware that Jenna had just come from laying flowers on her mum's grave. She might be feeling vulnerable right now, and Abi would never want to take advantage of that.

Jenna nodded. "Don't worry, you have the green light. Ten of them, in fact." She pressed their lips together again and this time Abi registered the taste of smooth, sweet chocolate.

When Abi drew her head back slightly and searched Jenna's face, she found a confused look. Perhaps she'd not expected Abi to be so gentle with her, the mood between them shifting back to something altogether more serious. A little colour rose on Jenna's cheeks as she focused on Abi's mouth, and her hands slowly crept around Abi's waist.

"I need a moment now," she whispered, her breath warm on Abi's cheek.

Their lips danced close to each other but didn't quite meet, and Abi's heart thumped, tantalised by the proximity and a desperation to end any teasing. Her hands prickled, compelled to run over Jenna's hips, up the taut muscles of her back, and through her hair.

Jenna seemed to know she had Abi in thrall as she teased her fingers gently under the bottom of her T-shirt and stroked her spine, smiling when she squirmed. "Sure you're okay there?" she whispered, nipping gently on Abi's bottom lip but only fleetingly. Her eyes flicked up to meet Abi's, once again full of trouble.

"I hate you," Abi replied, her eyes narrowing.

"No, you don't."

Jenna nipped again. Then again. Then the teasing became too much for them both and they were almost back to where they'd been on Friday night, only this time, it was Abi backed up against the wall and their movements were slower, more purposeful. Abi drew Jenna's body flush against her own. She dropped her mouth to Jenna's shoulder, kissing along the burn marks and tan lines, feeling the heat under her lips.

"I think we need to stop," Jenna whispered, as she melted into the kisses now travelling up her neck. "I'm all for outdoor sex, but maybe not at your aunt's house when your dad's in the garden, huh?"

She laughed, but Abi's brain had just exploded over the idea of outdoor sex. "Whu?" was all she vocalised, her head snapping up.

"Whu?" Jenna teased, her eyes widening as she mocked Abi's expression.

"You're still a pain in my butt."

"Mmm," Jenna mumbled, their mouths only inches apart. "I

know." She rubbed her nose along Abi's. "I hate to kiss and run, but I should probably go now. I really did only come to drop you the Thermos."

Abi smiled. "You came out of your way for the Thermos, did you?"

"Whatever are you suggesting?"

"The kissing was an entirely unplanned bonus?"

"Absolutely, I had no idea you were going to jump me like that. Would I call it a bonus, though?"

Abi rolled her eyes. Jenna had definitely initiated the kiss, but she wouldn't be drawn in. "On second thoughts, I'm going let you go before you spoil the moment. See you at training on Wednesday?"

"Yes." Jenna paused and chewed on her bottom lip. Then she drew in a deep breath before adding, "But first I need to admit to something. The real reason I came over was because I meant for the footgolf thing to be a date, and I realised I hadn't made that clear."

"Really?"

She nodded. "Yes. Have I made myself clear enough now, though?"

Abi sucked her teeth. "I don't know... maybe try reminding me all about the unplanned kissing thing? It might help."

With a hand gripping the centre of Abi's shirt to draw her closer again, Jenna pressed their lips together and quickly deepened the kiss. She let out a little moan of pleasure this time, but it stopped dead when Stanley interrupted them.

"Cut it out, you two!" he mocked in a childish tone from the kitchen. "Disgusted father in earshot."

Jenna looked down at the ground. "You heard that, huh?" she yelled.

"Yeah." Abi sighed. "He could sleep through my hard work, but not that. Go figure."

"Want to get out of here and teach him a lesson?"

"Absolutely."

\* \* \*

Everything was suddenly moving fast, except for Abi, who inched inside the front door of Jenna's house and gently clicked it closed behind herself. When Jenna had asked if she wanted to go somewhere, she'd presumed they'd grab a drink or something. She hadn't imagined for a second that they'd go back to her place, with all the implications that were now running through Abi's mind on loop.

New build houses were often magnolia boxes, but Jenna's was far from generic and lifeless. On every wall were photos in mismatched frames, showing family, friends, and special occasions. They nestled alongside art prints and shouty motivational quotes, and Abi read them as she crept along the hallway.

"You really smell," Jenna yelled matter-of-factly from the kitchen.

"Is that the honeymoon period over? Must be some sort of record." Abi untied her work boots, yanked them off her feet, then tucked them neatly in the open space under the stairs.

"I'm not complaining, I'm just wondering if you'd like to take a shower?"

A shower? Here? That meant taking off her clothes, and Abi's heart thumped. It had been a while since she'd been naked in someone else's house and the thought unnerved her a little. She guessed she couldn't sit around in her dirty work gear, though.

"In a sec," she said as she finally reached the kitchen, buying herself a bit of time to acclimatise. It was a standard affair with cheap units and a fake granite worktop, then a small dining area with double doors leading onto a patio. Abi peered through them, finding that Jenna's garden was much as it would've been when she bought the place. There was a patch of turf, one crooked raised bed with a few veggies in it, and a circular metal table, but not a lot else.

All the same, Jenna threw open the doors because it was a scorcher of a day, and stepped down onto the sandstone. "I hope you're not judging me based on my garden. I'm self-conscious now."

Abi laughed and joined her. "No, don't worry. I'm judging you, but it's not because of the garden."

It earned her a whack on the stomach, but at least broke the tension. Jenna reached for Abi's hand and clasped it, their fingers entwining. It made Abi's heart bang again but this time she smiled.

"Can I show you my cucumbers?" Jenna asked, already leading Abi across the grass.

"Is that a euphemism?"

"No, it's not. Behave."

Jenna released Abi's hand and crouched beside her planter, the side panel of which wobbled a little as she leant against it. The whole thing could use a bit of TLC but Abi resisted pointing that out. Instead, she nodded as she was shown every fruit and vegetable Jenna was attempting to grow, despite the soil being bone dry and some of the plant's leaves turning yellow and crispy.

"Shall we water this?" Abi offered, hoping the hint was subtle enough.

"Sure. I'll get the hose."

Abi waited while Jenna retreated up the garden and unwound a bright yellow hose pipe, coiled next to the outside tap on the other side of her kitchen sink. Then she turned to face the vegetable patch again and bent to pick out a few weeds, thriving despite the conditions. They'd only take nutrients from the plants Jenna wanted to grow. The familiar and comforting act helped Abi relax and her heart finally returned to a normal pace, until a jet of cold water against her back sent it into overdrive. For a moment, she couldn't catch her breath and grasped her chest, wondering if this would be the thing to finally finish her off. Then she gasped and shot from the ground, holding both hands in front of herself as a shield as she turned around.

"When you offered me a shower, I didn't think this was what you meant!" she yelled as she darted up the lawn and grabbed hold of the hose about a metre from the head.

"Don't you dare," Jenna warned, backing off and trying to pull the hose from Abi's grip. She hunched over, a devilish smile on her face, and wrestled to turn the water on Abi's face, but her hands were slippery and she lost control.

"You're in trouble now!" Abi turned the hose on Jenna and blasted her up and down at close range as she shrieked and then crouched down, almost reaching the foetal position.

"Stop!" Jenna begged, through bursts of laughter. "I'm sorry, okay?"

"You will be."

"I already am."

Once she was thoroughly drenched, Abi finally relented and wandered down the lawn to douse the vegetables, her clothes clinging tight to her body and leaving a trail of drips.

"I think we could both use a proper shower now." Jenna joined Abi and worked to strip off the T-shirt that clung to her torso.

Beads of water glistened on her shoulders and Abi glanced over once, twice, three times, before she could no longer hide her desire to kiss them. With the hose still pointed at the vegetable patch, she hooked her free hand around Jenna's waist to pull her closer and dabbed Jenna's tan lines, the water cool on her slightly sunburned lips.

"Hey," Jenna whispered, her palm finding Abi's cheek and tilting her head up. They kissed until the ground was so saturated that the stream from the hose sounded like rain falling on a puddle, and Abi had to turn it away. She pecked Jenna on the lips one last time and ran up the garden to turn off the tap, then wound the hose into place.

By the time she'd finished, Jenna was back in the house. Abi wandered into the kitchen, conscious that she was still dripping everywhere, but reassured that there was already a puddle on the vinyl.

She heard Jenna bound up the stairs and followed. When she reached the landing, Abi was handed a neatly folded white towel. Then Jenna exited into one of the rooms and returned with a pair of running shorts and a fresh T-shirt.

"Will these do?" she asked, holding them up. "You can't exactly put those clothes back on."

"They'll be fine," Abi assured her, taking everything and then glancing at each of the three doors.

Jenna seemed to catch her hesitation and pushed open the middle one. "Oh, right. You don't know where you're going." She pulled the light cord and an extractor fan hummed into life. "You can use the main bathroom and I'll go in the ensuite."

When Jenna darted off, Abi hung her things on the towel rail and rifled through the various potions on the shelf, selecting one of about a hundred shampoos which all looked like samples. Then she set about trying to extricate herself from her clothes, and plopped them in the sink. She shivered and ran the shower, relieved to find a strong, hot stream.

Once she'd washed and dried herself, she stood in a haze of steam and surveyed herself in the large mirror over the sink. She turned sideways, then flexed a bicep. Her physique wasn't at its pre-pandemic peak and there were stretch marks where she'd lost some muscle mass. She'd never been self-conscious of her body, but then it had never let her down so thoroughly before. Not that it seemed to bother Jenna in the slightest, judging by the way she'd raked her eyes over every inch of skin whilst Abi was changing yesterday.

"Are you alright in there?" Jenna called, rapping her knuckles on the door.

"Yeah!" Abi called back, pulling on the shorts she'd hooked over the towel rail.

"You're taking ages. I wondered if you'd slipped and seriously injured yourself."

"And you didn't think to check sooner?" Abi had just finished wrestling the T-shirt over her head as she spilled out onto the landing. "That's good to know. Have you got a bag I can shove my dirty stuff in?"

"You can put it straight in the washing machine and once you've done that, come to my room so I can sort your hair." Jenna ruffled the unruly mass. "Want me to dry it for you quickly?"

"You're going to wash my clothes and dry my hair?"

"Yes."

Abi did as instructed, running downstairs with an armful of wet, smelly clothing and quickly locating the washing machine. Then she ran back upstairs, her hair in disarray and splashing water all over the flimsy cotton T-shirt barely disguising her lack of bra. When she reached Jenna's bedroom, she stopped at the door.

"I'm back," she said quietly.

"Then come in, you idiot."

It was almost a relief to find that nothing much had changed between them. If Jenna stopped calling her an idiot, Abi realised as she inched open the door, she wouldn't know what to do. "Can you promise me that if one date turns into fifteen, you'll always hurl insults?"

Jenna laughed. "Absolutely. Now come over here, dickhead, and let me dry your hair."

With that, the rest of the tension Abi had felt at being in Jenna's house for the first time fell away and her shoulders dropped with it. She smiled and did as she was told, sitting on the floor in front of Jenna and leaning against the bed, whilst Jenna placed a foot on either side of her and bounced up and down on the mattress a few times to get comfy.

Abi liked it here. She liked being around Jenna. She liked how gently Jenna was touching her, after months of feeling like the world was a harsh and disconnected place. She closed her eyes as Jenna's hands ran through her hair.

"Don't go to sleep," Jenna warned over the hum of the hairdryer. She raked her fingers up the back of Abi's head so that her chin fell forward, and Abi wrapped her hand around Jenna's calf to stop herself doing just that. The skin there was soft and perfectly smooth, and she rubbed her thumb into it. Then, when the hairdryer stopped a few minutes later, gently pressed her lips to the inside of Jenna's knee.

"Thank you," she whispered, her mouth still hovering over the same spot. She dabbed again, then brushed her lips up a little higher.

"You're welcome," Jenna whispered back, still running her hands through Abi's hair. When Abi twisted and pulled herself to kneel, her fingers trailing around the back of Jenna's knee, her heart pounded. Their eyes met with an intensity that made so many parts of Abi's body come to life, it was like someone had dropped a match in a fireworks factory. The T-shirt had no chance of hiding how hard her nipples were, or the quickening of her breath. Still, though, she teased. Her middle finger traced the back of Jenna's calf, and then it stroked higher until Jenna's quads were rough with goosebumps.

"You okay there?" Abi asked, taking a firmer grip around the backs of Jenna's knees and pulling her forward slightly, so that she was flush between Jenna's legs. When she took away her hand, though, she realised she was the one shaking and balled a fist to stop it. Maybe she wasn't quite so relaxed as she thought.

"We can take it slow," Jenna whispered, holding Abi's fist in her palms and kissing her knuckles. "Why don't we go downstairs and watch that movie I promised you yesterday? Maybe also order a takeaway? I've only eaten a chocolate bar today and I'm starving."

Abi nodded. She didn't know what had precipitated the reaction, but she agreed they needed to take it a touch slower.

"What are you in the mood for?" Jenna asked when Abi still didn't say anything.

She knew they were talking movies and dinner, but Abi didn't care about that. What she wanted was to savour this thing with Jenna. To feel her warmth, and the weight of her. To smell her hair, and touch her skin, and lie with her while absolutely anything at all played out on the screen. She didn't know how to explain that, though, so she simply replied, "you choose."

## 18

# JENNA

*Slow. Slooooooow.*

Jenna shook her head and rolled her shoulders back. Now full of Thai takeaway, she was satiated in one way and her mind had returned to the other. She could do this, though. Absolutely. Having the woman she fancied like crazy wandering around her house barely clothed would present no challenge whatsoever. Even coupled with the deep, penetrating heat.

She pulled open the fridge and grabbed a cold can of lemonade, then held it to her forehead. It could really do with going elsewhere, but that might be a bit obvious.

"Do you want one?" she yelled to Abi, who was flicking through Netflix trying to find them a film after they'd argued extensively through dinner about whether British or American rom-coms were superior.

"I know this is weird given it's so hot, but I really fancy a tea. I've wanted one ever since you used that Thermos as an excuse to come and see me earlier. Is it too much hassle?"

Jenna laughed. "Your family love their tea, huh?"

"Yep. My dad thinks it's a fix all for everything. To be fair, I guess I owe him. If he hadn't forced you to take one with you last week, I might not be here now…"

Jenna flicked on the kettle, then wandered back down the hallway and poked her head through the living room door. "You think this wasn't going to happen without tea…? It's another thing that doesn't have magical powers." If it hadn't been the Thermos, there would've been another excuse.

Abi was sat on the floor, leaning against the sofa. She stopped scrolling and peered up for a moment, with an uncharacteristically mischievous look on her face. Jenna felt compelled to ask what had elicited such a reaction. It surely couldn't be a bog standard builders tea…

"Maybe I'll tell you in a bit," Abi replied, running her tongue over her bottom lip. "Or show you."

Suggestive tea was a new one on Jenna, but she'd take it. This was, after all, a brave new world of trying different things. Maybe that also meant they should deviate from both American and British rom-coms.

"Is there anything Australian on there…?" she asked, narrowing her eyes.

"Muriel's Wedding?"

In unison, they both screeched, "You're terrible, Muriel!" and then barrelled into laughter.

Jenna walked back to the kitchen and grabbed a mug, then dumped in a tea bag from the jar on the work surface. "Sold!" she yelled over the chugging of the kettle as it came close to boiling. "I love that film. It's an absolute classic."

"Agreed, but don't complain if I'm singing *Dancing Queen* all night."

"*All* night, huh?" Did that mean Abi planned to stay? They hadn't talked about what would happen next, but Jenna definitely hoped that Abi would spend the night. Even if they had to murder Abba songs into the bargain.

When she returned to her place in the doorway, this time with a mug of tea in hand, Abi was smiling. That was probably a good sign that she might be up for it. The nerves were understandable. This wasn't like going home with a random person who you wouldn't see again if it didn't work out. They would be left with the image of each other's naked bodies for the rest of eternity, and reminded of their mistake for seasons to come. Even so, Jenna had to admit that she was looking forward to seeing Abi's naked body. She could leave on the boots occasionally, though, if she wanted.

"What are you grinning at?" Abi asked when Jenna still didn't venture any further into the room.

"Me?" Jenna did her best to look innocent, despite her thoughts being anything but, and finally set Abi's tea down on the glass coffee table in the middle of the lounge. "I'm just excited for the film."

"Mmm. I'm not sure I believe you." After groaning and hoisting herself from the floor, Abi slumped onto the sofa and hitched up her knee. Then she patted the seat cushion next to her. "I need to know if you're a snuggler, because it might be a dealbreaker."

"Which way?"

"Guess."

Jenna laughed. It didn't take much guesswork at all. "You want me to stay away, right?" She sighed loudly and perched on the arm of the sofa. "Well, I guess it won't be too uncomfortable to sit here."

Abi reached over and grabbed Jenna's arm, pulling her sideways onto the sofa and then wrapping her legs around Jenna's torso. They both laughed again but it stopped dead when Abi cuddled Jenna more gently.

"Shall I start the film?" Abi whispered, before shuffling backwards to make space so they could spoon.

With her one free arm, she reached for the remote, which had become lodged underneath them in the melee. She didn't wait for a response, and she wasn't going to get one, because Jenna was already busy wriggling back against her. She didn't need any more invitation to get as close as possible.

It was a good job she'd seen this film at least a dozen times before, because Jenna was paying no attention to the opening scene of a bouquet spiralling though the air into Toni Collette's outstretched hands. She was too busy thinking about where Abi's hands were. How the one that'd dropped the remote onto the carpet and just slipped under the bottom of her T-shirt was gently massaging the little love handle she kept as a tribute to her love of half-time Haribo and pre-match fry-ups.

"She's a very underrated actress," Jenna said to disguise the fact that her hips had already twitched multiple times.

"Huh?" Abi replied absently. Perhaps she was similarly distracted.

"Toni Collette."

"Oh. Yes. She is. I really loved that she was cast in About A Boy. Big Nick Hornby fan."

"You read...?"

The stroking stopped and instead, Abi gave Jenna a gentle slap. "Yes, I read. Why does that surprise you? Just because I'm also amazing with my hands..."

Jenna giggled. "You reckon, huh?"

"Another thing I might show you later."

It would be great if she wanted to make a start on that little show and tell session now, and Jenna reached back to pull Abi's leg over herself. She stroked along the back of it with her fingertips. "How late were you planning on staying?"

"I don't know. This is your house, so it depends when you kick me out..."

Jenna laughed again and it bought her a few seconds to

decide how to reply. She didn't want to pressure Abi into anything she wasn't ready for, but she also really wanted them to spend the night together. "After you've made me breakfast...?" She bit her lip and waited for the reply, her heart fluttering with a touch of apprehension.

Abi's hand slid out from under the T-shirt and she used it to sweep the hair from Jenna's neck. Nuzzling in close to her ear, she whispered, "sounds perfect" and this time the fluttering spread lower. Jenna squirmed, pressing her legs tight together, but then Abi flipped her over onto her back and climbed on top so that she had no hope of dampening her desire. Sex wasn't the only thing she wanted from Abi but right now, the same impulse that had overcome her whilst backed against the clubhouse wall was riding rough. She wanted Abi to consume her, both literally and figuratively. She wanted to fulfil every fantasy she'd harboured of Abi pounding into her whilst wearing nothing but her work boots, then ransack the drawer of toys in the bedroom above.

Once again, though, she found herself holding back and letting Abi take the lead. She'd seemed shy, almost embarrassed, over the vibrator. Maybe asking her to strap up was a bit much for their first time. Especially given Jenna didn't own one and had no experience in that area. It was consigned to the 'want to try' pile of sexual acts, despite her impressive collection of vibrators.

She also had to admit that she was enjoying the intimacy of just lying on the sofa, cuddled up together. Despite joking with Abi, it wasn't actually something she'd done often with ex-girlfriends. Not recent ones, anyway. She struggled to remember the last time she'd shared any sort of tenderness and before she knew it, the topic was all she could think about. Shuffling with a little agitation this time, she imagined cuddling up with her first girlfriend, back when she was fifteen and before everything fell apart. Was that the last time?

There was something else niggling, besides the warmth of her embrace with Abi, and Jenna was trying to put her finger on it. Before she knew it, the warmth started to feel threatening. When she wriggled again, Abi dropped a soothing kiss on her shoulder, but she couldn't shake the discomfort. There was a rising urge to escape but instead, she pulled Abi's arm into her chest and hugged it there, then closed her eyes tight shut with the realisation that what she feared was another hard loss.

"Are you okay?" Abi asked, flexing her fingers.

"Yeah, are you?"

"Yep, but you're sort of crushing my hand."

Jenna released her grip a little but didn't let go. She raised Abi's fingers to her lips and kissed them, then settled in to watch the film, hoping it would be the first of many and knowing that she was prepared to take the risk.

*  *  *

It was still light when the final scene played, along with *Dancing Queen*, which they both wailed at the top of their lungs. Jenna sat up and waved her arms in time with the music, then decided she wasn't conveying enough enthusiasm so stood and danced around the living room with her arms still outstretched, until Abi was laughing so hard that she could no longer sing.

Abi gave up and grabbed her now empty mug from the table, still chuckling. "So, um." She gave it a little wiggle as Jenna turned off the TV. "What shall we do now?"

Jenna sucked her teeth and turned, placing her hands on her hips. Then she blew a loose strand of hair out of her eyes. "You want some more tea?"

"Sounds good. I mean, it isn't even dark yet..."

"That's true, so it's probably too early for bed. The only question is what we're going to do with our time. There's been food, we finally watched a film together..." Jenna tugged on the bottom of her T-shirt to waft some air onto her torso because it was still hot and dancing hadn't helped. They were in for a damp, muggy night, and she knew she wouldn't sleep. Not that she wanted to, in any case.

Abi had watched the rise and fall of Jenna's shirt and was still intently focused on her midriff. Then she snapped out of it and wiggled her mug again. "More tea, then?"

"Can I offer you a biscuit with it this time?"

"You can always offer me a biscuit."

Abi shuffled off the sofa and followed Jenna into the kitchen, where she was directed to a box of assorted biscuits in the cupboard directly above the kettle. They were never far from reach, and it meant that Jenna wasn't far from Abi's grasp, either. As Jenna filled and clicked on the kettle, then chucked a tea bag into the mug, Abi snaked an arm around her waist and craned to reach for the box.

"Hey," Abi whispered, lingering with the box of biscuits in her free hand. She dabbed a kiss on Jenna's temple.

"Hey yourself," Jenna replied, placing a hand on Abi's forearm to hold it on her own stomach. She was enjoying the closeness again.

Abi set the box down next to them and fumbled to lift the lid. "These are a bit fancy."

"They were a gift."

"Oh, yeah? Someone clearly knows the way to your heart."

"Too true. Worried you've got competition?"

"Always." Abi laughed and held up the little insert which explained the different types of biscuit in the selection box.

"These were from Jax." Jenna sucked her teeth again whilst considering how to get the best rise out of Abi. Eventually, she plumped for, "This could turn into quite a complicated little love triangle, couldn't it?" and then waited for the reaction.

As expected, Abi dropped the biscuit menu and tickled Jenna, who squealed but couldn't escape because she was pinned to the work surface. Maybe teasing again hadn't been the best idea. She snatched for breath and it was only when she stunned Abi by accidentally clouting her on the chin with a flailing knuckle, that Jenna could finally wriggle free. Unfortunately, though, it had come at a cost because Abi was bent over holding her face.

Jenna also doubled over, clutching her legs as she panted and tried to ease her cramping stomach muscles. "Are you okay?"

"Yeah," Abi replied, moving her jaw from side to side. "Have you considered taking up boxing?"

Still red faced but sufficiently reoxygenated, Jenna took Abi's face in her hands. "I'm sorry." She dropped a delicate kiss on Abi's chin. There was a bit of a mark but nothing horrific. "I didn't mean to rough you up."

Abi didn't seem to have taken it too personally because she wrapped her arms around Jenna's lower back and pulled her closer. "How are you going to make it up to me?"

It was a demand more than a question, and there was a firmness in her tone that Jenna had rarely seen lately. It was a glimpse at the confident Abi of old. She was never cocky or arrogant, only self-assured, and it was one hell of an aphrodisiac.

"I don't know," Jenna whispered against Abi's ear. "But I'm sure we'll think of something."

When she drew her head back, their eyes locked for a second, and then Jenna ran her hands through Abi's hair and kissed her. She didn't really want to talk or debate it, she just wanted to forget the day, the month, the year, and everything that had happened. She wanted to wrap herself up in Abi's safe arms again and leave no equivocation about her intentions.

Abi didn't waver again, either. She kissed Jenna back, even forgetting about the biscuits. Apparently, there was one thing more enthralling than tea, and it wasn't a chocolate coated ginger nut.

She ran her hands down over Jenna's bum, then her fingernails clawed gently along her lower back, travelling higher until the T-shirt rode up and had to be removed. Jenna flung it at the work surface and quickly resumed their kiss, which only became more fevered when Abi's hands were free to roam over Jenna's shoulders and stroke her sides. Their hearts beat hard against each other, the only sound besides the blood thundering over Jenna's ears coming in bursts when one of them grunted or allowed a moan to escape, until the kettle added a slow, bubbling crescendo where Jenna had overfilled it.

She was about to tug Abi's T-shirt over her head when it was launched across the room. Abi was one step ahead and spun Jenna around with dizzying precision. There was none of the hesitation she'd shown earlier. Her breasts pressed into Jenna's back as she flicked her thumbs over taut nipples, sending thrill after thrill to Jenna's clit. The warmth of Abi's mouth on her neck and ear lobe caused her entire body to glow and she closed her eyes, letting the heat consume her. Neither of them spoke, driven on instinct like they had been in the club car park. This time, though, they didn't stop.

Jenna put out a hand to brace herself on the work surface in front of her when one of Abi's hands slipped into the front of her shorts. Jenna bucked into her touch, her head twisting as her mouth sought Abi's. She reached her hand from the work surface to Abi's cheek, guiding them together, nibbling on Abi's tongue as Abi ran circles around her clit. Abi's other hand raked over Jenna's stomach, her sides, the tops of her legs, until they shook.

"Fuck, Abi," was the only thing Jenna said, because it was all she could get out. Her eyes still closed, she reached both hands behind herself and grabbed Abi's bum, pulling her tight. But with the click of the kettle, signalling that the water was boiling, Abi withdrew her hand and Jenna's eyes shot open.

Dazed and breathing hard, she shook her head. "Wh-why have you stopped?" she stuttered out, still shaky and needing to lay a palm on the work surface again.

When Jenna looked over her shoulder, Abi smiled casually. "Water's ready. I thought we were having tea?"

Was she taking the piss? "Bugger the tea, I was about to have an orgasm."

"Are you always this impatient?" Abi asked, nudging Jenna out of the way and pouring water over her tea bag.

Jenna wanted to reply but she'd tripped on the sight of Abi topless in her kitchen. For the first time, she could see Abi's breasts, casually on display as she stirred a spoon around her mug. They were tanned and pert, with a little mole on the left one, just above her nipple, which Jenna incidentally wanted in her mouth way more than tea.

Still dumbstruck, Jenna followed Abi down the hallway and into the living room, where she set down the mug and then relaxed on the sofa.

"What is happening here?" Jenna asked, hovering in the doorway. "Have I actually just been abandoned for a boring mug of tea?"

"Tea isn't boring!" Abi protested, sitting more upright. "Come over here and I'll prove it."

Now Jenna was thoroughly confused, but she had to admit to also being a little intrigued. She side-eyed Abi as she inched into the room, unsure why Abi had a mischievous glint in her eye again.

"Am I safe?" Jenna asked as she stood in front of Abi.

"Completely," Abi replied, placing a hand on either side of Jenna's waist and guiding her forward. She laid butterfly kisses across Jenna's stomach, then moved her hands lower and ran them over her quads.

It didn't take long before the throbbing between Jenna's legs verged on uncomfortable and she was going to lose her shit if Abi stopped again. Not wanting to offer the opportunity, she decided to go all in. She pulled off her shorts and straddled Abi's lap, grinding against her to get a little relief. Abi's hand crept higher up the back of her leg, then higher still, until Jenna was desperate to feel her inside. She wasn't even beyond begging this time.

"I really need you to fuck me some time soon," she said against Abi's ear, before swirling her tongue around the lobe and then giving it a little tug with her teeth. Blood pounded over every erogenous zone and when Abi sucked one of Jenna's breasts, she felt it in each inflamed part of her already hot and sweaty body.

When Abi finally complied and curled two fingers against her G-spot, Jenna let out a sigh of both relief and pleasure. She ground hard into Abi's hand, her enthusiasm matched as Abi's strong arm pounded her hard. Jenna grasped Abi's bicep, feeling it contract with every thrust, and then arched her back to allow Abi to consume her breasts again.

"I'm so close," she muttered, wrapping an arm around Abi's neck and pressing her mouth to the wet hair on her temple. Then she reached down with her free hand and held Abi's wrist, shuddering as she withdrew Abi's fingers and slid them back to her clit. "I can't orgasm just with penetration."

"Noted," Abi replied, before removing her hand entirely. Was she fucking serious?

"If we're stopping again, I'm going to hit you," Jenna said, her head slumping against Abi's shoulder.

"I just need a sip of tea."

"Really?!"

"Yes, really."

Abi held Jenna close with a hand on her back as she rocked them forward and grabbed her mug from the table. She took what felt like an eternity and Jenna was considering a strongly worded letter to the Yorkshire Tea company when she was flipped onto her back. She was about to protest when her legs were parted, Abi's hands wrapped around the backs of her knees, and her clit was gently sucked into Abi's warm mouth. No, not warm. Hot.

"Holy shit," Jenna breathed, squirming as Abi's tongue flicked across every swollen nerve ending. Why was Abi's mouth so hot? It took a moment for Jenna to realise that it was the tea, but she didn't have time to ruminate for long because she was soon writhing out her orgasm, her hands running through Abi's hair to hold her in the right spot.

Maybe tea wasn't so boring after all, and she'd be happy to confirm that after a few more rounds.

19

## ABI

"Dammit!" Abi cursed as her logo expanded across the page until it was partially out of sight. She'd been at it for almost an hour and her laptop risked a trip through the café window. The purpose of the outing was to relieve her stress, not add to it, but apparently location was not the root of Abi's technological issues. She'd all but given up and decided she needed help after all when Jax appeared in front of her, like some heavenly apparition.

"In a café at one o'clock on a Wednesday afternoon?" Jax sighed, resting her hands on her hips. "Man, you self-employed folks have it tough, don't you?"

"Shut up, I'm working very hard," Abi shot back. She jabbed at the keys, and then pushed the laptop over the table and folded her arms. The pout was an unnecessary touch, but she added it anyway, for emphasis.

"Still working on that website?" Jax sat down opposite and helped herself to a fresh cup of tea from Abi's pot. "Let me see." She swung the laptop around and then scrolled for a bit. "Stop being a martyr and let me help. It'll take an hour to finish. Max."

"But—" Abi got out, before realising Jax was right. She'd

wasted a monumental amount of energy and had a job to get to later in the afternoon. As work started coming in, it was becoming harder to find time. "Fine. There must be something I can do for you in return, though."

"Oh, there is. Let's do this in the clubhouse on Friday night, and you can buy me some drinks." She took a few sips of the tea she'd just poured. "See you at training tonight? Lots to go through before the first match of the season next Sunday."

Abi closed her laptop and dropped it into her rucksack. She was still deciding whether she wanted to play the match but she'd be at training, so she murmured a quick "mhm" and quicky changed the subject. "Have you decided who you're picking for captain yet?" The previous one had decided to retire and not return after the long break, so there was an open spot.

"Yep, but I'm not telling you who so don't even ask. You'll only blab to her."

"It's not me, then?" Abi laughed, partly with relief. She really didn't want the job. Even if she did choose to play, which she probably wouldn't...

"You'll just have to wait to find out."

"Jenna?" Abi pressed, even though she knew she was pushing her luck. She searched Jax's face for any kind of giveaway. "You have to admit she'd be perfect. She's dedicated, experienced, and everyone respects her."

Jax took another sip of tea and then narrowed her eyes over the top of the cup. "You're being awfully supportive. Think you might have missed the boat with her, though. Sorry."

She didn't look at all sorry. In fact, she looked like she knew a lot more than she was letting on, but Abi had no intention of spilling any information either. "Oh, really? That's a shame. Still, I suppose we shouldn't be gossiping about her behind her back. Whoever Jenna wants to date must be pretty incredible and it's her own business."

Jax grunted. "Hmm. I need to get back to work."

"And I need to get to the framing shop. I'll see you at training."

She could see that Jax was desperate to ask more about that, but Abi didn't give her a chance. She picked up her bag, slung it over her shoulder, and waved as she made a swift exit. Then she strode down the pavement and ducked into the framing shop on the high street. The bell dinged as she opened the door, and a white-haired woman looked up from the counter at the back.

"We've just finished it." The woman smiled and then turned to lift a package from the rack behind her. It was bigger than Abi had expected, but she supposed it had to accommodate a full flattened football shirt, from sleeve to sleeve.

"Looks great, thanks so much." Abi held it up, admiring the gold frame alongside the white of the England kit. Then, in blue, the number ten and the name 'Smith'.

"We're asked to frame more football memorabilia than you'd think. I don't remember a Smith on the England team for a long while, though."

"Kelly Smith OBE," Abi schooled her, emphasising the O-B-E. "One hundred and seventeen caps for the England Women's team. My friend loves her, so I got this to hang in her office."

"Lucky her. I hope she likes it."

*You and me both.*

Abi paid and then manoeuvred the frame out onto the street. She'd already messaged Jenna to make sure she was in town today and not off surveying the rest of her empire, so it was only a short walk from there to the barbershop.

This time, Abi knew to expect the overwhelming smell of 'modern man' and braced herself on entry. There were two stylists in the main room, but they were just stopping for lunch. Abi attracted the attention of a young woman in head to toe black, with a nose ring and a streak of pink hair. "Is Jenna about? She knows I'm coming."

"In her office," the woman replied cheerily enough, but without looking up from the floor as she swept it.

Abi made her way down the corridor and rested the frame next to Jenna's office door. Then she knocked softly and nudged it open. "Can I come in?" she whispered.

"Suppose so."

"Is it okay that I'm here? I don't want to crash in while you're working." Inching inside, Abi fiddled with the strap of her bag.

Jenna rolled back on her chair. "Don't be silly. Besides, you said you have something to give me. Gift bearers are always welcome."

Abi held up her index finger. "Wait there." She took off her rucksack, dumped it on the floor, and then strode out into the corridor. Halfway down it, she called back, "Close your eyes!"

"Should I be worried?"

When Abi arrived at the counter, the two stylists were just departing. They yelled out a quick goodbye and offered amused smiles as Abi fussed over the frame, wiping her hands over the edges to make sure it was clean and presentable. When it was perfect, she carried it down the corridor.

"Have you got your eyes closed?" Abi asked as she lingered outside the office door again.

"Yes, but I swear if I have anything splatted on my face, you're dead."

"I'm hoping the only thing you'll have on your face is a smile." Holding up the frame in both hands, Abi stepped inside and instructed Jenna to open her eyes. Then she waited expectantly for the response, her fingers sliding up the edges where her palms prickled with sweat. "What do you think? Thought it might brighten up your office."

"Is that your Kelly Smith shirt? You're giving it to me?"

"If you want it, yeah. I've come armed with the fixings to hang it behind your desk. What do you reckon?" After setting the frame against the wall, Abi grabbed her bag, unzipped it and pulled out her hammer. Then she rummaged around for the box of picture hooks she'd stolen from Petra's crap drawer.

Jenna laughed. "You're even going to hang it for me? I'm speechless."

"Then I've done the impossible." Abi tucked the hammer and hooks back in her bag, then picked up the frame, rounded Jenna's desk, and held the it against the wall. "You said you never got official shirts when you were a kid, so I wanted you to have this one. Is that okay?"

Laughing again, Jenna folded her arms and took a step back to survey the shirt. "It's more than okay. It's probably the most thoughtful thing anyone's ever done for me. Thank you."

"You're welcome." Her arms were beginning to shake, so Abi put down the frame, carefully propping it against the wall again, and shook out her hands. Then she noticed Jenna's glistening eyes and pulled her into a hug. "Are you alright?"

"Yep," Jenna mumbled into Abi's shoulder. "It's just been a big week already, and we're only halfway through."

"Did you hear from your grandparents?"

"I got a call from my gran yesterday evening. She wanted to let me know that they've made some money available in case I needed it for the shop. To be fair to them, they loaned me the extra cash I needed to open this place a few years ago and I think it's their way of saying they're here for me. They just don't know how to do it any other way."

"I'm glad you're able to see that and make some sense, but it's still okay to feel your feels."

"I know. Thanks." Jenna drew her head back and kissed Abi softly. "Hi, by the way. I missed waking up with you this morning. And yesterday morning."

Abi swept the hair out of Jenna's face with the back of her hand. Then she dropped a kiss on her nose. "You've only ever woken up with me once."

"I know, and it's not enough, but I appreciate you giving me some space yesterday. I'm actually going to have to kick you out of here soon, too, because I'm meeting your dad to go over final plans for the new shop."

"Are you definitely hiring him?"

"Yep. His was by far the cheapest quote and usually that would make me suspicious, but I trust him. The only catch is that he said he might not be able to start for a couple of weeks."

That rang true. His team were handling the big projects so that wasn't a problem, but Stanley was tied up with all the work he'd committed to at Ida's, and she was the one person who took priority over anyone else. No matter how much he wanted to help Jenna out for Abi's sake, Stanley wouldn't bump her. "Is that going to cause you problems?"

"It's not ideal, but it's still preferable to using someone else. And to be fair, it's partly my own fault. I dragged my heels a bit in terms of sorting out the shopfitting work because I was wavering over what to do. I can't expect people to be magically free just because I now want to move fast."

That was also true, but Abi had a feeling she could help all the same. As Stanley had already pointed out, Cass wasn't the only one with connections. "Will you make it to training after?"

"No, which is really annoying. First game of the season next Sunday and I hate to miss a session but I'm interviewing someone at half six when they finish work and I don't think I'll be done in time. What are you doing after, though?"

"I could be persuaded to go back to your house again." Because there was no way in hell they were going to Abi's bedroom at her parents' house. "I might be a bit less free over the next week or so, though."

"Really? Oh. In that case, I guess I need to make the most of it. You could make me some dinner and maybe give me a little massage…"

"Hang on, if I'm making dinner and giving you a massage, what are you doing in return?"

Jenna pursed her lips as she considered. Then she shrugged. "I'm letting you."

\* \* \*

"I'm home!" Abi yelled as she left her rucksack at the foot of the stairs. She wanted Stanley but, as luck would have it, she found her mum instead.

"I'm in the garden!" Petra called back. The door from the kitchen was open, and she appeared in the frame with a pair of secateurs in one hand, a can of pre-mixed G&T in the other.

"Where's Dad?"

"Where's Dad? Where's Dad? Always your father!" With each statement Petra snapped her secateurs, inching forward until she was in the kitchen and risked taking a chunk out of Abi's T-shirt.

With a nervous laugh, Abi took a step back. "Are you safe with those?"

The answer was likely no, but that never deterred Petra. She snapped the secateurs again a few more times for good measure and placed them on the table, then took a sip from her can. "He's taking a shower. Why can't I help, huh?"

"Unless you've changed profession, I need Dad." After a few moments, Petra set her can down as well and studied Abi's face until she was so creepily close that Abi had to look away. "What are you doing?"

"Trying to work out what is going on with you. You're…"

Petra's arms looped as she searched for the word, and then she clicked her fingers. "Happy. Is there a woman involved?"

"Maybe..."

Before Petra could say anything else, Abi jogged into the hallway because she'd heard the padding of footsteps above. Peering up with a hand on the balustrade, she found Stanley strutting towards his bedroom with a towel wrapped around his waist, mouthing words into a comb.

When he spotted Abi, he pointed at her and started belting out an old Carpenters song at the top of his voice. That man was such a juxtaposition, and Abi shook her head.

"Alright, hard man?" she asked when he finally stopped.

"Something told me you were going to be very interested in where I've just been. Am I correct?"

"You're correct. So long as we're talking about Jenna's shop and not whatever you've been doing in that bathroom." Abi took the stairs two at a time and stopped in front of her dad on the landing, where he was now using the comb for its intended purpose. "How did it go?"

"It went very well. She's going to drop a spare key to me when she gets them on Friday, I've lined up one of my guys for the electrical work, and I'm going to start the rest in about a fortnight."

"You can't do it any sooner?"

"Nope. I'm at Ida's, remember. I can't leave work half finished."

"What if I finished it for you?"

Stanley considered for a few seconds and then, without any preamble, answered "no" and exited to his bedroom. "Leave this to me and Jenna," he called back. "You just worry about your own business."

So much for friends in high places. The door shut and Abi scuffed her foot on the carpet. She felt overwhelmed by a compulsion to help, and by extension to argue, but she knew from his tone that Stanley's word was final.

Skulking back downstairs, Abi hopped out onto the patio and stuffed her hands into her pockets. Petra had resumed her pruning and her can of G&T.

"That was quick," Petra noted without looking up from the rose bush she was butchering. "Was he able to help?"

"No. He refused."

"That's unlike your father. I'm sure he would've if he could."

He could, but he didn't want to, and Abi was trying to work out why. She knew she needed to focus on her own business, but that wouldn't be affected by spending a few more evenings at Ida's. It had come to something when Abi was so perplexed that she turned to her mum for advice.

"You were right, I have been seeing someone, and Dad's doing some work for her," she explained, resting on the low wall that marked the start of Stanley's vegetable beds. "I asked if he could start the work sooner if I finished at Ida's but he basically told me to mind my own business."

"I see. Well, it is his client, regardless of your personal relationship."

"I know, but he's the person who said that her ex wasn't the only one with connections and that I should use them. Now I just feel completely useless."

Petra said "I see" again but didn't follow it up this time. She squinted at her roses, and then into the can of G&T. "I need another drink. Would you please get me one?"

Abi huffed as she pulled herself back off the wall. She took the empty can when Petra held it up, and then carried it into the kitchen. When she returned, she found her mum had downed tools and was now sat at the patio table, her face inclined to the sun.

"Come and sit with me." Once Abi had scraped out a chair

and sat down, then cracked the ring pull, Petra continued to probe. "Tell me why you feel useless. What is this about an ex-girlfriend?"

Were they going to talk about Cass again? Abi had already done this with Stanley. She knew she felt insecure but she was over it now. Jenna had made it entirely clear that there were no longer any romantic feelings between them, Abi knew she was just struggling because her own world had been turned upside down, and she'd made peace with Cass after the gnome incident. Hadn't she?

"It's nothing," she replied, wondering who she was trying to convince. Cass was taking Jenna for a fancy meal on Friday night, at a place she'd wanted to go for ages, meanwhile Abi was only going to a freebie footgolf session. There was still a part of her wondering how she could possibly compete. "Okay, maybe it's something. I just wish it wasn't. I need to get over myself."

"How so?"

"I keep worrying because her ex-girlfriend is really successful and I'm back in my parents' bedroom at thirty-three, but I thought I'd worked through it. I guess now I'm annoyed with myself that it's come up again."

Petra laughed. "Oh, Abi!" she chastised. "Anyone can throw money around. If she doesn't want you exactly as you are, then maybe the question is why you want to be with *her*. So invite this woman over some time and try to stop worrying about it."

Abi nodded. She knew this. She'd never twisted herself or begged anyone to show interest in her before, and it frustrated the hell out of her that she'd drawn herself into doing that. "I'm trying not to worry. I didn't think I was." But apparently she was kidding herself, and Stanley had more than likely clocked her motivations. It was why he'd said no.

"Have you spoken to her about this?"

"No," Abi admitted. There had been a lot of honesty from

Jenna recently but she didn't know about the gnomes. Or what had precipitated that reaction.

"Then I think you have your answer. It's going to keep coming up until you speak with her about this. It is a good sign if you can communicate clearly and she shows help and understanding. It's also a good sign if she agrees to spend a night here." Petra shrugged and reached to take a sip of her drink. "It will prove that your circumstance is not an issue."

Abi agreed with most of that but she was still unsure how she felt about Jenna staying, because as surprisingly useful as she'd found this little heart to heart, Petra had form. "Thanks, Ma. That was actually... helpful."

"Don't sound so surprised! Things will turn around, I promise. You're back at football now and work is picking up. Just give it some time."

"Actually, I'm not sure I'm going to play this season," Abi found herself admitting. She held her breath, waiting for a torrent of protests, but let it out when none came.

"You cannot help if you're still unwell," Petra said with surprising calm. Or was it? The one thing she feared more than anything was Abi getting ill again. "But we will all be there watching, in any case. You will still be a part of the team even if you're not on the pitch."

"Do we all need to go if I'm not playing?"

"What does it matter, then, if you're not playing?"

"I guess."

Petra's shoulders lifted and her eyes twinkled as she grinned. "This is exciting."

"Is it?"

"Yes. Usually it is your father you confide in, but now it is me."

Abi went to correct the error because Stanley already knew most of it but then she stopped herself. Petra was beaming, and

## 20

# JENNA

Cass raised a flute of Champagne and a hundred bulb lights refracted in the bubbles. "Congratulations. I'd forgotten we'd have the new shop to celebrate when I booked this."

Jenna raised her glass to meet Cass's. Then she set it on the table and leant back, surveying the room for about the tenth time that evening. It had been a beautiful meal, even if the portions were way too small, and Cass had even managed to pay attention for most of it. No deals, no favours, no jibes. It had been nice. "Thank you for booking this."

Cass smiled. "You're very welcome."

She'd left her phone face down on the side of the table after paying for the meal and gave herself away by glancing at it too many times in a row. She was clearly desperate to turn it over, and Jenna laughed. "You can look at that if you really want to. Don't worry."

"I saw a message come through when I paid. Jax wants me to meet her."

Jenna tried to quirk an eyebrow but probably only looked a bit demented. "Oh yeah?"

"Yes. She says she's in the clubhouse with Abi and wants me to collect her."

Now Jenna's interest was really piqued because she couldn't shake the nagging feeling that Abi had lost interest, given her declaration of non-specific unavailability. They'd enjoyed a late night rendezvous after training on Wednesday night, and could be headed towards another, and that reassured Jenna a little. On the other hand, though, she didn't want to end up as the person Abi only met up with for sex. It was a real bind.

"Shall we go after this?" Jenna picked up and wiggled the Champagne bottle. By "we" she meant she'd finish it herself, because Cass was driving.

Cass relaxed back into her seat and sipped at the remaining Champagne in her glass. "Fine. Have it your way." She regarded Jenna with a wry smile. "I take it there's a compelling reason you're so desperate to see Jax tonight."

Jenna laughed. "Oh, yes. I'm desperate to see Jax. You know how I feel about her. She's the light of my life."

"Nothing at all to do with a certain gardener…?"

It elicited a blush and Jenna looked away, deciding that for now she'd like to divert the subject ever so slightly. "Speaking of her, I don't suppose you'd mind leaving a review on the new Facebook page we set up?"

"I'm sure I can manage that." When Jenna slid Cass's phone across the table towards her, Cass chuckled. "You want me to do it now?"

"Please." There was no time like the present, and Abi had been dire at prompting other people to do it.

Once Cass had written the review and Jenna had checked she was happy with it, they made their way out to the Mercedes. Jenna squinted and pulled down the visor as Cass started the engine, and they crunched down the long gravel drive of the old manor house.

"You know," Jenna ventured cautiously. "Given this is only a bit of fun, you and Jax are spending a lot of time together."

"Well, we're having a lot of fun."

"How do you know it's only fun, though?"

Cass laughed. "Because we've talked about it."

Talking was something Jenna probably needed to do with Abi, too, but she was a little scared. What if it *was* just a sex thing for her? The squint turned into a frown, just as Cass glanced over.

"I feel like there's something on your mind."

There was, but could Jenna really have this conversation with her ex-girlfriend? "Are you sure we can talk about this stuff? I mean, I know we're a cliché, but..."

"Try me and if it's uncomfortable, I'll hit the brakes."

"A very sensible suggestion." Maybe they were both growing, because usually Cass shut down any situation where there was a looming threat to her comfort. All too often, it had left Jenna feeling needy and like she was being a bit of a burden. Again.

"Sensible is my middle name," Cass joked. It was another surprise to find she'd gained a sense of humour.

"Okay, well I've been spending time this week with the woman I asked on a date. Things have felt good, I've enjoyed us getting closer, but then on Wednesday she told me she might not be able to see me much for a while. Right after giving me a very meaningful gift. So I guess I'm just confused as to her intentions."

"That's understandable."

"Right!" Jenna held out her hands and stared at her palms, as if trying to weigh things up. "I don't know whether I'm just worrying for nothing. We've only really been seeing each other a week and it should be fine to not spend every moment together. But on the other hand, I've had this ridiculous compulsion to check my phone every few minutes since then and I feel really on edge. Like I'm just waiting for a the axe to fall."

Cass considered for a second as she stopped for a behemoth to let a Range Rover pass them on the narrow track. When she pulled off again, she glanced sideways and asked, "Can I be honest?"

It sounded ominous but Jenna didn't have much choice. "Shoot."

"You need a lot of reassurance." There was another sideways look, no doubt to gauge the reaction. Then Cass returned her eyes to the road. "It's not a bad thing so please don't take it that way. But I do think you need to be with someone who is understanding of where your anxiety comes from and is prepared to make you feel safe. I always failed, Lord knows, but that doesn't mean Abi will, so give her a chance and be honest. Tell her what you want, and what you need, and see if she can be that person for you."

"Abi," Jenna whispered. She was surprised Cass had been so candid and acknowledged who they were talking about, but she wasn't sure why. Cass was no idiot, and she had her problems with facing emotional issues but she wasn't completely incapable. Just scared, probably, but in a different way.

"Yes, Abi," Cass repeated. "The person who you're the most genuine version of yourself with. The person I watched you worry over when she wasn't messaging back and you knew she was unwell. The person you're currently scared is going to let you down like everyone else."

Jenna nodded.

*Yes. That Abi.*

\* \* \*

'That' Abi was sat in her usual spot opposite Jax in the clubhouse when they arrived. Her laptop was open on the bar, and Abi was banging her head into her arms as she slumped forward, narrowly missing her half-finished pint. By all accounts, this latest attempt to finish her website was going well.

"I thought you were going to fix this?" Jenna asked, pointing at the screen.

Jax sighed. "I have. It's finished. I just made the mistake of trying to show her how to edit it, and things took a turn."

Jenna's first instinct was to stroke Abi's hair and comfort her, and she had to quickly do something else with her hand, so she pushed Abi's shoulder instead.

"Hey!" Abi protested, her head shooting off the bar. "That was a bit mean. What did I ever do to you?"

Nothing yet, but it was early days.

"Stop being dramatic."

Abi seemed to clock that Cass had glided in behind Jenna and finally straightened, giving her a nod. "Good to see you." She was becoming a better liar, but at least she was making the effort. "I'm just popping to the bathroom. Feel free to take my stool."

She jumped down and jogged towards the toilets but Cass didn't accept the invitation. She continued to linger, not quite in the group.

"I like what you've done with the place," Cass said surprisingly genuinely, searching the room and then pointing to the pool table. "Would you like a game?"

Jenna frowned for a second. She couldn't quite picture Cass playing pool in the clubhouse. It was a weird clashing of two worlds and she wasn't entirely sure what to make of the request. Could Cass even play pool? She had no idea. The only thing she knew for sure was that she didn't want to get stuck here. She wanted to speak with Abi. Alone.

"Umm," she replied, glancing at Jax. "I'm actually feeling quite tired. You two play, though. I'll watch."

Jax shrugged. "Fine. I need to ask you about something

quickly whilst Abi's out of the way, though, so come and help me rack up."

If it was Abi related, Jax would get full attention. "What's up?"

They all wandered towards the pool table and Jax crouched to collect the balls. "Has she said anything to you about not playing this season?" The balls were placed on the table, one by one, and Jenna began moving them to the triangle. "I've asked her about it a few times but she's being evasive."

"No." The sinking feeling Jenna was currently experiencing was partly hunger due to the size of her dinner, and partly something else. They'd been speaking all week and getting closer, but Jenna had no idea Abi was even considering not playing. It was another mark in the 'about to be dumped' column.

"Hmm," Jax mumbled. "Okay. Don't suppose you'd mind talking to her?" She glanced up at Cass, who was rolling her shirt sleeves and seemed to mean business. "Subtly, though, because I don't want her to know I've spoken to you about this or think she's been ambushed. Then find a way to make sure she plays. I know she'll regret it otherwise and we need her."

Jenna nodded. She doubted whether she had the sway. In fact, she was currently doubting a lot, but she'd have the conversation if one presented itself, and she wouldn't drop Jax in the shit. "Sure. Maybe I'll ask her to drive me home. Give you two some space, and see if it comes up." Although right now, she wanted to clarify more than just whether Abi would play football this season.

Abi returned as Jax was placing the last ball on the table. "Are we playing doubles?" She rubbed her hands together and smiled at Jenna, seeming to have flushed her worries about the website down the toilet. "Want to be my partner?"

"I would love to be your partner, but would you mind driving me home instead?"

Abi frowned. "Yeah, of course. Are you okay?"

"Yep." Jenna checked that Jax was occupied setting up her balls and Cass was busy chalking a cue. Then she mouthed, "Thought we could have some alone time."

The frown on Abi's face quickly mellowed back into a smile. "Of course I'll drive you home. Can't have you all tired around a pool competition. We both know how that'll end."

"Too true," Jenna agreed, not taking the bait.

"Enjoy your date tomorrow," Jax yelled after them as they made their way towards the laptop still open on the bar. It caused both Abi and Jenna's heads to snap around. "Let me know how it goes."

Jenna didn't reply and nor did Abi. Instead, they threw the laptop into Abi's rucksack and both made a swift exit into the car park. Once away from prying eyes, Jenna was relieved to find Abi's attention was a bit more enthusiastic.

"You look fantastic," she said, holding open the passenger door of her van. "I've never seen you all dressed up before."

Jenna stroked her hands down the arms of a white shirt, paired with braces and tailored trousers. "This old thing? I just threw it on."

"Like hell you did. Modesty doesn't suit you but that outfit does. You looking smoking hot."

"I've been experimenting with my look. I'll consider this a success."

Abi shut the door, dumped her bag in the back, and then hopped into the driver seat. "How come you've been experimenting?"

"Why not?" Jenna shrugged and clicked on her seatbelt. "I'm embracing change in all areas of my life."

"Oh yeah? So, what can we expect next?" Abi asked with an air of amusement as she turned the key in the ignition and the van reluctantly stuttered into life.

"That's the beauty part. No one knows. Even I don't. Life is a great big open road of possibility right now."

"I should buckle up, then?" They reached the end of the driveway and Abi peered left and right. "Am I actually taking you home or was that just a ploy to whisk me away?"

Jenna considered for a second. "It was a ploy. Can I take you somewhere?"

"I think I'm doing the taking, but sure."

"Great. Drive us to the village shop first."

"Yes, boss."

It was less than a minute before they pulled up in front of the little grocery store, and Abi cut the engine. She waited while Jenna ran inside, then frowned when Jenna spilled out of the shop a short while later and a large bag of crisps rolled off the pile of goodies in her arms. She'd gone in for a few essentials and come out with a week's worth of groceries. It was a common mistake.

"Have you got pre-match nerves or something? I thought you'd already eaten?"

Jenna just about managed to twist and lower the food into the footwell before a punnet of strawberries and a bottle of Prosecco met their doom on the pavement. "I have but I'm still hungry. The portion sizes were tiny." Plus, she was feeling a little nervous. Not that she intended to admit it. At least if everything went wrong, she had comfort food.

"Where are we going?" Abi asked as they pulled out of the bay.

"To my top secret seduction spot."

"Hate to tell you, but if you take every woman there, then it's not top secret."

Jenna shoved Abi's leg. "Thanks for the tip." Her hand lingered and she rubbed Abi's knee, grinning when Abi stroked her fingers. Right now, she needed the reassurance.

"You'll need to give me some idea where we're going because

I'm the one driving," Abi pointed out.

"Left at the end of the road."

Abi followed Jenna's instructions and they drove for about a mile out of the village, until Jenna suddenly yelled at her to stop. Abi hit the brakes and lurched forwards, then checked the rear view mirror.

"A bit of warning next time?"

Jenna laughed. "Sorry. It's hard to see the gate. It's just that bit of dirt track behind us."

Abi shoved the van into reverse and it squealed backwards, then bumped across a patch of dry grass. "Here?"

"It'll do."

They both exited the van and Abi picked up the strawberries, a bag of crisps, and the bottle of Prosecco, while Jenna grabbed an old hoody from behind her seat. Then she followed through a narrow gate down a footpath marked by a weathered green sign until they reached a field with views in all directions across yet more fields. The countryside rolled for miles, broken only by rows of trees, a patchwork of yellow and green as far as the eye could see. Besides the village behind them, and the rustle of birds in the hedgerow, there were no signs of life.

A haze shimmered on the horizon, beating out the last golden rays, and they both stared at it without speaking.

After a few moments, the snacks still clutched in her hands, Abi whispered, "This is beautiful."

"Yep. I started coming out here at the end of that last awful lockdown. It was my escape place." Back when she was trying to work out why she had everything she'd ever wanted, but was still miserable as fuck.

Jenna laid out the hoody, then sat on it and crossed her feet over as she rested back on her elbows. She inclined her face to the soft sunlight, closed her eyes, and smiled, trying to hold onto those peaceful vibes. She hoped her happy place wasn't about to become her sad place. "You definitely don't have hay fever, right?"

"No. Even if I did, I'd risk it. I can see why you wanted to escape out here."

Abi set the bottle and crisp bag next to the hoody but kept hold of the punnet. She laid down next to Jenna and rolled to prop herself on her side, then prised off the lid and took a strawberry, twisting out the stalk before holding it to Jenna's lips.

"You can stay if you're going to feed me." Jenna took a bite and sent juice trickling down her chin. After wiping it with the back of her hand, she shuffled to face Abi, took out another strawberry, and ate it. "Need to be careful of these trousers. They're now my best ones."

"Is that why you're sitting on my hoody?"

"Yep." Jenna laughed and picked up another strawberry, lobbing the stalk over her shoulder and holding the berry out for Abi to take in one mouthful. "I can't share it because there isn't space but I will share these. I wouldn't usually, but I like you better than all of the others."

"Exactly how many women have you had out here?"

"At a rough estimate? Twenty-seven."

Abi shoved Jenna so that she rolled over onto her back, giggling. "I'm just one in a long line, then?"

Jenna let out another stutter of giggles as she propped herself on her side again, so that they were facing. "You didn't know about my reputation? I bring all my mates here for a trial run. Some people spent lockdown nurturing sourdough starters, I did that." She reached out her hand, searching for Abi's, and held it. Then, after a few seconds, she dropped it abruptly. "Oh! I've just remembered I've got some good news for you." She pulled out her phone, swiped at the screen for a few seconds, and then held it up. She knew she was stalling, but this was legitimately important. "You have your first five star review on Facebook. Cass just posted it."

Abi squinted. "Cass left a five star review?" She pointed at her own chest. "For me?"

Jenna spoke slower. "Yes. For you. Abi. The gardener who did a great job for her." She returned to normal pace and slotted the phone into her pocket. "It looks so much better. I don't understand what's shocked you. This is something you need to ask every client to do."

There was a long pause, and Abi's squint became more pained. "I'm surprised she wanted to give me a review because I fucked up on something. It was dumb, and I apologised, and I finished the work for free, but to be honest I don't think I deserved her leaving me five stars. It was kind of her to do that."

"What did you do?"

Squirming, Abi drummed her fingers on the side of the strawberry punnet. "I smashed two of her gnomes." She peered up, looking guilty as all hell.

"Was it an accident?"

Another long pause, before a sheepish "no."

"Okay." Jenna's head tilted a fraction as she continued to stare at Abi. She'd expected the conversation might go in many directions, but not this one. "So, why did you intentionally smash them?"

"Because I was jealous."

"You were jealous of her hideous gnomes?"

"No, of course not! I hate the things. I was jealous because —" Abi huffed and moved the punnet from the space between them, setting it behind herself. "I was jealous of you."

"You were jealous of me, how?"

"Not jealous *of* you. Because of you. Because—" There had been a lot of 'because,' without the actual because, and Abi was becoming progressively more uncomfortable. She laced their fingers together again, and then admitted, "you went home with Cass after the party." She finally looked up, meeting Jenna's gaze. "I get that we weren't really anything to each other, and a kiss didn't change that, but I did. I felt jealous, and I'm sorry. I'm also sorry for fucking things up when you got me the job with Cass. Can you forgive me?"

Jenna couldn't help but laugh a little. "It's between you and Cass, and it sounds like you sorted it out with her. Although I'm not sure how I feel about you replacing those bloody gnomes. You'd think she'd take the hint." She was more interested in the fact that Abi was questioning what was going on between them, and decided to take the plunge. "Do you agree we're something to each other now?"

"I really hope we are, yeah."

"Then why do you look so nervous about admitting you were jealous?"

"Because I've really struggled lately and I think there's still a part of me worried that I'm not good enough for you. I can't buy you fancy meals and I don't drive a Mercedes. I've got ambitions with my business but they stop a long way short of world domination."

"Has this got anything to do with why you told me you're not available next week?"

"Kind of. I wanted to help you out, like you've helped me, and so I told my dad I'd finish the work at Ida's so he could start on your place sooner. He said no, though. Think he knew why I'd offered."

"Do you want to know what story I was telling myself?" When Abi nodded, Jenna squeezed her hand and let out a quick chuckle. "I was worried you were going to end things with me."

"Why on earth would you think that?"

"Because I know I seem really confident, and I am, but I also have a lot of insecurities underneath all of this hotness. You think maybe you can understand that?"

Abi laughed. Then she nodded. Then, finally, she said, "Yeah, I think I can. I've never felt this insecure before, I'm usually pretty at ease in relationships, and it sucks."

"Yeah, it does suck. So maybe we need to be more honest with each other when we're feeling that way. I had a great time tonight but what I'm most looking forward to this weekend is our first official date."

Abi smiled and dabbed Jenna's nose with a kiss. "Me too. Are you sure you want to play more football, though?"

"Absolutely. This isn't football, this is..." Jenna pursed her lips before settling on "non-competitive relaxation time."

Abi scoffed. "I'm not sure you know what non-competitive relaxation time looks like, but I'm looking forward to it all the same."

## 21

## ABI

The following day, Jenna quickly proved Abi right. She crouched low to the ground, squinting from one eye with her tongue stuck out to the side, umming and ahhing for longer than lining up her shot warranted. In the end, Abi lost patience.

"Who do you think you are, Nick Faldo?"

Jenna peered over the top of her sunglasses and frowned. "Who?"

"Never mind. Can we hurry this along?" They'd been at it for half an hour and only reached hole three of eighteen. "I'll starve to death before you make it around all the holes."

The frown on Jenna's face broke as she sniggered. "Probably. I am *very* thorough." She stood up and struck the ball with the side of her foot, sinking it into a wet hole in the ground with a plop. Then she wiped the ball clean on the grass and tucked it under her arm, staring down the next part of the course. "Chop chop." She nudged Abi in the ribs. "You're the one who needs to catch up. What's the score again?"

Abi reached for the card in her back pocket, not that she needed to read it because she knew she was woefully behind already. Footgolf was exactly like regular golf, and that extended to her complete lack of ability. She could tee off fine and boot the ball down towards the hole but didn't have Jenna's accuracy with putting and kept overshooting the target.

She glanced at the scorecard, then tucked it back in her pocket and slipped off her trainer, tipping it to pour out the accumulated bunker sand. "I can confirm I've had a lovely day at the beach."

While Abi put her trainer back on, Jenna walked about twenty metres downhill from where they stood, searching for Abi's latest over hit ball. "You're going to need to put a bit of weight behind this to get it back up. Otherwise, it'll keep rolling down again."

"Yes, thank you for that basic physics lesson," Abi replied as she joined Jenna and playfully shoved her out of the way.

"Alright, don't get shitty with me just because you're losing."

"I'm not getting shitty because I'm losing. I expected that, but I don't need coaching over every single hole."

"There's a relief."

Jenna kept her mouth shut long enough for Abi to get the ball up the slope and move it in increments until it also plopped into the water-filled hole. By the time they made it to the next part of the course, though, her lip had tooth marks where she'd bitten into it so hard. She placed her ball, ready to tee off, and then faced Abi with her hands on her hips.

"What?" Abi enquired with a sense of trepidation. She knew that mischievous look all too well.

"Nothing!" Jenna replied, her eyes widening. "I just thought you might like some help to redeem yourself."

"Excuse me, but I don't need to *redeem* myself. I'm here to spend time with you and have fun, although now I'm wondering why." Knocking Jenna's ball out of the way, Abi put her own down instead.

"Hey, don't kick my ball away!" Jenna retaliated by booting

Abi's ball, but her typically overzealous approach backfired when it surged towards the pond. "Oh shit," she yelled, running after it and stuttering to a stop just short of the water's edge. She pointed at the ball as it bobbed across the surface. "Think we have a problem."

"You mean *you* have a problem?" Abi shouted back. She laughed as Jenna knelt to stretch her arm out over the reeds and rushes, because the ball only floated away. "You know you don't officially win if we don't finish, right?" That seemed to be enough for Jenna because she stood up, tore off her trainers and socks, and waded into the pond. It sent Abi peeling into more laughter, and she ran down the bank to make sure Jenna wasn't about to drown herself. "I was only joking, you idiot!"

"Joke away. A pond won't defeat me." Now in as far as her knees, Jenna caught hold of the ball and held it up as she slipped and slid, trying to keep her balance. She emerged, her feet and ankles brown with mud. "Told you."

"I didn't doubt it for a second." Grimacing, Abi watched as Jenna flicked a foot across the top of the pond to wash it. The thought was there, but the action had little impact. "That's... disgusting."

"If you can't deal with me at my worst, you don't deserve me at my best."

"That's great. Did you get it from a coaster or was this one Pinterest?" Abi doubled over when Jenna thrust the ball at her stomach.

After raising her middle finger in Abi's face, Jenna strode back up the bank. "To make this easier on you, I'm going to play the hole barefoot."

Abi reached the teeing area just as Jenna approached her ball and pelted it down the course. "You mean because you've left your socks and trainers by the pond and you're too dirty to put them on, anyway?"

"Yes. That too."

They finished the hole with Abi coming in way over par again and then retrieved Jenna's trainers before moving on. Fourteen holes later, the early afternoon sun had burnt them both to a crisp, and they were the only group still to finish. Everyone else was filling in feedback cards and enjoying lunch in the clubhouse, and Abi rubbed her stomach as it grumbled.

"We're still eating, right?" She was sure they'd mentioned the free buffet ended at three o'clock when handing out balls and scorecards. It was already two.

"Relax. We can get you some food in a minute." Jenna set down her ball and stuck her tongue out to the side as she surveyed it. "This won't take long."

She was true to her word and in three strokes had potted her ball. Stood back with it under her arm, she raised a hand to shield her eyes because the sun was high, and she'd tucked her glasses into the neck of her T-shirt. Abi lined up her shot and then took a deep breath as she whacked it hard down the green. The ball curved on the breeze and looked as if it might end up in the bunker again, and Abi twisted her body like Fred Flintstone in a bowling competition.

"Hard luck!" Jenna yelled from behind the hole, but then the ball bounced once, twice, and rolled in. She threw hers at the floor and jumped up and down, her glasses falling at her feet and almost crushed with the excitement. "What the fuck! You got a hole in one!" She ran up the green, her grin wide and her eyes sparkling with unbridled joy. "I can't believe you did that when you're so crap!"

Abi had been enjoying the arms that had just flung around her neck in congratulations but faltered with that last bit. "Er... thanks?"

"You know what I mean," Jenna whispered in Abi's ear, still

clung on and bouncing up and down slightly. "That was amazing."

"I was going to say it was more luck than judgement, but since you only believe in talent and hard work, I guess it must be supreme levels of skill."

Jenna stepped away, flushed and smiling. "And you did it all without your lucky shirt. Who would've thought."

"Alright," Abi shot back, shoving her as they walked down the green to retrieve the balls and Jenna's sunglasses. "It's not like I ever said that shirt had magical powers. It means a lot to me, that's all."

"I know it does. I'm only teasing you."

"Well, do you have to always tease me? You could try just being nice to me!"

Jenna frowned. "I really am sorry. Are we okay?"

Abi shot her a reassuring smile. "Of course we are."

Jenna returned the smile and then snatched a quick kiss before sprinting off. When Abi reached the hole a few moments later, she had her sunglasses tucked safely back into her T-shirt and a ball under each arm.

Jenna tilted her head and frowned. "Would some food make it up to you?"

Abi's stomach gurgled in agreement and they both laughed, ambling across the peaks and troughs of the golf course until they reached the door to the clubhouse. It had the ambience of a log cabin, with rough wooden cladding, exposed beams, and the scent of cut pine. An upmarket cabin, though, with plush wingback chairs and ornamental rugs. Hanging from the high ceiling were large pendulum lights, and on the far wall above the dormant fireplace was a mantel filled with trophies.

"This is fancy for footgolf," Abi whispered, as Jenna dumped their balls in a bag by the door.

"Special privileges," she whispered back. "This is the proper clubhouse for the golfing members. You wouldn't get access to this if you were a regular punter paying a tenner for a round of footgolf."

Abi nodded and followed Jenna to a long table on the far side of the room. On it were plates of finger foods: canapes, sandwiches, cheeses, salad, fruits. She went to grab a plate from the stack at the end, but a lad wearing what looked like his dad's Sunday best interrupted them.

"Can I get you a drink, madam?"

Abi frowned down at her shorts and T-shirt. She'd worn the same kit she would've put on for training and wasn't sure it warranted a *madam*. "Sure. I'll take anything soft, please." While the task distracted him, she stacked her plate high.

"Calm down," Jenna said with a quick laugh as she nudged Abi's shoulder. "This isn't an all you can eat breakfast at a Premier Inn."

Hovering over a third bread roll, Abi glanced sideways at Jenna. "It is free and all you can eat, though, right?"

"Yes. This could be a great opportunity to do a bit of networking, though, so just... go steady."

"Do you ever stop?"

"What do you mean?"

"Can't we just switch off from work for a bit and have some fun?"

"We're having fun! Well, I am, anyway. I can't vouch for you." Jenna wore a look of mock-offence, but it broke into another amused smile as the waiter returned and Abi looked from him to her heaped pile of food.

"Thank you." Abi balanced her plate in one hand and took the glass bottle of Pepsi. "I bet you can't go the rest of the day without mentioning work." Considering for a second, Abi set down her bottle on the edge of the table and took a bite of cheese. Then she pointed the stick of cheddar at Jenna. "Or even the next hour."

"You can't expect me not to talk about work. I got my keys yesterday. It's huge!"

"Fine. You can talk about that. I don't want to talk about networking, though. I want to talk about..." Abi trailed off and smiled at how cute Jenna looked when she was indignant.

"What?"

"I want to talk about how proud I am of you."

Jenna raised the back of her hand to her cheek and turned away. "Abi..."

"I'm serious!" She set down her plate and then leant in for a kiss. "I'm glad you asked me on a date."

"Me too. Even if we have ended up sleeping together multiple times before we got to it..."

"Do we get to sleep together officially now?"

"Are you inviting me home with you?"

Abi considered for a second, then jumped in before she chickened out. "Yeah. I am."

\* \* \*

This time, when Abi crept up the driveway with Jenna lagging behind she was doing it for a joke. Mainly. Stanley's car was on the driveway and she hadn't cleared it with her parents for Jenna to stay, but they had said she was welcome any time, and Petra had actively encouraged Abi to extend an overnight invite. On that basis, she'd presumed it would be okay.

"I might start to take it personally," Jenna teased, hooking her finger into the back of Abi's shorts. Unlike the last occasion where they'd been in this position, though, she pulled Abi back and then hugged her from behind. "Relax."

Abi dropped the large duffel bag they'd collected from

Jenna's on the way and it thumped to the ground. She'd spent a lot of time getting ready, including a full outfit change, and it was a little suspicious. "I'm worried you might be moving in." Abi turned so they were facing. "How much stuff have you brought with you?"

Jenna laughed and readjusted her grip around Abi's waist, to account for their new position. "Enough. Including a few surprises to help you get in the mood here later." She dipped her mouth to Abi's and kissed her slowly, her eyes still open and glinting with mischief.

Abi's heart beat hard against Jenna's. Now she really wished they weren't here. "Are you sure we can't just get a hotel room or something?"

Shaking her head, Jenna playfully slapped Abi's bum. "No. You can't afford it and there's no need. Now let's get inside and be nice."

After kissing her one last time, Abi submitted to leaving the embrace and grabbing Jenna's bag again. Then she took a deep breath and braced herself. When she opened the door, she could hear Petra's rapid intonation against the backdrop of more Carpenters classics. Thankfully, they were coming from the stereo this time and not being sung into a comb.

"I hope you know what the full force of my parents will entail," Abi said to Jenna as she removed the key from the lock and swung the door shut behind them. She paused and listened to what her mum was so irate about. There was something about the weather forecast for Brighton and then she moved on to hats, but after that it stopped dead.

"Abi, is that you?" Petra yelled from somewhere upstairs. A shuffling noise followed, and then she appeared at the top of the stairs. "Oh!" Her face lit up when she spied Jenna. Then she rushed back into the bedroom. "We will be down in a moment!"

Abi rubbed a hand over her brow, but Jenna had only

grinned through every second of the experience so far. The music cut and Petra came bounding down the stairs, with Stanley following more slowly behind.

He shook his head when he reached the entrance hall, and placed a hand on Petra's shoulder. "I'm taking your mother for a meal tonight. Give you two some space." Abi was so grateful for her dad in that moment, she could hug him, until he added, "Make sure you've got clothes on by ten, though."

Jenna laughed when Abi's whole body crumpled in on itself. "Noted. Thanks. Have a good evening."

Stanley steered Petra towards the front door as she resumed her chatter about clothing options for their weekend away. When they'd safely exited, Abi sighed heavily.

"And you wonder why I'd rather stay at your place and want to get out of here," she said, picking up the bag and leading Jenna up the stairs. Again, she was half joking. It was pretty sweet of her parents to leave their own home just so she'd be more comfortable.

"I think you're seeing this all wrong," Jenna replied when they were on the other side of the bedroom door. She snatched the bag from Abi and instructed her to sit. Curiously, she also had Abi's work boots in hand. Abi had missed that until now. "Think of all the scandalous things we can get up to."

"Scandalous? What are we going to do, take up seats in the House of Parliament and then cheat on our wives with our secretaries?"

It won Abi a laugh, but Jenna was undeterred. "Hey, whatever turns you on. But I thought that tonight, we'd expand on this whole open and honest thing and I'd show you what turns *me* on."

Now Abi was intrigued. What *was* in that bag? And why did Jenna have her boots? "Are you trying to tell me you haven't been turned on so far? Because if so, you're one hell of an actress. Maybe life as a politician is for you after all."

"Put these on," Jenna instructed, although she didn't look entirely sure of herself. She threw the boots at Abi's feet and then shuffled from one foot to the other. Was she nervous, or turned on, or both?

Abi did as asked, intrigued to find out either way. "Are you about to ask me to water your vegetables again?" She was trying to put Jenna at ease, and smiled up as she tied the second lace. It was odd to see her this way. She never seemed to mind voicing her opinion, but for some reason, this was tripping her up. "You look very cute right now."

"I'm not trying to look *cute*. I want... sexy."

"You're always sexy as hell to me."

"Good save."

"Thank you." Abi straightened and then gestured to her boots. "So, what now?"

Jenna faltered big time. She looked down at the bag, then back up at Abi, her face flushing crimson. Then she took a few steps forward, paused, and slumped onto the bed. The bag hit the ground with another clunk.

When she still hadn't said anything a few seconds later, Abi put a hand around her back and kissed her shoulder. "Are you okay?"

"Yes," Jenna replied, rubbing her hand over her brow and letting out a little laugh. "Sorry. I had a plan but it's sort of... fallen over."

"You had a plan? For tonight?"

"There was something I wanted to try. With you. So I bought something. A... toy."

She said the last part quietly and Abi reached down to part the bag's zip with her free hand. "A toy?" When Abi caught sight of what was inside, she was the one who laughed this time. "Ah,

I see. A *toy*. You want us to use this?" Abi rubbed Jenna's back when she only nodded. "Feeling a bit shy?"

She leant sideways into the embrace. "Yes. Don't tease me."

"As if I would. You've not used one before?"

"Nope. I've sort of let other people take the lead in this area, unless I'm on my own of course, but I felt like I could tell you what I want. Seems I can't, though…"

"I don't know, I'd say you've made it pretty clear what you want, what you really really want." Abi wriggled free and crouched by the bag, smiling when Jenna continued humming The Spice Girls *Wannabe*. She never had explained about her favourite album, but Abi wasn't minded to ask right now. She was too busy rummaging around in the bag to get a better look. "How do the boots fit with this?" Abi dangled the harness from her finger and took the dildo she imagined Jenna had intended them to use it with, and held it in her other hand.

Jenna became more matter of fact now. "I wanted you to wear them. Together."

"Interesting. A little *Lady Chatterley's Lover* roleplay? Or were you going for the German porn film vibe, and I'm coming over to mend your fence?"

"I mean, either works." Jenna shrugged, her mouth twitching as she tried to hide a smile. "So long as the end result is you wearing nothing but the boots and that harness." She ran her tongue almost imperceptibly over her bottom lip, but Abi caught it. "What do you think… boss?"

The full storyline of Jenna's fantasy was beginning to dawn on Abi, even if it mixed genres a little. She stood and threw the harness, then the dildo, onto the bed. "I want you to undress. But leave your underwear on. I'm going to take that off myself."

Jenna stood and pulled the T-shirt over her head to reveal a black lace bra. Then she unbuttoned her jeans and wriggled out of them, and it soon became clear they were part of a matching set. At least it explained what had taken so long when Jenna went into her house earlier.

She kicked her clothes to one side and then fussed with the bra strap, but Abi was lost somewhere around the top of Jenna's strong quads as her tan graduated to creamy skin and lace. Her hands twitched and she balled her fists for a second, then rounded the bed and pulled open the top drawer of her cabinet. She returned with her new vibrator, and a mischievous smile played across Jenna's mouth. The fiddling stopped.

"What are you going to do next?" she asked, her eyes dropping to the small pebble vibrator turning in Abi's hand.

"I'm not going to do anything until I'm ready." Abi took a step forward, entering Jenna's space. She smelled of jasmine and orange-blossom and Abi could feel the heat radiating from her skin as she leant close into Jenna's ear and whispered, "I want you to take this and tell me what you've imagined. What's made you so hot." She nipped briefly on Jenna's lobe and slowly slid the vibrator into the front of her underwear, turning it on as she added, "All the ways I've fucked you and what it's felt like."

She wanted to take a step back and watch but Jenna's hand pressed over her own, guiding it a little lower. Instead, Abi lingered against Jenna's ear and nipped it again, deciding that encouraging her could be just as fun. She was eventually allowed to remove her hand, and trailed her fingertips over Jenna's bum, half exposed by the skimpy underwear, and then over the goosebumps on the backs of her legs.

All the while, Jenna ground gently into the vibrator, her other arm wrapped around Abi's waist to draw her closer. She kissed Abi's throat, not in the frenzied way she had when they were backed up against the clubhouse, but slowly nipping a line up to her ear so that it sent successive tingles down Abi's spine.

By the time she'd reached the lobe, Abi had almost lost it. Playing anything cool was impossible when she had Jenna in her arms, wearing nothing but a few strings of lace and grinding herself into a vibrator. A little moan and the warmth of Jenna's breath made her shiver and the hand that was still trailing now curled into Jenna's hip.

"I've been watching you work for weeks," Jenna teased with a whisper. Apparently, they were going down the *Lady Chatterley* route. Not that Abi was fully following the narrative right now. She was just trying to hold out long enough to give Jenna what she wanted. "I've imagined your strong arms. Your hot, sweaty body on top of me."

The vibrator had become so wet that it slid out of Jenna's grip. Abi took it as a sign and threw it onto the bed, then pressed the heal of her hand against the damp lace, as both of Jenna's arms wrapped around her neck and they finally kissed. Long, deep, passionate strokes of Jenna's tongue as her hands tangled in Abi's hair were only punctuated by breathy moans as Abi stroked more firmly, replacing her palm with her fingers.

Blood thundered first in her chest and then lower, urgency building with every touch until she couldn't take it anymore. She pushed Jenna back abruptly and she ended up sitting on the end of the bed, breathing hard. The insides of her thighs glistened and Abi wanted desperately to run her tongue up them, but she knew that wasn't what Jenna wanted. Instead, Abi fumbled with the button of her shorts and lowered them over her boots, then quickly relieved herself of her T-shirt and underwear.

Stood naked at the foot of the bed, besides her feet, she paused. Jenna's eyes raked over her body and then met Abi's. Jenna bit her bottom lip as Abi more slowly reached for the harness, slotted in the dildo, then stepped in. She tightened it over her hips and then stopped again, once more enjoying how much this was turning Jenna on. Her chest rose and fell quickly, flushed with desire as well as the usual sunburn and smattered tan.

Abi rounded the bed and opened the drawer of her cabinet a second time.

"What are you doing," Jenna asked, back to sounding a little unsure of herself.

"I'm getting some lube," Abi replied, pulling out the strawberry flavoured variety and applying it to the length of the dildo. "Lube makes everything better."

"Oh, okay. No arguments here." There was a little burst of nervous laughter and Jenna laid back, propping herself on her elbows.

"I don't want to ruin the mood in any way," Abi said as she knelt between Jenna's legs and then rested back on the heels of her boots. "But if you don't enjoy this and want to stop at any point, you'll say. Right?"

Jenna nodded, her eyes firmly fixed on the phallus between them. Then she wriggled out of her underwear and flung it to one side, before realising what she'd done and looking up with a guilty expression. "Sorry, I didn't have permission for that. Am I in trouble?"

Abi lowered herself between Jenna's legs, spreading them wider, and positioned the tip of the dildo tantalisingly close to her opening. "Don't worry," she muttered, wearing a smile and placing a hand either side of Jenna's head. "I still hold all the power here."

It was tough to tell which fantasy they were playing out now. Did Jenna want the boss or the gardener? Either way, she wanted Abi to fuck her. That was clear. She ran both hands flat over Abi's breasts and then rubbed her thumbs into Abi's nipples, turning the tables so that it was now Abi's hips struggling not to twitch. Then she clawed her nails along Abi's back, urging her on. In the end, it was too much for either of them and they both exhaled with relief as Abi slowly slid inside, pinning Jenna to the bed with her hips.

"Fuck," Jenna moaned breathily.

"You like that?" Abi whispered as she withdrew and repeated the action. She did it again, and again, until Jenna begged her to speed up. "I thought I was in charge here?"

Jenna's fingers dug into her bum as it prickled with sweat. Jenna was struggling to get her words out, her other hand once again rubbing over Abi's chest. Then she took both away, threw them above her head, and finally got out, "You're in charge. Fuck, you're in charge."

"Good," Abi replied as she picked up the pace, snapping her hips so that their flesh slapped together and Jenna let out an anguished cry. It shot right to Abi's clit, which already throbbed with every thrust. She wasn't sure whether the tops of her legs were soaked with Jenna, herself, or the lube anymore. All she knew was that she was so wet that she was struggling to stop the dildo slipping out.

Eventually, it did, and Abi fumbled to unbuckle the strap before wriggling free and casting it aside. A breeze hit the fierce heat underneath and made her shiver again.

"Why have you stopped?" Jenna just about got out before it merged with another strangled moan because Abi's mouth had just closed around her clit. "Oh, fuck," she called out, her delicious quads squeezing around Abi's head.

She tasted of the strawberry lube but Abi barely had the chance to enjoy it before Jenna's hips bucked wildly and then came to rest, her legs still holding Abi in place. It was only when a few more gentle nibbles on her clit made her squirm and roll away that Abi was freed. She crawled up the bed and then grasped Jenna's hip to pull her closer as she languished on her side, sweaty and heavy limbed.

"So," Abi asked after their breathing had settled to a more normal rhythm. "How did that measure against the fantasy?"

Jenna laughed and reached a hand over her shoulder to gently tap Abi's face. "Not bad. I'll write you a proper performance review later. Shall I also send you a list of all my other fantasies, now the lines of communication are open?"

"Sure. I'll file them with my secretary."

There was a long pause, before Jenna said, "Hang on, isn't that me...?"

"Afraid so. Guess you'll just have to keep talking."

## 22

# JENNA

Halfway through rolling onto her side, a hand grabbed Jenna's waist to pull her closer. "What time is it?" she mumbled, flopping onto her back. "Come to think of it, what day is it?"

"No idea, and Wednesday," Abi whispered. "You know we've ended up spending every night together since Saturday?"

"The second most lesbian thing I've ever done, huh?"

Jenna laughed, but then her face turned serious as Abi stared at the freckles on her chest and traced them with her index finger. They had training later and it was the last session before their first match of the season, but Abi hadn't said anything yet about whether she intended to play. In fact, she'd entirely avoided the subject, even dipping out of all the WhatsApp banter on the team group chat about who would be made captain, and Jenna was running out of time to broach a conversation. Her last ditch effort was due to arrive in the post today, and she hoped to God that it worked.

"Are you training tonight?" Abi asked, as if she could read Jenna's mind.

It took her by surprise, and her eyes widened. "What?"

"Training," Abi repeated with a frown. "Sorry, I was speaking English then, wasn't I?"

Jenna smiled. "Cheeky. Yes, I am training." She considered her next move carefully. "The temptation to sack off football later is strong, though, and I don't say that lightly. Not with the first game of the season on Sunday."

"I'm probably not playing anyway, so I would definitely be up for that."

"What?" Jenna stopped dead, her mouth hanging open in mock surprise. It was tough to tell if she'd pulled it off or she was about to be caught out by her hammy acting. "What do you mean you're not playing? Has Jax dropped you because of that red card the other week? I'll fucking kill her."

After adjusting the pillows behind her back, Abi shuffled to sit, seeming not to have notice how far Jenna had over baked her response. "No, she hasn't dropped me. I quit."

"You quit?!"

Abi winced when Jenna's eyes widened in horror again. "Well, I haven't quit. I'm still training and I'll be around the club but I'm done with playing competitively for now. I'm going to tell Jax tonight." When Jenna grumbled under her breath and then pulled back the covers, swinging her legs around and folding her arms, Abi asked, "What are you thinking?"

"I'm trying to remember whether there's any bacon left."

"Oh." Abi also swung her own legs off the bed. "I'll go to the shop quickly." She kissed the side of Jenna's head and got up.

"You don't need to do that... but if you're going, can you also get some orange juice? And bread?"

Abi laughed. "Yes, boss. Maybe I'll also buy your half-time sweets for Sunday, too. Since you've clearly had better things to do than shop."

"Follow me." Jenna grabbed Abi's T-shirt from the floor and flung it at her. Then she led them out of the bedroom, down the stairs, and along the hallway into the kitchen as Abi tried to wrangle it over her head. When they reached the line of cupboards, Jenna pulled open a deep drawer stuffed with dozens of bags of sweets.

"Holy shit," Abi muttered, running her hand through them so that they rustled. "What are you planning to get out of this season, league promotion or diabetes?"

Jenna swiped Abi's arm away. "They're not for you. Players only. You've waived that privilege."

"I see. It's like that, is it?"

"Don't know what you're talking about." After bumping the drawer shut with her hip, Jenna grabbed the kettle from its stand and began filling it. She'd hit her stride now. "But it might have been nice if you'd told me."

"Ah. I guess you're right about that. I'm sorry."

"So you should be."

Abi looked down at herself. "Why am I wearing a T-shirt and you're not?"

"Because the police don't like for you to go to the shop without clothes. Gets them all arresty. Don't think you can change the subject, though. You're picking up bad habits from me."

"No, okay. I'm sorry. It's just... I don't know. I want to play but I don't think I'm ready."

Now Jenna had Abi exactly where she wanted her, and she'd also heard the well timed snap of the letterbox signalling that the post had just arrived. "How will you ever be ready if you don't play, though?"

Jenna left Abi to stand and fidget while she went to check what had landed in her hallway. She'd paid a huge premium for super-fast dispatch and delivery, and she'd be annoyed as all hell if her silver bullet wasn't there.

"What if I mess up again, though?" Abi called down the corridor.

"It doesn't matter if you mess up. We just want you to play. *I* want you to play. And I know *you* want to play," Jenna replied as she bent to rummage through the junk mail and bills until she found what she was looking for. With a quick "aha" she left everything else where it had fallen in disarray on her mat and carried the plastic wrapped package back to the kitchen.

"Who even are you?" Abi asked, looking up and down Jenna's naked body.

"Someone who cares about you a lot." She chucked the package on the table and then placed her hands on her hips. "Look, I'm not going to say I don't mind about winning or give you some bullshit about how it's the taking part that counts. It'd be hypocritical and you know me too well. I can honestly say, though, that I think we're a better team with you on the pitch. And that it might take some hard fucking work to get back to fitness, but playing will get you there a lot faster than moping and telling yourself these stories about how this is all inevitable and you just can't do it anymore. It's not inevitable. And you can. It's a choice to give up, it's not fated."

"Let me guess, we're about to have a talk about how you don't believe in luck or the universe," Abi said, folding her arms to match Jenna's stance. "I already know that but I don't think you understand how wrecked I felt after that friendly. And how much every little thing that went wrong or was out of place in the clubhouse made me want to run and hide. I've been battling against it for weeks, trying to tell myself that if I just push it out of my head, by the time we get to the game, I'll feel fine again. It hasn't happened, though."

Tears glistened on Abi's cheeks and Jenna wanted to hold her right now, but she had something she hoped would bring more comfort. "Close your eyes."

"What?"

"Just do it," Jenna said, offering Abi a smile in the hope it might soothe her temporarily. "Please. I promise I'm not going to splat your face."

Abi grumbled but did as she was told, pressing her eyes tight to make a show of them being shut. "Still doesn't sound safe, but fine."

"Keep them shut," Jenna warned her, tearing open the package on the table. She took out the garment from inside, unfolded it, and then pulled it on over her head. Once she'd straightened it out and admired her work for a second, she instructed Abi to look.

Abi inched open her eyes as far as a squint, then she laughed and they shot fully open when she saw that Jenna was wearing a shirt from the new kit. "What are you doing?"

Jenna turned and thumbed over the back of the shirt, to the number eleven. "I couldn't get Jax to give you your old shirt number but I was able to get a new one printed. This is a replica lucky shirt, for private use. And right now, I'd say it's your *very* lucky shirt."

"Yeah? How do you figure that?"

"Well, for a start, I'm in it and I'm wearing nothing else. For another thing, this is me acknowledging that whilst I don't think a shirt holds any magical powers, I do see how important your old one was and how many memories you had in it." She shrugged, hoping Abi got the sentiment. It didn't feel quite up to the level of handing over a framed football shirt you'd owned since you were a kid, but Jenna was pretty impressed with herself for coming up with the idea.

"I don't know what to say," Abi replied, her arms dropping to her sides. She laughed again, then shuffled forward a few inches. "I'm lost between thinking this is really sweet and really hot, but also knowing that you have a very obvious ulterior motive."

"Won't deny that," Jenna said with another shrug. "You know

I want you to agree to play, but the shirt is yours either way."

"Do we get to have sex either way? Because you look..." Abi blew out a long jet of air as her gaze travelled over Jenna's bare legs, the tears long forgotten.

"No can do, sorry. You need to fetch breakfast because we both have to work. I'll let you consider this whole package, though, " Jenna said as she gestured up and down her own body. "Whilst you're sweating in those sexy boots of yours later."

\* \* \*

It was Jenna who ended up sweating because Wednesday was another scorcher of a day and she had to spend it conducting yet more interviews. Not just for staff, but she'd arranged to meet a couple of freelance therapists who had expressed an interest in renting space. Football training started at seven and she was still sat in her office chatting to a masseuse at six-thirty, so the race from there to the playing fields was a fraught one. She wasn't in kit yet, she hadn't had time for dinner, and she hadn't even had time to pee since late morning.

When she pulled up in the car park, Abi and Jax were inflating footballs using an electric pump attached to Abi's van. Jenna ran past them and ignored every attempt to greet her, desperate for only one thing: a toilet.

"Training hasn't started yet, buddy," Jax called after her.

"I know," she yelled over her shoulder. "Emergency!"

When she returned, relieved but still feeling like a hot mess in a sweat-stained blouse with hair matted to her forehead, Abi was stood next to Jenna's car and Jax was laying out cones on the field. "Are you okay?"

"Yep," Jenna replied, making vain attempts to push her hair back behind her ears. It'd be fine when she had her sports headband on. "Just a bit... busy."

Abi smiled. "Have you eaten?"

"Not since the bacon sandwich you made me this morning."

"I know we should probably spend a night apart, but would you like me to cook you something later?"

Yes, they probably should spend a night apart, but yes, Jenna would like for Abi to cook her a meal. The alternative was probably another supermarket salad, and she didn't relish the thought.

"We could always agree to spend tomorrow and Friday night apart...?" Jenna offered, her face scrunching because she knew they really were becoming a stereotype.

"Deal. I'm at Ida's tomorrow night anyway." Abi shrugged and then, after a few moments of consideration, she added, "Although to be fair, I'm not sure you calling me after a late gym session and asking me to come over for sex really counts as quality time together, so I'm not counting Monday or Tuesday." She didn't seem to have minded, though, and a smirk played across her mouth. "When I was at the shop this morning I also bought the ingredients for cookies. Maybe we could bake them."

That sounded like heaven. Those cookies had been a long time coming. "Well, you do owe me," Jenna pointed out as she popped the boot of her car and pulled out her kit bag. "Are you sure we can't just sack off this session and go straight to the cookie dough part?"

"Oh, I see! You just want my dough. Absolutely not. First game of the season on Sunday, remember?"

"Does that mean you're playing...?" If so, Jenna's dinner options weren't all that was looking up.

Abi glanced at the playing fields, where Jax had moved on from her cones. There were ladders, hurdles, resistance bands, and all manner of other torture devices. "Jax was just asking me the same thing. I was sort of dodging her question. I guess, though."

That didn't sound convincing, but Jenna got the notion that she was close to success. "What would swing it from *I guess*, to hell yes?"

"I was going to say a kiss," Abi said quietly. "But that's just me being opportunistic. Right now, I'd quite like Jax to put some of that equipment away. Otherwise, I'm not sure I'll make it to Sunday."

Jenna felt the same, but she wasn't going to let Abi take them off topic. She was the master of that particular skill and Abi wasn't getting a diversion past her. "You can have a kiss later. If you're playing."

"So much for it being my decision, huh?"

"It is your decision. Guess it just depends how good my kisses are."

She left it there and slammed her boot shut, then rounded the wall towards the patio in front of the changing rooms. Some of the other players had congregated and were once again discussing the captaincy, but she didn't have time to engage.

She ran into the changing rooms and peeled off her blouse, changed into her training kit, and stepped back out wondering if she had another odd combination of socks. They appeared to be red and pink, and she was so focused on her mistake that she'd completely missed the team meeting going on in front of her. That explained why everyone was hanging about.

"Excuse me," Jax shouted from her position atop one of the benches on the patio.

Jenna waved. "Why, what have you done this time?"

It won her a scowl from Jax but a laugh from every other member of the team, including Abi. She was leant against the wall of the clubhouse, and shouted, "probably stolen someone's wife again."

"Or their will to live," Jenna added, pointing to the assault course of fitness equipment littering the playing fields.

"There you two go, cracking me up again." Jax folded her arms. "Are you done now?"

Jenna looked at Abi. "I don't know, are we?"

Abi shrugged, the same smirk re-emerging. It soon became clear why. "Given she was just announcing you as captain, we probably should shut up and stop teasing her."

"Me?" Jenna asked, her eyes shooting down to her socks again because they'd just prickled with tears and she wasn't sure why. She honestly hadn't expected that and thought Abi would get the role, partly as a tactical ploy to keep her playing but also because she was one of the longest serving members of the team. Jenna was so convinced that she even started arguing.

"Do you not want the captaincy?" Jax asked, still stood on the bench with her arms folded when Jenna had reeled off at least half a dozen reason why Abi would be a better choice.

"No, it's not that. It's just..." Glancing at Abi and seeing her mouthing "shut up and accept" on repeat, Jenna laughed. "Sorry. Was actually just a bit of a surprise."

"I don't know why," Abi said out loud this time. "You're going to be an awesome captain."

Jenna blushed, and it wasn't helped by Jax shouting "get a room" because that was exactly where her own mind had gone. It was sweet of Abi to throw her support behind the decision, even though she was missing out. Thanking her for that would have to wait, though, because no one knew how close they'd become—even with Jax's daft joke—and going public wasn't a topic they'd yet broached. Banging Abi up against the clubhouse wall again would probably cause more shock than the captaincy announcement.

\* \* \*

"Are you coming into the bar?" Jax asked as she dragged a bag of balls behind herself. She had on her sunglasses and a relaxed smile, which only made Jenna want to punch her. Would it hurt to appear at least a little sorry for putting them all through that hell? Instead, she seemed to have enjoyed it. "I want to hear about how your date went."

Jenna waited for Abi to reply and hoped it was in the negative. She was hungry and wanted the meal she'd been promised. She'd also done a good job of dodging Jax's repeated messages about the date. Thankfully, Abi was busy puffing on her inhaler and provided yet another diversion.

"Are you okay?" Jenna asked, placing a gentle hand on Abi's back. She nodded furiously as she took a second drag. "All the same, I think we should get you home."

"Probably," Abi replied once she'd exhaled. She seemed to have caught on the real reason Jenna was desperate not to stay, because she began to smile the minute Jax turned away from them and headed in the direction of the shed.

Jenna stroked Abi's fingers but withdrew her hand quickly when Jax glanced back to double check Abi was definitely playing on Sunday.

With a double thumbs up, Abi smiled again and then began a slow amble up the field, towards the car park. She had her bag slung over her shoulder and shifted it to the other side so they could walk closer, the back of her hand stroking up and down Jenna's arm after she'd done the same.

"Hey," Abi whispered.

"Hey yourself," Jenna replied, wishing she could just hold Abi's hand. What did it really matter if people saw them? They couldn't dodge Jax or the rest of the team forever. "So, what are you cooking me tonight?"

"I don't know. What's your favourite meal?"

"That lemongrass seabass I had from the Thai restaurant the

other Sunday."

Abi scoffed. "In that case, we're getting takeaway."

"I thought you were cooking!"

"And I thought you were going to say something... normal!"

Jenna brushed her little finger along Abi's. "How about beans on toast?"

"Now *that* I can manage."

When they reached the car park, Jenna followed Abi to the back doors of her van. Once they were propped open to allow Abi's kit to be thrown inside, she stole a kiss in the relative privacy, and then dropped her own bag on the gravel.

"So, shall I meet you back at my place?"

Abi peeked around the door of the van, then laughed and lifted Jenna clear of the ground, giving her a far more effusive kiss. "Yes," she replied, as Jenna slowly slid down her body. "Try not to miss me too much."

"Get over yourself."

Jenna playfully slapped the top of Abi's arm and then pushed her away, but the truth was, she did miss Abi every time she wasn't around. She'd been like a giddy teenager since their date. How was it possible to feel so safe and wanted so quickly? She guessed it was because they'd already known each other for years. Abi was already the person that, as Cass had rightly pointed out, she was most herself around and who put her at ease.

"I really wanted a hug when Jax told me I was captain," she admitted, tousling the wisps of damp hair on Abi's neck. Then she dabbed another kiss on Abi's lips and grabbed her bag from the ground, rummaging for her keys in the side pocket. "See you in ten?"

Abi nodded, then tilted her head, smiled, and waved as Jenna backed off towards her car.

When they met again it was on Jenna's driveway, and Abi did the same thing.

Jenna creaked open the driver side door of the van. "Are you coming in or are you just going to sit there waving at me like an idiot?"

"Oh baby, seduce me with your honied words." It took a few moments for Abi to lift her own legs out of the footwell. "I wanted to move but I'm not sure I can." She took a hold of the seat with one hand, and then placed the other on the chassis. "If this goes badly and my legs don't remember how to stand, just leave me and save yourself."

Jenna laughed. "I can't. I'm relying on you for dinner and cookies." She held onto the door to stop it swinging closed and breaking Abi's hand, because she was hoping to make us of it later.

There was a long, low groan as Abi hoisted herself into a standing position and then her eyes widened as they met Jenna's. She paused for a second, her knees still slightly bent, before slowly releasing her grip on the van.

"I think I'm okay," she said, taking a few stiff steps forward.

Jenna swung the door shut. "Are you sure? Because right now it looks like you've shit yourself."

"I'll be fine after a shower. Let me just get the cookies in the oven first."

Her priorities were in good order, at least. "You do that while I make the beans on toast. It can be a team effort."

It took Abi an age to make her way to the kitchen, wash her hands, and bend to search through all of the cupboards. Jenna could have helped, of course, but where would be the fun in that? Instead, she stuck bread in the toaster, set some beans to heat in a pan, and then stood back and folded her arms because Abi had sneaked out a packet of Haribo and was munching them in between tasks.

"Excuse me, I thought I said they were only for players."

Abi chucked another in her mouth and then beat together the contents of her mixing bowl. "I figured since I agreed to play on Sunday, I was now allowed sweets."

"But it isn't half-time."

"Have a heart," Abi said, making a show of how the stiff mixture was making her arm hurt. She set down the bowl and poked her bicep, adding a little pout for sympathy.

"Fine," Jenna relented, picking up her wooden spoon from beside the hob and giving the beans a quick stir with a lot less effort. "Don't tell anyone you're getting preferential treatment, though. I get to pick my vice-captain and I won't be accused of nepotism."

Abi grabbed a large bag of chocolate chunks, tearing open the top. "That's a shame because I haven't even had a chance to bribe you yet." She tipped them into the mixing bowl. "Won't the cookies do it?"

"I don't know, I haven't tasted them yet. They might not be as good as your aunt's. You could be a completely crap baker." Which would be a crying shame because Jenna was enjoying having Abi bake for her. Jax was wrong and the provision of cookies was a totally valid criterion when entering a new relationship.

"You know, she's not actually my aunt," Abi said casually, stealing one of the chocolate chunks and sucking it into her mouth. Then she returned to slowly mixing her dough.

"What?"

"Ida. She's not my aunt, she's actually my gran."

Now Jenna was thoroughly confused, and shook her head. "She's your gran?"

"Yep. Had my dad when she was a teenager. He was raised as her brother and they keep up the pretence to outsiders, but I guess you're not an outsider anymore if you're my girlfriend and

I'm sharing her best cookie recipe, so... there you go. I know your big family secret and now you know mine."

"Scandalous," Jenna replied, although that wasn't the part of Abi's story that had most interested her. "*If* I'm your girlfriend, huh?"

Abi stopped and turned. It was tough to tell if she'd gone red from the mixing or what she'd just said. "Um, well yeah. If you want to be my girlfriend. At some point. If we... talked about what this is. And..."

"If I stop fucking around with those other twenty-seven women and make a commitment?"

"Yeah. Then."

Jenna tapped her foot on the floor. "Hm. The thing is, I just feel like I need more romance than that. Y'know? A declaration of your intentions." Which was a bit mean given how much she'd struggled to even ask Abi on a date. Despite the ease of relations between them, there was no way she felt confident enough to make the first move and pin this down. There were some habits that were hard to break.

After a few moments, Abi grabbed a couple of sweets from the bag of Haribo and slowly dropped to one knee with an agonised expression on her face. Then she held up a gummy ring and Jenna's eyes widened. That was too far.

"You're proposing to me?!"

"Fuck off, I haven't lost my mind! I would definitely like you to be my girlfriend, though. I know we haven't been seeing each other all that long but this feels right to me and I want to see what happens. Just the two of us. Exclusively and all in. Open to the world about the fact that we're a couple."

A smile crept across Jenna's face at the last bit. "I don't know. What are your prospects like?"

Abi laughed but the motion jarred her back. She clutched it, grimacing as she gurned through a barely audible, "Terrible."

"Okay then." Jenna swiped the gummy ring and shoved it in her mouth.

"Hey!"

"What?" Jenna murmured. "Was I not meant to eat it?" She took sweet back out, all sticky and mangled, and deposited it in Abi's palm.

"I'm kneeling here with green gunge in my hand, in agonising pain, and I've also been completely overlooked for vice-captain, so why do I feel like the luckiest girl in the world?"

"Because you've got the best girlfriend in the world?"

Abi laughed again. "That must be it. Now help me off the floor so I can finish your cookies."

## 23

## ABI

"Heaven preserve us," Abi muttered, shielding her face and sliding down the passenger seat as they pulled up in the club car park. Jax had just stepped out of the clubhouse but shrunk back at the sight of the rear window descending. She almost crumpled in on herself entirely when Petra stuck out her head, channelling Audrey Hepburn in a pair of square-framed sunglasses.

Stanley bumped Abi's shoulder with his fist, which she knew meant 'relax, your mother means well', but it was of little comfort. Not when this same scene had played out many times before and never ended well.

"Do we have to go through this every time?" she whispered back.

Abi popped open the door and shook her head for Jax's benefit. Getting words in wasn't an option because Petra was blathering so fast that it was hard to tell which language she currently spoke. It had something to do with an international friendly she'd watched earlier in the week, and tactics for the game, which Jax took with a nod and good grace. Until they all caught the words "I can help you from the sideline" and it elicited a ripple of laughter.

"Ma, that's sweet, but I'm not sure Jax needs an assistant."

"I don't know." Jax took a few steps forward and raised her hand to shield her eyes as she stared out across the field, where the opposition were already warming up. "You might be useful today. It'll be a tough game."

"Absolutely not. She's not helping. It's enough that she's here when I'm pretty sure I said not to come."

Petra climbed out of the car and slammed the door shut. "You said we couldn't watch you play but you accepted that it was fine if you *weren't* playing." She smirked as if that was check mate and she'd been waiting for an opportunity to point it out.

"But I *am* playing," Abi replied as she also hoisted herself out of the car. "So your argument has kind of failed."

"No, okay. Well, you probably weren't playing when we made plans, and I'm not changing them on a whim."

Abi laughed. It was another of those slightly delirious, totally resigned ones. There really was no point in trying to argue with her mum because she had an answer for everything. Besides, it was kind of cute that this meant so much to her parents that they'd planned their entire dirty weekend in Brighton around it. They'd arrived home with only minutes to spare and insisted on bundling Abi into the car with them.

Petra looked a little hurt, under all the bravado, so Abi put her arm around her mum's shoulder and kissed the side of her head. With that simple act, Petra's mood righted itself, and Abi returned her attention to the real job in hand. She opened the boot of her dad's car, pulled out her bag, and tried to shake off a far more pervasive sense of dread. It was worse than anything Petra had managed to stir up during their short journey.

"We can go if you like," Stanley said quietly as he sidled up alongside.

"It's fine, don't sweat it."

"Okay, love. Just go out and enjoy the game."

That was a the plan, and Abi nodded.

Leaving Petra to bend Jax's ear, she rounded the building and stopped in front of the changing rooms. The sound of laughing and shrieking inside elicited a smile and she wondered for a second whether the racing of her heart might have *just* tipped over the line into excitement.

Abi pushed open the door and the chaos continued around her. She picked her way across a sea of loose socks and bits of discarded tape, and Jenna scooted over to make space for her. Then she nudged her shoulder against Abi's.

"Hey," she whispered. "Are you doing okay?"

"I'm actually pretty good. I was just thinking about how the only thing that matters is us all being back together."

Jenna laughed and shoved Abi's knee, probably just as an excuse to touch her again. The goofy grin on her face was a total giveaway. "Very wholesome. I kind of agree, but I kind of also want to win, so can this kumbaya crap wait until you've broken some more ankles?"

"I will be breaking no ankles today, thank you very much." Taking a deep breath to ground herself, Abi delved into her kit bag and pulled out her shirt. She'd have to make peace with it and maybe Jenna was right. This season was a chance to make some new memories, and the number four shirt could prove even luckier than the number eleven. Only Abi had the power to decide.

She changed and returned to her seated position, both feet firmly on the ground as Jax entered the changing room with the little square of paper holding her fate. She would have to make peace with whatever that said, too. Even if it meant she was benched again or in defence.

"Are we ready?" Jax bellowed.

"Sir, yes sir!" Jenna yelled back with a salute.

"At ease, soldier."

The defensive positions were reeled off and Abi's heart sank a little when Jax omitted her name. It seemed the most likely place for her to start, which was why she didn't initially register when Jax then added, "Abi, I want you back on the left wing." It was only when Jenna's hand wrapped around her leg and gave it a squeeze, that she shook her head and paid attention.

"Earth to Abi," Jax said, waving the sheet of paper. "Are you actually with us?"

"Er, yes. Of course. Sorry. I heard." Trying to keep from smiling, Abi shuffled and cleared her throat. "I can do that. Sure."

"Good, I hope so. Jenna's up top on her own and we're relying on good service from the wings." The piece of paper flapped as Jax clapped her hands together to rally the team. "I want us to set the tone for the rest of the season, right here and now. Let's get out there, warm up like we mean it, and play like we haven't just spent the past two years sat on our arses."

A cheer erupted from the changing room and then the players began to follow Jenna out. All except Abi, who was still dumbstruck.

"You all set, bud?" Jax asked whilst cleaning up some of the tape and other crap from the floor.

The last player filed out behind her and Abi rooted around in her bag, digging out her spare inhaler and tucking it into the pocket of her hoody. "Yeah..." She *was* set but couldn't help wanting to ask why Jax had played her. She could adjust to a lot, but not a pity party.

"That's not convincing. I need you on your game. Do you need me to play one of the teenagers instead?"

"No!" That was too far. It was a niggle and Abi definitely wanted to start, but her depleted ego could use a little reassurance. "I guess I'm just wondering why you've decided to give me my place back. I'm happy about it but I don't want any favours."

"I'm not doing you a favour. You never lost your spot in the first place, I was just using the friendlies to try out a few new things. As if I was ever going to start one of the kids in a game like this, but they have to get experience somehow."

"Oh."

Pre-empting what Abi was about to say, Jax threw a bunch of detritus in the bin by the door and then turned back with her hands on her hips. "You'd know that already if you'd let me talk to you rather than keep running off or changing the subject. You've been spending far too much time around Jenna."

"Not possible," Abi muttered under her breath. Then she slung her hoody over her shoulder. "Right then," she said, puffing out her chest and trying to send her body a notice of intent. "Let's have at it."

\* \* \*

Abi's body got the memo but it took a while for her brain to catch up. She was marginally less fucked than expected by half-time, but the team hadn't created many chances and Abi knew she was partly to blame for sitting too deep. For someone who hadn't wanted to play as a defender, she'd certainly spent a lot of time loitering in her own half.

Fifteen minutes into the second half, she was still chickening out and passing off the ball rather than carrying it up the pitch. She just couldn't seem to get into gear, despite a sugar injection from a handful of cola bottles, and Jenna's frustrations began to surface.

"Run with it!" she yelled when the perfect opportunity presented itself. There was acres of space, the opposition winger was knackered and ambling, and Jenna gesticulated wildly. "Go!" she urged, staying tight on the last defender, drawing her forward and eking out a pocket behind her to run into if Abi didn't bottle it.

Abi knocked the ball into the space and ran after it, then did the same past the right back. She prayed that she didn't scuff the cross this time and Jenna seemed to see the hesitation because she ran towards Abi and pointed at her own feet. Abi obliged immediately and then carried on running, overlapping Jenna, receiving the ball back on a reverse pass that put her in behind the defence.

She was now through on goal and the only person she had to beat was the goalkeeper, who was running towards her at speed and closing down the angle. The last thing Abi heard was Jenna shouting "shoot!", before she let rip and tried to slot the ball into the right hand corner. The ball rebounded off the post and out for a goal kick and Abi's fists balled with frustration.

"Better," Jenna shouted as she ran back into position. "You can do it, I have total faith!"

That was a slightly better kick up the arse than simply yelling instructions, and Abi's hands unclenched themselves. She jogged back to mark her player and await another chance. Or, as she suspected might be the case, create one.

They were playing a team who had just been relegated from the league above and it was a level of intensity The Blues weren't used to. Especially after a long break. What they did have was experience, and this week Abi knew that meant keeping her head. She took a few deep breaths and focused herself, trying to read the player she'd battled against for the past seventy-or-so minutes. Every time she received the ball she was doing the same thing with it, trying to hit her striker with a pass in over the top of defence, and each time, she did so with her right foot. If Abi could stop her from using it, she could neutralise a big threat. She also knew she was more likely to get past if she forced the player to defend on her weaker side.

When Abi next received the ball, she put her theory to the test, making a run up the wing but then cutting inside. Jenna once again read her intentions and pulled the defender who was marking her away from the goal to leave Abi with a clear line of sight, so long as she could hit a shot on target from long range before cover arrived.

Once again, Abi heard Jenna's cry of "shoot" but this time it was accompanied by the same calls from the crowd. All seven of them.

She shot as instructed, hoping to guide the ball into the top left hand corner, but once again she was denied.

"Oh, for fuck's sake," Abi muttered to herself when the ball hit the crossbar. This time, though, it rebounded into the eighteen-yard box and landed at the feet of a waiting Jenna. The net rippled, and Abi threw her arms into the air as if it were her own goal. She'd certainly take the assist.

A few seconds later, Jenna's arms flung around Abi's neck.

"You stole my goal," Abi whispered against her ear.

"Shouldn't keep hitting the woodwork," Jenna whispered back. "We'll work on that, but not bad."

"Not bad? That's such a supportive thing to say."

"I know. You're so lucky to have me. Maybe I'll be your charm rather than the shirt." Jenna laughed and let go, turning to grin back at Abi as she ran towards the middle of the pitch. The celebration was over and she'd want them to go for another.

Despite doing so, no more goals came. In fact, they were fortunate to hold onto their narrow lead and ground out the victory with absolutely no style whatsoever. Not that it mattered. They'd won and it was all anyone would remember.

As Abi trudged off the pitch, exhausted and elated in equal measure, Jax high fived her. "Awesome, buddy. Told you it'd all come together."

"Think I deserve a pint and a big fat sausage for that performance."

"Hey, what you get up to in your own time is your own business. Your mum is inside sorting the food so I doubt you'll have long to wait."

"My mum?" Abi shook her head but couldn't help smiling. "I'll go and give her a hand."

After jogging up the field whilst dragging one of her legs behind herself, Abi stumbled into the clubhouse. The glorious smell of chip fat was already floating through into the bar, and it made her stomach grumble. She'd been too nervous to eat before the match but was now ravenously hungry.

"Ma," she said as she pushed through the kitchen door to find Petra tipping chips from baskets into serving trays. "You don't need to do this. We have a rota."

"I know I don't need to do anything," Petra replied, still focused on her task.

That was true. She was trying to be helpful. And supportive. "Thank you. Can I help?"

"Yes, please carry these through." Petra gestured to the row of serving trays she'd lined up on the work surface, filled with chips and sausages.

"Fine, but please don't do any more. I'll clean up. Will you just come into the bar and have a drink with us?"

"I'll let you buy me a gin and tonic, yes."

Abi had just carried out the last tray when the first players filtered in. She ran back into the kitchen to grab some paper plates and the condiments, then set those alongside and headed for the bar. She definitely owed her mum that G&T, plus a pint for her dad and Cokes for herself and Jenna. The last drink was just being slid towards her when a hand landed on her shoulder.

"Well played, love." It was Stanley, and he'd taken his beer before it'd even been offered. "Do you need me to take your mum home after this drink?"

"Nah. She's okay."

Stanley laughed and sipped his pint. "Looks like Jax is taking the heat, anyway." He nodded to her position, backed up against the wall near the toilets whilst Petra gave a highly animated assessment of her tactics. "We won't come every week but it's meant a lot to watch you play again. She was beside herself when you were ill. It was like watching her with that newborn again."

Abi chugged a few mouthfuls of Coke, trying to clear the lump that'd just formed in her throat. She'd not really considered what it must have been like for her parents. "I really do appreciate you guys."

"I know, love." Stanley slapped her shoulder again but walked away when Jenna came bouncing up behind them, high from the win or more Haribo. It was tough to tell.

"That was *so* good," she enthused, wrapping her arms around Abi and hugging her back. "I didn't want to say anything and make you even more stressed, but some of those girls were the bitches from my old team so I'm doubly glad we stuffed them."

Stuffing was a bit of a stretch, but Abi wouldn't argue. "I said I'd always take vengeance on your enemies." Without even thinking, she took hold of Jenna's wrist and guided her forward, then hooked the arm around her waist. "You were pretty good today."

"Pretty good?!"

"Okay, very good. We make a great team."

"I won't argue with that."

When Abi gave Jenna a peck on the lips, she could see from the corner of her eye that Jax had caught it because her mouth dropped open. Fortunately, though, she was still trapped by Petra. Abi was doubly grateful for her mum right now.

"Do you want some food?" she asked, knowing they'd both be on the same page.

"Yes, I—" Jenna stopped abruptly and her head banged

against Abi's shoulder. She let out a long, anguished groan. "I forgot to sort out the ketchup. It was all going so well..."

"Wait here."

Abi left Jenna with the drinks and jogged out to the changing rooms to grab her bag. When she returned, she dumped it on the floor and then reached in to produce two large bottles of tomato ketchup. "I have you covered," she said, holding them up.

"You are my actual hero. Do you know that?"

Jenna gave Abi a far more enthusiastic kiss, and this time, Jax didn't let Petra stop her. She strode over and wrenched one of the bottles from Abi's hand, set it on the table, then stood with her hands on her hips. "I knew it."

"You knew nothing."

"I knew *everything*. Come on, tell me I'm right. I can't wait to hear, in detail, how everything I said to you both was spot on."

Jenna had begun piling a paper plate with chips but she stopped and peered over her shoulder. "Hang on, what have you been saying to Abi?"

Jax's gaze fell to the floor. "Err."

"Err?"

"Well, I might have mentioned once or twice about how great you two would be together, and how I can see she's crazy about you, but she was dragging her heels!"

"Was she now?" Jenna set down her plate, that little mischievous glint back in her eye, and it was trained on Abi. "Why were you dragging your heels?"

"You know why. We talked about it," Abi replied with a shrug. "I didn't think in a million years that anything would happen between us. You're incredible. I'm very lucky."

The mood was shattered when Jax stuffed two fingers in her mouth. "Yuck, what have I done?"

"Shut up," Jenna shot back. "Let her finish explaining how

incredible I am." Her arms wrapped around Abi's neck, her lips dabbing Abi's nose. "I think you're pretty incredible, too." Her foot shot out, kicking Jax in the shin when she made vomiting noises again. Messing with their star striker was a bad idea. "Unless you've got something nice to add, be quiet."

Jax huffed. "Fine. I really am pleased for you guys. All those break up messages and ridiculous fantasies about someone who'd bake you cookies, and I knew she was under your nose the whole time."

"The cookies were delicious," Jenna confirmed, turning to let Abi hug her from behind. "And now that we've worked things out, we can help you."

"You can do what?" Jax's panic stricken face said it all.

"Absolutely," Abi joined in, knowing full well they were only winding Jax up. "Find you a nice woman who bakes. Someone homely. A nice apron."

"Sounds like your mum," Jenna added with a quick laugh.

"Think she's taken, sorry. Hmm, there has to be someone, though. What about Cass?" It was meant as a joke, but the way Jenna and Jax exchanged looks and then their eyes darted around the room told Abi everything she needed to know. "Okay, message received. Should've known you've already been there. Is there any woman in a ten mile radius who hasn't been in your bed?"

"Sure!" Jax exclaimed. "There's you two, for a start. We can change that, though, if you like. Threesome?"

Jenna rolled her eyes. "Down, tiger."

"You know I'm only joking. Maybe I'll have to start revisiting women I've already slept with. Not for a relationship, though. I'll leave that to you guys. There's only one woman I'd ever have settled down for, and she's long gone."

"I feel like there's a story here, hang on." Jenna unwrapped Abi's arms from around her waist and picked up her plate of

Printed in Great Britain
by Amazon